Surpise View

Robert Coon

Note for Librarians: A cataloguing record for this book is available from Library and Archives Canada at www.collectionscanada.ca/amicus/index-e.html
ISBN 1-4120-9595-6

Printed on paper with minimum 30% recycled fibre.
Trafford's print shop runs on "green energy" from solar, wind and other environmentally-friendly power sources.

Offices in Canada, USA, Ireland and UK

Book sales for North America and international:
Trafford Publishing, 6E–2333 Government St.,
Victoria, BC V8T 4P4 CANADA
phone 250 383 6864 (toll-free 1 888 232 4444)
fax 250 383 6804; email to orders@trafford.com
Book sales in Europe:
Trafford Publishing (UK) Limited, 9 Park End Street, 2nd Floor
Oxford, UK OX1 1HH UNITED KINGDOM
phone +44 (0)1865 722 113 (local rate 0845 230 9601)
facsimile +44 (0)1865 722 868; info.uk@trafford.com
Order online at:
trafford.com/06-1351

10 9 8 7 6 5 4 3 2

Surprise View is a real place. It is a clifftop viewpoint just off the narrow road which leads up to Watendlath, from where magnificent views of Derwentwater may be enjoyed by all. It is owned and managed by the National Trust. There is no hotel there and I hope there never will be. Neither is there a motor repairs garage on the road between Keswick and Borrowdale.

The story is set in the mid 1990s.

Surpise View

a story of
vigilantism, sadism, love & passion,
at a luxury country house hotel
in the English Lake District

One

There are several reasons for visiting the Lake District, thought Oliver, as the wind rushing over the top of the little windscreen whipped at his hair. Sightseeing, walking, climbing and water sports are the most common, of course. Some people are escaping the stresses of everyday life, if only for a few hours, while others are seeking the beauty and tranquility to be found there, perhaps to practice their creative talents of writing, painting, or photography.

Then he thought that the reasons must also include murder and suicide, as he recalled the reports in the *Cumbria Star*, some of which he had written himself, on the trials and inquests that had followed such sudden deaths.

There were the *Lady in the Lake* murders which, as well as making the headlines in the *Cumbria Star*, were also reported in the national press, after the bodies were discovered in Wastwater and Crummock Water. The husbands of both women had already been convicted of their murders.

Suicides, Oliver remembered, did not always make the headlines, although they were usually reported in the *Star*. Every year people drive to the Lake District, sometimes for long distances, to find a secluded beauty spot, before connecting the hose which they have brought for the purpose, from the exhaust pipe to the inside of their car. For that is the usual method. Often the location is chosen for some cherished memory of happier times.

Oliver was contemplating these thoughts as he sped northwards in his Lotus Elise. But morbid as they were, he was beginning to feel his inner knot of anxiety loosen and his mood lift, with every mile that passed. Now, as he sped along on this warm May day, it seemed incredible to him that only a few months ago he had been contemplating suicide himself.

The acrimonious rows, the separation, having to find somewhere to live at short notice, the solicitors' letters and the bitter wrangling over the divorce settlement, coming as they did so soon after the accident, had all taken their toll. His work had begun to suffer and, as his depression deepened, for the first time in his life he had contemplated killing himself. He worked out how he would do it, then one evening after he had drunk more wine than usual, he took the hose from his vacuum cleaner and held it alongside his Ford Mondeo. Satisfied that it was long enough, he found a roll of adhesive parcel tape.

Once he had decided the method, he kept visiting the scene in his mind. Would the hose be long enough and would the tape make the gap at the top of the window airtight? Would the engine overheat and catch fire and burn him before he was dead? Who would find him? Would a police officer notice his Mondeo in the little carpark and spot the hose? If so, might he use his baton to break a window and then resuscitate him? Or would someone walking their dog early the next morning see the car and the hose and, fearful of what might be inside, hurry away to phone the police?

The shock of realising that he was becoming suicidal stunned Oliver into making an appointment with his doctor. As he left the surgery holding a prescription for a course of an anti-depressant, it occurred to him that the long-suffering G.P. probably heard problems like his every day.

As the anti-depressant began to take effect, Oliver's mood slowly lifted until he was able to make a fresh appraisal of his life.

NOT YET FORTY, HE WAS a successful freelance journalist with a growing reputation, whose articles now appeared in many glossy magazines and weekend supplements. He had done well, considering that when he had moved to London five years ago he was virtually unknown.

He had wanted to work in newspapers from an early age and had not wavered in this ambition. In due course a good degree in journalism had got him the offer of a job at the *Cumbria Star.* This suited him, as he would be back among friends in his home county and living with his parents again. Oliver appreciated his home comforts and they would be pleased. Four years in student accommodation had been long enough and he did not have a steady girlfriend, or anyone else to share somewhere with.

The *Cumbria Star*, whose head office is in Keswick, is the Lake District's main local newspaper. Oliver's years with the firm were happy and successful. He became a good friend of the editor, an old-fashioned newspaper man called Ron Formby, who was nearing retirement age and who, apart from his National Service, had spent his entire working life with the newspaper. With Ron's support and guidance, Oliver made good progress – assistant reporter, reporter, experience in the advertising, photographic, accounts and printing departments, then senior reporter and main feature writer. He was a hard and willing worker who was prepared to put in long hours and become involved in the local community. Finally, when he became the *Star's* youngest-ever assistant editor and was able to introduce some ideas of his own, there was a slight improvement in the circulation figures.

One of Oliver's interests was antique furniture, which came from his parents who had built up a modest collection at their house at Loweswater. To obtain some experience during his second summer at university he had worked at the London office of a glossy magazine which featured country houses and stately homes. While he was there he also became interested in fine art.

His interest in these things continued to grow after he started at the *Cumbria Star*, when several of the features he had to write were on big country houses in Cumbria. He enjoyed writing them and the favourable response they received encouraged him to enrol at evening classes in architecture and interior design. He made up his mind that if he ever left the *Star* he would specialise in writing articles on country houses and stately homes.

It was while he was in Essex following up a news story with a Cumbrian connection that he met his future wife. Until then there had been only two girlfriends and they had not lasted long. This time it was different and after a brief courtship, which involved a lot of to-ing and fro-ing between Cumbria and Essex, they decided to get married. They discussed their future together, when she told him that she did not want to lose her job in London by moving north. For several months Oliver had been thinking that while he would be quite happy to spend the rest of his life in Cumbria, he should be more ambitious. He knew he was a good writer and could at least double his income by becoming a freelance journalist in London.

He talked it over with Ron, who thought he was making the right decision, adding that he would be missed, both professionally and personally, at the *Star*. It was, therefore, with mixed feelings that he addressed his letter of resignation to the managing director. Before leaving Cumbria, he wrote to several London editors to introduce himself and received some encouraging replies.

The wedding in Essex was, as planned, a modest affair for just the two families. Oliver's parents drove from Cumbria, to see their only child married and to meet his in-laws. They were delighted, but sorry that he was moving so far away. Of course, they were hoping to become grandparents in the fullness of time. After the reception, Oliver and his bride set off for a weekend honeymoon touring Devon and Cornwall in the Mondeo. They had decided that on their return they would continue to live in her flat, until they had found somewhere bigger.

The bad news was written on the faces of the two Essex police officers who were awaiting their return. They had been looking for Oliver for two days. His mother and father had been killed in a car crash in the Lake District, on their way home from the wedding. His father had swerved to avoid an oncoming car, which was travelling at high speed on the wrong side of the road. Their car had hit a tree and burst into flames. The other car, which had been stolen earlier in the day from a nearby village, had not stopped and had been found a few miles away, abandoned and burnt out. The Cumbria police were still looking for its two young male occupants.

Oliver's wife was unable to accompany him to Cumbria because of her work, so he was obliged to set off alone. On his arrival at Keswick he went to the police station and met the two traffic officers dealing with the accident. They were sympathetic and efficient. Unfortunately, the two youths had not been caught, but the Cumbria police were doing all they could to find them. They told him that car crime was becoming a serious problem in the county.

Visiting the scene of the accident on Whinlatter Pass and then having to identify his parents' bodies in the mortuary were difficult, as was returning to their empty house at Loweswater where he had decided to stay until after the funeral. He made the necessary arrangements with the funeral directors, then met his parents' solicitor, who, as their executor, had their wills. She confirmed that apart from two modest gifts to charities, Oliver was the sole beneficiary and said that it was in order for him to put the house on the market.

After the well-attended, sad little service and interment at Loweswater church, where his parents had been regular worshipers, he returned to Essex. The solicitor and estate agent kept in touch from Cumbria and eventually the house was sold and his parents' estates wound up. The solicitor's cheque, while not making him rich, certainly made him financially secure.

Oliver began to work long hours, spending most of the day at his new home writing, with trips into London to meet editors and to properties in the home counties to research his articles. Gradually, as his reputation as a feature writer grew, they began to appear in more titles on the news stands. He realised that as far as his career was concerned he had done the right thing by moving south.

His marriage, however, soon began to go downhill. At first he made an effort, but it was not long before both of them realised they were incompatible in too many ways. They were still living in her flat, as they had not got round to finding somewhere bigger. Neither of them had wanted children right away, but by now there was little likelihood of such an event, as both were working long hours and were usually exhausted by the evening. There were frequent arguments, usually bitter and occasionally violent, followed by long brooding silences.

One evening, after she came home from work, a row developed which was worse than the previous ones. She screamed at him that he was a bore, was always working, did not do his share of the housework, was not interested in holidays, in finding a bigger house or even in sex. When he began to remonstrate she hurled something at him, so he slapped her face. She screamed that their marriage was over and told him to get out of her flat, because she had met someone else at work who wanted to move in with her.

Oliver was shocked, because he had not suspected anything like that. He stormed out of the flat and drove to a nearby hotel, where he spent a miserable, sleepless night. The next morning he returned and, finding that she had already left for work, let himself in and collected his things. Then he went in search of somewhere to live.

As the wind continued to blow his dark hair about on the journey north in the little Lotus, he remembered that after six months of despair, it had taken just four weeks for the anti-depressant to take effect and soon he was able to resume his work.

****

It was almost a year after the divorce that he received the message from the editor of *Venues*. She would like to discuss some business with Oliver and could he call in? Yes, Oliver certainly could and would be pleased to do so. *Venues* was a new, up-market magazine, which was doing well and for some time he had been wondering how he could get a foot in the door.

He was shown into the editor's modern office. She was a tall, fashionably dressed young woman who greeted him enthusiastically. "Thanks for coming in at such short notice," she said as they shook hands.

When they were seated she smiled at him across her desk and handed him a newspaper cutting. Under the heading 'PM chooses top Lake District hotel' was a photograph of an attractive sandstone building standing on a cliff top. "I was wondering if you would be interested in taking on a feature on this place for us? I'm hoping it will be our lead story in the next issue. You might have heard that the Prime Minister and his wife are to spend a weekend there next month. It happens to be their wedding anniversary, which should add to readers' interest. You've acquired quite a reputation for this sort of thing."

Oliver looked again at the photograph then laughed. "Yes, I'd love to. I'm a Cumbrian and I know Surprise View quite well. When I was a student I took my parents there for dinner on their silver wedding anniversary, which almost broke me at the time. It's very exclusive and extremely expensive." He did not mention that the other reason for his sudden laughter was the sheer irony of the situation. Surprise View was just a mile up the narrow road from Ashness Bridge, where not long ago he had planned to end his life in the little carpark.

For the next half hour they discussed the feature, as well as his fee and expenses. He noticed two rows of framed covers of *Venues* on the wall behind the editor's desk. He counted twenty-three of them and realised there was one for every month that the magazine had been in business. He wondered if the twenty-fourth issue would contain his feature.

As they parted, the editor said "If this feature is the success that I'm hoping, we may be able to offer you something long-term."

"I'll certainly do my best," Oliver assured her. It struck him that things were looking up. Not only would the fee be his biggest yet, but he was getting full expenses for staying at Surprise View as well!

****

Oliver was recalling that fateful meeting of a year ago and the subsequent events as he continued northward. Although his article had been a huge success, his visit to Surprise View had unsettled him and the memory of it would not go away. He wanted to go back, if only for a few hours, to remind himself of everything that had happened.

He also knew that he needed a change. Although his mood had lifted, he was beginning to realise that he did not like living alone in the south and was missing Cumbria more than he had ever imagined. He decided to take a week off work and spend it there, visiting old haunts and looking up old friends. Not only would it give him an opportunity to review his life and plan his future, but the following Monday would be the anniversary of his visit.

That evening he phoned Ron Formby at his home near Keswick. The mild Cumbrian accent of his old friend reminded him of the happy years he had spent there. "My word, it's good to hear you again, Oliver. You seem to have gone from strength to strength since you left us. You're becoming quite a household name."

They chatted for a while, then Oliver told Ron of his discontent with living alone in London. "To be perfectly honest, Ron, if there was a half decent job for me in Cumbria I would jump at it. Now that you've finally decided to call it a day, have they made any decision about your successor?"

"Not yet," replied Ron. "But the M.D. is planning to advertise for applicants soon, then he'll make a short-list for interview. However, he was so impressed with you while you were here that if you're interested in the job he might just forego all the usual rigmarole and give it to you."

"Yes, I'm very interested and will appreciate it if you'll tell him so. I'm taking a week's holiday in Cumbria from this Saturday and could meet him while I'm in the area. I thought I might stay at Surprise View, for old times' sake. It would be nice if we could get together for a chat."

"I'd like that very much." Ron paused, then added "But you can't have heard about Surprise View. It didn't re-open at Easter and it's still closed. They haven't taken on any seasonal workers, although I believe some of the key staff are still living there. One of the partners, Ginger Rutherford, died in the autumn and the other one is ill." There was another pause. "I tell you what, why don't you come and stay with us? Marjory's cooking won't be up to Surprise View standards, but it will save you a small fortune and we'll enjoy having you"

"Thanks Ron, that's very kind of you. Yes, I'd like that very much, although it sounds a lot of trouble." Oliver heard Marjory's voice in the background.

Ron chuckled. "Marjory says it's no trouble and the spare room will be ready for you on Saturday. Also, I haven't to be rude about her cooking!"

"Tell her I'm looking forward to it" said Oliver. He was excited about having a break in Cumbria and the possibility of getting Ron's job on his retirement, when he would be moving back there to live. Then he added "Its strange about Surprise View. There was no hint of this last year. The owners seemed in remarkably good health and spoke of their intention of carrying on the business for ever and a day. I think I'll call in and see what its about while I'm in the area."

OLIVER'S THOUGHTS RETURNED TO THE JOURNEY. He had been driving for more than three hours and needed a rest. When he crossed from Lancashire into Cumbria he turned into the first motorway services, pulled up the hood and locked the Lotus. He went into the restaurant, bought a salad and a coffee and found a table. As he ate a late lunch he was feeling ridiculously happy to be back in his home county and began to recall his memories of it.

Of course it was not called Cumbria until the boundary changes of 1974, when the two old counties of Cumberland and Westmorland came together and took in the Furness district of Lancashire and part of the West Riding of Yorkshire as well. Oliver knew that many local people still felt a greater affinity towards their old county and wondered if the mountains and lakes were partly responsible for these parochial attitudes, by placing physical barriers between communities.

He had been born and brought up in Cumberland, the larger of the two old counties, to the north-west of what is now Cumbria. Westmorland was the smaller, to the south-east. The Lake District National Park at the centre of Cumbria, was previously shared between the two. Keswick was in Cumberland, while further south Ambleside and Windermere were in Westmorland.

Oliver was remembering the boundary changes and the resentment they had caused, when he noticed a woman at a nearby table reading a newspaper and recognised the masthead of the *Cumbria Star.* It always pleased him that although the paper was over a hundred years old, the masthead had not been changed. He had already made up his mind that if he got the job he would resist any attempts to do so.

His eyes moved down the front page and from where he sat he could just read the larger print. The main story was about a factory closure and job losses in West Cumbria. Underneath was a report on a tourism boom in the Lake District. His eyes continued to the next heading: "Whitehaven youth disappears – Cumbria police confirm nine local youths now missing." The words below were too small to read, so he decided to ask Ron what it was about.

He finished his lunch and returned to the carpark. As he put down the Lotus' hood he reckoned the final part of the journey through the Lake District, his favourite, would take another hour. As he rejoined the motorway and changed up through the gears, he realised he was feeling happier than he had for years. He was looking forward to seeing the Lake District again, not least because he knew it always looked its best in the late spring and early summer and the forecast for the next few days was good. He was also looking forward to meeting Ron and Marjory again and to hearing about the MD's reaction to his interest in the job.

Oliver was also hoping to do some flying while he was there. Flying a light aircraft had been a hobby since he had obtained his private pilot's licence at Carlisle Airport eight years earlier. After qualifying, he had bought a share in a Piper Cherokee there, in which he had spent many happy hours flying over what he considered to be the most beautiful part of Britain. It had been a relaxation for him while working at the *Star* and sometimes he had taken friends along too. On moving to Essex he had kept up his licence by occasionally hiring an aircraft from a nearby flying club, but the flat countryside north and east of London was not as appealing as Cumbria and the airspace was more congested. He particularly wanted to fly over the Lake District again and had brought his licence and log-book, together with his photographic case. He decided that when he got to Ron's house he would phone his old flying instructor at Carlisle Airport and hire an aircraft for a couple of hours the next day.

As he contemplated these pleasant prospects, his only disappointment was not being able to stay at Surprise View. But he knew that a week there would have been an extravagance and now he was looking forward to staying with Ron and Marjory. Nevertheless, not re-opening the hotel for the season did seem odd. He made up his mind to drive up there on Monday to see what he could find out, as that would be the anniversary.

Two

"I'm quite sure Surprise View couldn't have done better than that." He wasn't just being polite, because it had been an excellent meal with lively conversation.

Marjory laughed. "I'm glad you enjoyed it, Oliver. It's wonderful to see you again and to have someone to cook for. We haven't had a dinner party for ages. Now, I'll go and make some coffee. I expect you two will want to talk shop."

When he had pulled up outside three hours earlier, Ron and Marjory had come out to greet him. Ron knew that Oliver was anxious to hear about the job and when the opportunity arose he said "The MD was tickled pink when I told him you were interested and wants to discuss it with you. Can you be at the office at ten o'clock on Tuesday?"

The pleasure showed on Oliver's face. "That'll be fine, Ron. My only plans are to go flying tomorrow and visit Surprise View on Monday."

"Good. I don't anticipate any problems. He thinks very highly of you and since you left he's been following your progress and looking out for your work. He particularly enjoyed your feature on Surprise View in *Venues*. Between you and me, if all goes well on Tuesday, he's hoping to appoint you there and then, which will save him the trouble of advertising and interviewing a lot of applicants."

"Well, I hope you're right. It would be great to be back with the old firm again, but I won't count my chickens until they're hatched."

The two men talked for a while, bringing each other up to date with events. When Oliver's parents had been killed Ron had reported the accident in the *Star* and also written him a personal letter. Now he said "I was sorry your marriage didn't work out, Oliver. Splitting up is difficult enough at the best of times, but coming so soon after the accident must have made it very hard for you."

"It did, but I've just about got over it. I got in a low way and couldn't work for a while until my GP put me on anti-depressants, then when *Venues* asked me to do the article that bucked me up as well."

"The modern anti-depressants seem to be very effective," said Ron. "I know it's none of my business, but what went wrong?."

Oliver considered for a moment before replying. "Things weren't right from the start and they deteriorated pretty rapidly. We discovered too late that we didn't have a great deal in common. However, I think the main reason was that we were both working long hours and by the evening we were too tired to have a normal relationship."

"Not many young women had careers when Marjory and I were married. I suppose nowadays most couples need both incomes, but it does seem to be behind a lot of the divorces."

"Fortunately, there were no children to get hurt, because we'd decided to wait until our careers were more established and had found somewhere bigger to live."

"I take it there isn't anyone else yet?." There was a twinkle in Ron's eye.

Oliver smiled. "Not yet. I meet plenty of attractive women through my work, but I don't seem to get round to asking them out. The divorce might have undermined my confidence and the fact that I no longer like living in London doesn't help," he replied. But he knew he wasn't telling Ron the complete truth, because there was a woman who now dominated his thoughts for most of the time, although he had met her only the once. Then the subject changed to the *Cumbria Star.*

"The paper hasn't changed much since you left us" said Ron. "There are some new faces, but most of the old team are still with us. I'm sure they'd be pleased to see you return as the editor. The circulation figures are the major headache. As our faithful older readers die, it isn't easy to find younger readers to replace them. There's so much alternative access to the news nowadays that the younger generation can't be bothered to read the local rag."

"The editors of local newspapers have to be up to all sorts of tricks to keep up their circulation figures. The latest one is to send their photographer round the pubs and nightclubs on Saturday nights to take groups of youngsters cavorting with their friends while dressed in their glad-rags and binge drinking. Then they run a full colour page of the photographs in the next issue. The youngsters not only buy the paper to see themselves, but many call in to order prints as well. It might be good for business, but in my book someone should do something good, bad or at least noteworthy to get their picture in the local paper, not just get drunk. The MD suggested the *Star* runs such a page, but so far I've resisted it. However, perhaps I've been running things for too long."

The two men continued to talk about the newspaper until Marjory brought in the coffee and rejoined them. Ron poured three glasses of port and for half an hour they chatted and laughed, as they retold anecdotes about the *Star*. Then Marjory returned to the kitchen.

When they were alone again Oliver said "By the way Ron, I noticed a report in this week's *Star* which sounded a bit odd. It was about a youth who's gone missing from Whitehaven, and eight others who are missing from across the county. That seems a lot for Cumbria. I remember there were always one or two people disappearing, but usually they turned up alive and well, or occasionally, dead or injured. Do you know much about it?"

"It is rather strange" replied the editor. "I happen to know that the police are becoming worried and are stepping up their enquiries. I'll tell you what I know, if you like." Oliver nodded."

"About four months ago an eighteen year old youth didn't return to his home in Keswick after going into the town one Saturday evening. His parents reported him missing a couple of days later. Exactly two weeks later two brothers aged nineteen and twenty-one disappeared in Workington under similar circumstances. The following Saturday a seventeen year old from Maryport was reported missing. The next week a twenty-three year old disappeared from Carlisle and two weeks after that a fifteen year old from Whitehaven. Then there was a sixteen year old from Carlisle, followed by an eighteen year old from Cleator Moor and now this one from Whitehaven. That's a total of nine, all on Saturday nights."

"As you say, missing persons usually turn up safe and well. Either there's been some domestic trouble or they've taken off with someone. Occasionally they're found injured or dead, having been in an accident or topped themselves. Two years ago a local woman who had gone missing was found wandering about in Blackpool suffering from loss of memory. However, despite all the police enquiries and quite a lot of publicity in the local papers, as well as on Radio Cumbria and Border Television, not one of them has turned up. No reported sightings or anything."

"What sort of lads are they? Have they anything in common?" asked Oliver.

"That's what makes it so strange," replied Ron. "When a person goes missing, we report the information given to us by the police – usually the name, sex, age and a physical description. These nine are all young males aged between fifteen and twenty-three, single, unemployed and from poorer homes in the local industrial towns and villages, mainly in West Cumbria. However, what the police have not told us, but I happen to know, is that they have all been in trouble. They are what most people would call dropouts, layabouts or toe-rags, but a more polite, collective term would be the underclass of our society. At school they were poor attenders and low achievers, who turned out to be troublemakers and criminals who will steal anything to finance their drugs habit. They all have criminal records for theft, drugs, violence and public order offences."

"And they simply vanished off the face of the earth?"

"Apparently so. They all disappeared on Saturday nights, having set off into their respective towns for their usual Saturday night's entertainment, which was to cause trouble, commit damage or steal something. Then they simply vanished. Within a few days, according to the degree of concern felt by their families or friends, they were reported missing."

"How extraordinary," said Oliver. "And the police have followed up all the usual lines of enquiry?"

"They didn't take it too seriously at first. I suppose when a person is reported missing they consider their vulnerability, so a child, young woman or elderly person will get a higher priority than a physically fit, street-wise, young man. These lads are all known to the police as local troublemakers who are street-wise and capable of looking after themselves. However, when the first five had not been found and the fifteen year old was reported missing, some awkward questions began to be asked and the Head of CID took over the enquiry."

"That makes sense, as the towns involved are in three different police divisions, if I remember rightly," said Oliver.

"That's right, so the Detective Chief Superintendent is now handling them all from police headquarters at Penrith. The usual missing persons enquiries have been made and descriptions of the youths circulated to police forces nationwide, although none of them is believed to have travelled far outside Cumbria. It was thought there might be a connection between the disappearances and the high levels of crime and disorder in parts of Cumbria at the moment. I expect you remember that crime, vandalism, and anti-social behaviour were on the increase when you left?"

Oliver nodded. "Yes, things were getting pretty bad in West Cumbria and Carlisle."

"Well, it got much worse and has become a serious problem, particularly in West Cumbria. The industrial towns and villages on the coast have always had a reputation for high levels of crime and disorder, which is why it became known as the Wild West. Over the years the shipping and coal mining at Whitehaven, the iron ore mining at Egremont and Cleator Moor, the iron and steel industry at Workington and more recently the nuclear reprocessing plant at Sellafield, attracted workers from outside the area. They included many Irish, which resulted in some pretty serious sectarian riots." Suddenly Ron slapped the arm of his chair and laughed. "Of course, you wrote an article on the Irish in West Cumbria, so you probably know more about it than me."

Oliver smiled "You've got a good memory. Researching it was most interesting, but I can only remember the main events now. The iron, steel and shipbuilding centres of West Cumberland attracted many working-class Irish settlers during the second half of the nineteenth century. Most came from Ulster, being the part of Ireland nearest the ports of West Cumberland. The Catholics settled in the iron ore mining community of Cleator Moor, which soon became known as 'Cumberland's Little Ireland', while the Protestants went to Whitehaven and found work around the docks. Living conditions in the poor, overcrowded courtyards became so bad that there were frequent outbreaks of cholera and typhus. After one epidemic the Government's Chief Medical Officer of Health wrote *"I found such an amount of human wretchedness and misery in Whitehaven that few people in better circumstances would believed existed."*

"So many Irish settled in West Cumberland that the area became a microcosm of expatriate Ulster life, seeing some of the worst sectarian and anti-Irish riots outside Glasgow and Liverpool. In 1864 there was rioting in Barrow when the Irish navvies building the docks there came under attack. Then 1871 saw serious disorder in Whitehaven, when the well-known Protestant preacher and rabble rouser William Murphy was attacked after one of his anti Roman Catholic lectures, by Catholics who had come by train from Cleator Moor, which also sparked off sectarian fighting in Workington. Seven Catholics were given hard labour and the following year Murphy died from his injuries. Sectarian feelings continued to run high and on the 'Glorious Twelfth' of July 1876 a large number of Catholics attacked the Orange parade in Cleator Moor. But the most serious violence was the Cleator Moor Orange Day riot of 1884 when a Catholic was shot dead by a Protestant armed with a revolver. An army detachment had to be put on standby in Carlisle when the police almost lost control of the situation."

Ron nodded. "Fortunately, the Irish troubles are now confined to West Cumbria's history, but the area still has a lot of hard men. The rise in unemployment following the closure of some of the traditional industries, which began about thirty years ago, has caused a lot of resentment. The biggest losses were the coal mines at Whitehaven and the iron and steel industry at Workington."

"I remember the iron foundries closing in Workington. That must have been a severe blow to the area."

"It was. As jobs dried up and drugs appeared on the streets, more and more young men turned to crime. Burglary, robbery, criminal damage, car theft, ram-raiding and anti-social behaviour seemed to become the new youth culture of West Cumbria, being particularly bad around Workington. So many stolen cars were recovered by the police that they had to use the empty bus factory at Lillyhall to examine them. Police cars had missiles thrown at them in high speed chases and two officers were badly injured when one was rammed. There were even reports of officers being followed from the police station after work by criminals intent on targetting their homes and families. Matters became so bad that the M.P. for Workington asked a question in the Commons about the policing of the town. As a result of all the insurance claims, Workington postcodes were in the highest risk band for a while."

"The police thought all this might be behind the disappearances – the missing lads might have been involved in accidents in stolen cars, or simply driven out of the area, that sort of thing. But so far everything has been negative."

"You may remember you sent me to work at the Workington office for a few months soon after I started at the *Star*. Even in those days there was a lot of crime and disorder down that way," said Oliver.

"A few weeks ago the window of our Workington office was broken one Saturday night. Just for the hell of it, it seems, as there was nothing of value in it. And there's graffiti everywhere. The young hooligans responsible are all on drugs of one sort or another, which can make them violent. Usually they start by sniffing glue, then graduate onto something harder. Cannabis is still popular which, when combined with alcohol, can cause paranoia and violent behaviour, especially in youngsters who already have personality disorders."

"I had no idea things were so bad. People imagine West Cumbria to be a quiet backwater. Where does public opinion lie?."

"As you know, most Cumbrians, particularly those in the Lake District and to the east of the county, are law-abiding citizens who strongly disapprove of all this. The two biggest towns, Carlisle and Barrow, have always had housing estates where crime is a problem and people accept that, provided it doesn't get out of hand. Generations of the residents of Appleby, the respectable old county town of Westmorland, have had to endure crime and disorder for a week every June when travelling people have descended on them for the annual horse fair. However, in West Cumbria there is a reticence and an ambivalence about the present state of affairs that I find disturbing. You would expect condemnation, even outrage from the usual quarters, with letters of protest appearing in the local newspapers."

"I suppose people are afraid to be heard complaining," said Oliver.

"I agree, there's a lot of fear of intimidation and violence, especially on the housing estates. But I also think that the older generation has a strong sympathy for the younger ones who can't find work. As you just pointed out, the loss of the iron and steel industry was a major blow to the area. For a hundred years it was the main employer, as well as being a benevolent and patriarchal one. Families saw generations of their menfolk start as apprentices and continue to work there all their lives."

Oliver nodded. "Maybe they're hoping that serious disorder will influence political decisions and lead to the return of well paid jobs. The amount of crime there at the moment sounds very unpleasant. One expects those levels in some of our cities, but not in Cumbrian towns and villages so close to the Lake District. How are the police coping with it?."

"Despite its small size and the large area it has to cover, the Cumbria Constabulary is rated highly, having a particularly good crime detection rate, and in the annual inspection of the forty-two police forces it usually comes out near the top. However, they seem to be up against it in West Cumbria at the moment. I believe this is due to the public apathy and because much of the crime is relatively low-level and has so far not justified the cost of additional resources."

"Well, it looks as though they're going to have to do something about it."

"The Chief Constable recently promised to crack down on the main offenders and has made a start by buying some of the latest fast traffic cars."

"It will be interesting to see how effective they are," observed Oliver.

"Quite apart from the crime, statistics show Cumbrians to be a pretty wild lot, although there are only half a million of us. In recent years the *Star* has printed the results of national surveys showing Cumbria to have very high rates of binge drinking, suicide among young men, fatal road accidents and homophobic and racist attitudes. Also sexual activity, with the average Cumbrian managing it 165 times a year, and sexually transmitted diseases, although these could be a matter of cause and effect."

Oliver laughed. "Perhaps Cumbrians have nothing else to do on all the wet evenings. But to be fair, ever since women and children worked down Whitehaven's coal mines in appalling conditions, the people of West Cumbria have never had an easy time of it. There's always been high unemployment and the area has never experienced any real prosperity. When I was at the *Star* a government report was published showing it to have some of the worst pockets of social deprivation in the country."

Ron nodded. "It seems that almost every week the *Star* reports the loss of another employer in West Cumbria. The biggest remaining one is Sellafield, but because the nuclear industry has become such a political hot potato even its future is now uncertain. Occasionally, a new firm starts up, but it's usually a case of one step forwards and two back, so the number of well-paid jobs in the area continues to decline."

"West Cumbria has always struck me as having a lot in common with Liverpool," said Oliver. "But you can't blame the people for feeling bitter. Ever since Whitehaven ceased to be an important trading port West Cumbria has suffered from its remoteness and inaccessibility. It desperately needs better roads and communications if new employers are to be attracted to the area."

Ron nodded. "There is an unfortunate dichotomy in Cumbria at the moment. On the one hand we have large numbers of rich people wanting to retire and recreate here. On the other the communities that have lived here for generations are seriously under threat, because Cumbria is now the only county whose economy is not only in decline, but is no better than those of former iron curtain countries. It's partly due to this scenario that big economic, social and cultural divisions have arisen between Cumbria's industrial communities and the more affluent parts of the Lake District, although as the crow flies they're only a few miles apart. I expect this was brought home to you last year when you visited Surprise View?"

Before Oliver could reply Marjory had rejoined them. "Where will you be flying tomorrow, Oliver?," she asked.

"If the weather's good I'll go down the coast to St. Bees Head, then across the Lake District to Penrith and back to Carlisle. That used to be my favourite route. But if it's not so good I'll give the Lake District a miss, because my old flying instructor used to warn me about the clouds with hard centres. You're both welcome to come if you like."

Marjory and Ron laughed. "Thanks all the same, but I had too many frights in the RAF," said Ron.

Oliver stood up. "If I get the opportunity I'll take an aerial photograph of your house for you. Now, if you don't mind, I'll say goodnight, because I've had a long day. Thanks again for that wonderful dinner."

Three

His former flying instructor welcomed him with a grin. "It's good to see you again, Oliver. How long is it since you moved away?."

"Its good to see you Jim. Three years, believe it or not. I've often intended to pay you a visit when I've been in Cumbria, but I always seem to run out of time."

"You've couldn't have chosen a better day for some local flying. The visibility is excellent. It's a good job you kept up your licence, or you'd be having to do a complete refresher. However, the rules require me to make sure you're still competent, so we'll have to do some circuits together before you can go off on you own again. No-one has booked *Yanky Mike* for this morning, so I've put you down for a couple of hours. I thought you'd rather fly the old girl than one of the school aircraft."

"Thanks Jim." Oliver was pleased. *Yanky Mike*, or G-AVYM, was the Piper Cherokee he used to fly at Carlisle Airport. It has been based there longer than any other aircraft and its 180 HP engine is more powerful than those in the basic trainers.

"If you do the pre-flight checks, I'll join you shortly," Jim told him.

Oliver left the instructor in the flight office and as he walked through the hangar he admired the assortment of privately-owned aircraft which are kept there, including some rare vintage types.

Yanky Mike had been pulled outside and was standing on the apron, its smart blue and white livery gleaming in the sun. He climbed onto the wing, opened the door and got into the left seat, then looked at the instruments and the controls and felt a thrill of excitement when he realised that little had changed. He found the check-list and began to work his way down it, checking everything inside and outside the aircraft. When he had finished he strapped himself in.

The aircraft rocked slightly as Jim climbed onto the wing and got into the right-hand seat. "Right, lets go," he instructed briskly. "See if you can remember the Carlisle procedures. They haven't changed much."

They put on their headsets and Oliver continued down the check-list, reading each one aloud so that Jim would know he was doing them properly. "External check completed, door closed, brake on, seat and belts OK, switches on, ailerons and trimmer OK, flaps OK, fuel on, carburettor heat OK, circuit breakers OK, rotating beacon on."

He was ready to start the engine. "Mixture rich, throttle set, engine primed." He looked out to make sure there was nobody near the propellor, then opened a small flap in the perspex canopy and shouted "clear prop" through the opening. He pressed the starter and the propellor began to spin as the Wycoming engine burst into life. He continued to read aloud the checks: "starter warning light out, oil pressure OK, throttle 1200 rpm, fuel pressure OK, alternator OK, suction OK."

Jim's voice came through the headset. "Right, call the tower."

Oliver pressed the transmit button on the control column. "Carlisle, Golf Alpha Victor Yanky Mike, radio check and taxi, two on board in the circuit."

"Golf Alpha Victor Yanky Mike, Carlisle radio check five, taxi holding point runway 25, QNH 1016 QFE 1009," replied the air traffic controller.

Oliver wrote this data on a pad, then repeated it to the ATC. He set the atmospheric pressures on the two altimeters – the one at 1016 millibars to give his height above sea level and the one at 1009 millibars his height above the airfield.

He released the handbrake and began to taxi across the apron towards the taxiway. When he reached the main runway he stopped at the holding-point and carried out the power checks. When the instruments showed correct readings at high revs he did the pre-take off checks. Finally satisfied, he called "Golf Yanky Mike ready for departure."

"Golf Yanky Mike, backtrack, line up runway 25," came the ATC's reply through the headsets.

Oliver released the handbrake and taxied along the runway in the opposite direction to which he would be taking off. He continued as far as the white '25' number painted on the ground, before turning Yanky Mike through 180 degress.

"Golf Yanky Mike, cleared take off, surface wind 250 at ten knots."

He was now facing into the light wind which was blowing straight down the runway – ideal for taking off and landing. He opened the throttle fully and as the speed of the aircraft picked up he pressed the rudder bar with his right foot to keep it on the centre line of the runway. When the airspeed indicator showed 90 knots, he eased back on the control column and felt the wheels leave the ground.

Maintaining the pressure on the rudder, he climbed to 500 feet, made a 90 degree left turn and continued climbing to 1000 feet. He levelled out, reduced engine revs to cruise and adjusted the trim. He made another 90 degree left turn then called "Yanky Mike downwind."

"Yanky Mike, report final."

Conscious of Jim's presence beside him, he continued to fly parallel to the runway until he was was well beyond it, while all the time checking his height and heading and looking out for other aircraft. He made another 90 degree left turn, reduced power, put on one stage of flap and decended to 500 feet. Turning left again and heading straight towards runway 25, he applied the second stage of flap and adjusted his speed. "Yanky Mike final, touch and go," he called.

"Yanky Mike, cleared touch and go, wind 250 at twelve knots," replied the ATC. The wind speed had increased by two knots and he had clearance to touch down and immediately take off again.

As the runway numbers loomed up he pulled back and let the aircraft stall the last few feet onto the centre line. When he felt the wheels touch he opened the throttle fully, removed the flap and took off again.

As they climbed again Jim said. "Apart from losing a little height when you turned onto the downwind leg that was good. Do one more and if you don't cock it up you can go off on you own."

Oliver completed the second circuit without fault and landed. As he taxied back to the apron the two men chatted through the headsets. Oliver looked round at the buildings of the former wartime RAF station and observed "Carlisle Airport hasn't changed much. I thought there were plans to develop it and re-introduce some passenger services."

Jim's voice came back. "There are, but it needs a new main runway and as usual it comes down to money. The trouble is there are only half a million people in Cumbria and Newcastle Airport is quite close. However, the goverment has said that because our major international airports are getting so busy it wants to develop more of the regional ones, so there's hope for us yet."

At the entrance to the apron Oliver had to give way to a departing aircraft. It was an unusual type with centrally mounted twin-engines and push/pull propellers. As it taxied past he noticed the emblem of the Cumbria Constabulary on its side.

"Have the Cumbria police got their own aircraft now?," he asked in surprise.

"Yes. They bought it recently and keep it here," replied Jim. "It's used for searches, tracking stolen cars, people on the run, that sort of thing. I suppose it can prevent the dangers of high-speed car chases. It has heat-seeking cameras and other special equipment. One of the instructors here flies it.

When they need it in a hurry they phone up and he gets it ready, then two or three police officers arrive by car and off they all go. They've had some successes with stolen cars in West Cumbria and located missing persons and a criminal on the run. A helicopter would be more suitable, but I don't suppose the Cumbria Constabulary can afford one."

They reached the apron and Oliver applied the handbrake and reduced the engine revs to minimum. Jim took off his headset and undid his straps. As he got out he shouted to Oliver "Enjoy yourself, but keep a good lookout for the military," then added with a grin "remember the saying – 'there are old pilots and there are bold pilots, but there are no old, bold, pilots'."

Oliver smiled at Jim's words of caution. "I haven't forgotten," he called after him, as he stepped off the wing.

He taxied back to the runway, then felt a thrill of excitement as, for the first time in three years, he took off alone from Carlisle Airport. He looked around for the familiar landmarks and identified them. Turning north-west, he levelled out at 2000 feet and headed for Gretna. Once again he was beginning to relax in *Yanky Mike*, pleased that it was still flying well. He pressed the transmit button and called "Yanky Mike, departing the circuit to the north west."

"Yanky Mike, report rejoining."

The sky was cloudless and the visibility excellent. When he looked around he could see for miles in all directions. He turned west and followed the Solway Firth along its Scottish side. The Lowland hills to his right and the more distant Lake District peaks to his left looked beautiful and appeared closer than they really were. Ten minutes after leaving Carlisle, Dumfries came into view. He circled the old Scottish town at 2000 feet, then turned to the south-east. As he headed back for the Solway Firth, he could see the Cumbrian coastline twenty miles ahead and the Lake District a further twenty miles beyond.

With ten miles of sea to cross he climbed to 4000 feet to give himself enough height to reach land in the event of an engine failure. He levelled out and pointed 'Yanky Mike" towards Silloth on the English side and when he could see the big wartime hangars on Silloth airfield he reduced power and began to decend towards them.

Oliver was interested in old airfields. RAF Silloth had been a training base for bomber crews in World War II and so many Hudson bombers came down in the Solway Firth that it became known as Hudson Bay. He spotted the little church and the two rows of war graves that he had once visited, where many of the aircrew are buried.

As he skirted the town he identified the course of the old railway line which, in the days when Silloth was a popular resort, connected with the main lines at Carlisle. He levelled out at 2000 feet and, keeping out to sea, headed down the coast. The pretty seaside village of Allonby passed below the left wing as Maryport appeared ahead. For a few moments he looked down and studied the old fishing port and modern marina.

The urban sprawl of Workington with its commercial docks came into view and he noticed for the first time the clusters of wind turbines which now surround this industrial town. From his vantage point the glorious backdrop of the Lake District looked very close. He recalled his conversation with Ron and found it difficult to believe that there could be so much crime and disorder in this part of Cumbria. And that business of the nine youths who had gone missing on Saturday nights seemed very strange indeed.

He was once again feeling completely relaxed in the aircraft he had so often flown in the past. He carried out an instrument check then looked round the cabin. Nothing had changed. He noticed the empty cigar-lighter socket and smiled, remembering that when he first joined the syndicate he smoked cigars while flying *Yanky Mike*. One day he found the lighter missing from its socket, confiscated, he imagined, by another member who objected to the smell of smoke.

Whitehaven and its old harbour now lay ahead and from the air he could see the symmetrical layout of the streets of this Georgian planned town. In the seventeenth and eighteenth centuries Whitehaven was one of England's busiest ports and ship-building, coal mining, rum smuggling and slave-trading are all part of its romantic history. He noticed the recent improvements to the harbour area, to encourage the tourism on which Whitehaven now depends.

If flying conditions had not been so good, Oliver would have skirted the northern fells of the Lake District and returned to Carlisle over Cockermouth and flatter ground. But because the visibility was excellent and he wanted to see the Lake District and *Surprise View* from the air, he decided to fly straight across to Penrith, then follow the M6 back to Carlisle airport.

From Whitehaven he continued down the coast to St. Bees Head at 2000 feet. As he rounded the old lighthouse on the sandstone cliff, the domes and towers of the Sellafield plant came into view further south. Just beyond them lay the seaside village of Seascale and further down the coast Millom, Barrow-in-Furness and Walney Island were visible. Out to sea the Isle of Man stood out very clearly.

Giving Sellafield a wide birth he turned inland and increased the engine power. He needed to reach 4000 feet, to be well above the highest peaks and yet a safe distance below the commercial airways. As he gained height the glorious panorama of the Lake District began to unfold before him, the shades reminding him of the picture on the big box of Cumberland coloured pencils he had been given as a child.

Egremont appeared ahead and beyond it the remoter western lakes. To his right was Wastwater, with its dramatic backdrop of screes and Scafell Pike. It is claimed that the Wasdale valley has the deepest lake, the highest mountain, the smallest church and, since the regular winner of a tall story competition lived there, the biggest liar in England! To his left was Ennerdale Water and beyond it Loweswater, Crummock Water and Buttermere, three smaller lakes in a straight line which point towards the centre of the Lake District.

As he continued to climb, other lakes came into view: directly ahead was Derwentwater, "The Queen of the Lakes," with Keswick at its northern end. He wanted to have a good look at *Surprise View*, on the clifftop on its eastern side. At 4500 feet he levelled out, throttled back and trimmed the aircraft to fly straight and level, relieved there was little turbulence from the mountains. As he had used more than half the fuel in the left tank he changed over to the right. Then he switched on the auto-pilot, which would keep him flying at the same height and heading as he studied the ground.

It was like looking at a huge relief map. Beyond Derwentwater to the east lay Thirlmere, Ullswater and Haweswater. To the south the smaller lakes of Grasmere and Rydal Water and beyond them, stretching into the distance, Windermere, England's largest lake. Running parallel and a short distance west was Coniston Water, Windermere's smaller sister. Much further south Morecambe Bay was visible. To the north he could see Bassenthwaite Lake lying between Keswick and Cockermouth. This is sometimes claimed to be the Lake District's only lake, because all the others are waters or meres!

His eyes followed the twisty, narrow road from the southern end of Bassenthwaite Lake across Whinlatter pass, until they found Crummock Water and Loweswater. For a moment he stared at the two pretty, smaller lakes remembering how, as a boy, he had rowed his father up and down them as he fished for trout. Then they focussed on the tiny village of Loweswater nestling between them and found his parents' house where he was brought up, and the little church and the churchyard where they were recently buried.

His eyes moved back across Whinlatter Pass and found the bridge and the bend where it happened. There was a darker area in the grass in front of the big sycamore tree and he realised with a shock that this must be new grass growing where the ground had been scorched. He clenched his fists and tears came to his eyes as he imagined the two youths abandoning them in their blazing car.

His fists slowly relaxed again as the scene of the tragedy disappeared below the left wing and he lifted his eyes to the panorama ahead. As well as the sixteen lakes, he could make out many of the Lake District's 463 tarns, some of them high up in the fells. Sparkling in the sunlight on this glorious day, they looked like jewels in some fantastic setting. He studied the contours of the land, trying to put names to the higher peaks. From the air the remoteness of some of the places was evident and he felt a sudden pang of guilt as he remembered how little he had walked in the Lake District, always preferring to go by car or, as today, by aeroplane. Then he smiled as he remembered being told that this is a sign of a true Cumbrian.

Derwentwater was now directly ahead and his eyes searched its eastern side at the southern end for the Lodore Falls. When they found the white cascade they followed it up the vertical cliff.

Yes, there it was! Surprise View! As he stared down at the elegant Victorian building, his thoughts went back to the unforgettable events of a year ago.

Four

As soon as he had got back to his flat from the meeting with the editor of *Venues*, Oliver had phoned Surprise View. He knew that the hotel was still owned and run by the elderly couple who had founded it in 1950. He wanted to introduce himself, explain about the feature and ask for their co-operation in giving him the information he needed to write it.

A well spoken woman answered. He gave his name and asked to speak to one of the partners. After a moment she said "I'm putting you through to Bunny Liddle, Mr. Mills."

He did not have to wait long. A man's voice, cultured and clipped but also friendly said "Bunny Liddle here, we've been expecting your call, Mr. Mills. We've just heard about the feature from the editor of *Venues*. It all sounds terribly exciting."

Oliver had wondered if the editor would contact the owners and was relieved that she had, as it saved him the trouble of having to explain everything. The partner continued. "We're all absolutely delighted at Surprise View and of course we'll give you our full co-operation. It will be a wonderful advertisement for the old place and give our staff no end of a boost to see themselves in *Venues*."

"That's very kind of you," said Oliver. "One night should be enough, preferably this weekend if that's alright. I'll arrive after lunch, meet everyone, then take some photographs and do some of the interviews before dinner. The following morning I'll do the remaining interviews and perhaps take more photographs, then leave before lunch."

"Sounds marvellous, old boy. Sunday will be best for us. Ginger Rutherford and I and the key staff will be here. We have a room with a lake view for you. We're fully booked with guests and diners, so you'll be able to see us in full swing. I'll send you one of our brochures which you might find useful."

"Thanks, Mr. Liddle. Sunday will be fine. I'll look forward to it," replied Oliver.

He was not just looking forward to visiting Surprise View and describing it in his article, but also to the break from routine. He would be in the Lake District again and the drive there would be fun. He remembered that the Mondeo was not only getting quite old, but now it reminded him of the darker times that he preferred to forget. Like many men, he had always harboured a desire for a sports car and had particularly admired the Lotus Elise. Aware that he could now afford one, he phoned the local dealer and arranged a test drive.

He immediately fell in love with the little yellow roadster and there and then agreed a part-exchange deal. He told the dealer about his journey to Cumbria and was promised that if he arranged the payment and the insurance in the meantime, the car would be ready for collection on Sunday morning.

Sunday turned out to be a beautiful day and after breakfast he set off in the Mondeo to collect it. The dealer was as good as his word, for when he arrived the Lotus was standing outside the showroom, gleaming in the sun. The dealer explained about the servicing and handed him the documents and keys. Oliver transferred his few pieces of luggage into the little boot, then stowed away the hood. As he drove away, he raised a hand in farewell to both the dealer and the Mondeo.

He intended to take his usual route to Keswick: the M25, M1, M6 to junction 36, then the A591 through the Lake District. He was particularly looking forward to this last part of the journey. His confidence in his new car grew as he became familiar with its controls and handling and by the time he had reached the M1 he was doing his normal motorway speeds. Even at eighty-five there was little wind noise with the hood down, but the rush of air over the windscreen was a novel experience. He felt that it was blowing away not only the cobwebs, but all his unhappy memories as well.

The more he drove the Lotus, the more he delighted in it. He had read a glowing report about it in a motoring magazine, which had named it the sports car of the year and praised its features, including the lightning response and excellent steering, gearchange, brakes, handling and roadholding which make it hugely enjoyable on twisty roads. Oliver was looking forward to driving it in the Lake District.

By the time he turned off the M6, he was feeling as though he had been driving the little roadster for years. In the distance he glimpsed Kendal, "the old grey town," then over the brow of a hill Windermere – both the lake and the town. He was feeling particularly happy because the Lake District was looking its best and the traffic was light. He followed the road along the lakeside and through

Ambleside, before negotiating the series of hairpin bends between Rydal Water and Grasmere.

He was delighted that as far as handling was concerned the report had not exaggerated the Elise's merits. On Dumail Raise he moved into the overtaking lane and shot past a long line of slow-moving traffic, touching eighty before the summit. He smiled to himself as he remembered that in the early days of motoring passengers had to get out and push their cars up Dunmail Raise.

As he began to descend the other side he remembered something else about Dunmail Raise. The Victorian writer and critic John Ruskin, on learning of the plans of an early railway company to build a line from Windermere to Keswick over Dunmail Raise, had written from his Coniston home complaining of *"the certainty of the deterioration of the moral character in the inhabitants of every district penetrated by a railway...I don't want to let them see Helvellyn while they are drunk."* And Ruskin a social reformer, too!

Thirlmere came into view and for a few minutes he enjoyed straightening out the bends along its tree lined shore. St John's-in-the-Vale extended away to his right, then at last, at the top of a hill, Keswick and Derwentwater came into view. He negotiated the tourists walking in the narrow streets of Keswick and as he took the road out for Borrowdale, he realised he had made good time and would not be expected at Surprise View for at least another hour. He had not eaten since leaving Essex so he decided to buy a sandwich and find somewhere quiet where he could relax for an hour. He needed petrol and remembered a little garage a mile or so along the Borrowdale road, so he decided to fill up there and buy his lunch at the same time.

As he pulled onto the forecourt the garage appeared to have changed little since his parents had called there for petrol when he was a child. It had retained its neat, well-run appearance and the freshly whitewashed stone workshop, big enough for two big cars or three smaller ones, looked as though it had not changed since the 1930s. He thought the circular enamel sign bearing the name "Barr's Garage," now starting to rust at the edges, would be a collectors' item. The only visible change was that perhaps thirty years ago the two ancient hand-cranked petrol pumps which had been used to fill his parents' car had been replaced by electric ones with pointers.

Set back behind the garage was a neat bungalow in an immaculate garden. A modern breakdown recovery vehicle, bearing the red lettering "Barr's Breakdown Recovery, Keswick" on yellow bodywork, was parked in the driveway. The little kiosk was well stocked and when Oliver came to pay for his petrol, sandwich and bottle of mineral water he was served by a pleasant, middle-aged woman, who wished him a good journey. As he was about to get back into the Lotus a middle-aged man wearing a clean overall and carrying a bucket approached him.

"Good afternoon, sir. It's a lovely day." He had a deep, rich voice and as he began to wash the little windscreen he asked Oliver "Are you on holiday?"

"No, on business, I'm afraid. I'm staying just up the road at Surprise View."

"You couldn't have chosen a better hotel, sir. We get a lot of their guests calling in here, some of them very famous people, too. They come from all over the world. The owners are a charming couple who have done a lot for the local community."

"I expect you see quite a lot of the owners and staff, being so close?"

"Oh yes, we have a very good relationship. Bunny Liddle and Ginger Rutherford have been our customers since they arrived in 1950. They always bring their cars to us for servicing. The staff and guests call in for petrol, too. There, that's got rid of the dead flies for you. I hope you enjoy your visit."

"Thanks very much" said Oliver, getting into the Lotus. The friendly reception had impressed him and he imagined that the man and the woman must be Mr. and Mrs. Barr. As he drove off he noticed two young men working on a car in the workshop. They looked smart in clean overalls and were of strikingly similar appearance, being of the same height and muscular build, with fresh-faces and wavy hair that was almost golden. He wondered if they were the third generation of the Barr family to work in the family business.

Just before the turning up to Watendlath he pulled into a small carpark surrounded by trees and switched off the engine. As he ate his lunch he listened to some classical music and thought about the job ahead. When he had finished he opened the boot and took out his photographic case and briefcase. He checked his camera, then opened the briefcase and took out the brochure which had arrived in the post.

Oliver already knew quite a lot about Surprise View. As a child at Loweswater he was always fascinated to hear about the famous people who stayed there, the fine foods and wines they were served and the enormous prices they paid. As he grew up, the hotel's reputation for luxury, its exquisite cuisine and breathtaking view continued to grow. His first visit was as a university student, when treating his parents to dinner on their silver wedding had made a substantial inroad into his savings. But he had not seen much of the place then because it had been dark, neither had he encountered the owners.

Later, when he was at the *Cumbria Star*, he sometimes reported the visits of royalty, film and rock stars, politicians, footballers and other famous people, as well as the presentations of several awards to the hotel. When he moved south he would occasionally read about Surprise View in a newspaper or magazine when some celebrity or other stayed there, or when it received yet another award. Recently, there had been several reports about the forthcoming visit of the Prime Minister and his wife.

Although he had already read the brochure from cover to cover, Oliver wanted to be sure that he had all the facts at his fingertips, so he began to turn the pages again. The cover featured a high quality colour photograph of the west side of the hotel. It was an elegant, three-storey Victorian building built of sandstone, with arched windows, gingerbread eaves and gables, nestling among trees on a cliff top. Towards its southern end an enormous bay window was built out almost to the cliff's edge and from this an elaborate veranda extended along the west side. Part of Derwentwater was visible at the foot of the cliff and he wondered if the photograph might have been taken from a boat.

The first page was taken up with the statement *"Surprise View is a world-famous country house hotel set in the beautiful English Lake District."* Below this the names of the owners were given as Captain Bernard (Bunny) Liddle, M.C., twice mentioned in dispatches, and Celia (Ginger) Rutherford, M.B.E.

On the next page was a short history of Surprise View. In 1882 a wealthy Carlisle mill owner had built a substantial house beside the track leading up to the hamlet of Watendlath. He named the house after the spot, which, because of its unexpected breathtaking view across Derwentwater, had been known since Victorian times as Surprise View.

After World War II the house came on the market and was bought in a dilapi dated state by a young couple called Bunny Liddle and Ginger Rutherford. They restored it, built an extension and in 1950 opened it as the *Surprise View Country House Hotel*. Their intention was to run a small, high-class hotel in a beautiful location, where they could cossett discriminating guests in luxurious surroundings and provide them with the best foods and wines. From what he had heard, Oliver thought they had succeeded in all respects.

On the following pages he studied more views of the hotel, as he tried to work out its internal layout. The original house, which was south-facing, was square with an impressive Victorian frontage. Five steps led up to a columned entrance with an arched window on either side. He remembered the entrance door leading into the hall and a reception desk on the left. On the west side of the building was a large bay window overlooking Derwentwater, which he guessed would be built onto the drawing room, which he remembered led off from the left of the hall. However, he couldn't remember what was on the right of the hall.

The extension had been built onto the back of the original house and extended northwards. On its western side a long window and three smaller windows were visible behind the veranda. He remembered a long window in the dining room and thought the smaller ones would probably be the kitchen. Running along the first and second floors were five arched windows. Oliver guessed there would be the same number on the east side, making a total of twenty guest bedrooms, with a central corridor running between them to an emergency staircase at the back. He thought that the original bedrooms, the windows of which were visible at the front of the building, would be used by the owners.

Satisfied that he knew enough about Surprise View to discuss it, Oliver set off to check in. After half a mile a sign for Watendlath appeared pointing to the left. He turned off the main road across a cattle grid and followed the narrow road up through steep, rocky woodlands. After half a mile he came to Ashness Bridge, an old pack-horse bridge not much wider than the Lotus, where he had to slow to a walking pace. As he looked back it occurred to him that the view of Ashness Bridge against the backdrop of Derwentwater, must be one of the most famous in the world.

Just past Ashness Bridge was the little car park where sightseeers leave their cars before walking back to admire the view and take photographs. He glanced into it and saw that today it contained only three cars. It seemed impossible that not long ago he had planned to drive here from Essex in the Mondeo, with the hose from his vacuum cleaner and the reel of adhesive parcel tape. He shook off the dark memory and continued up the hill.

A mile above Ashness Bridge he came to another steep, wooded area and a tall beech hedge appeared on his right. Set back in it were two tall, black, wrought iron gates on sandstone pillars. Across their middle the words *SURPRISE VIEW COUNTRY HOUSE HOTEL* had been formed in the wrought iron and picked out in white.

He turned in through the open gates, past a lodge on the right which looked lived in, and drove slowly along a tarmac driveway between the glorious colours of majestic rhododendrons and azaleas. He passed a secondary driveway which led off to the right and was marked 'private', before coming to a tall hedge. Just beyond the hedge the hotel itself came into view.

Five

Surprise View looked just as elegant as it had done in the brochure. At the front of the fine sandstone building the tarmac driveway widened into a parking area for guests, which was surrounded by immaculate grass borders and flower beds. In the centre and directly opposite the columned entrance stood a tall flagpole, at the head of which a Union Jack fluttered proudly in the summer breeze as the sunlight reflected off its fresh white paint and gold finial.

Oliver parked at the end of a row of cars next to a magnificent new Rolls Royce. He got out and identified it as a new Silver Spur Turbo Saloon. For a few moments he stood and admired the metallic blue coachwork and gleaming chrome and the Spirit of Ecstasy sculpture mounted on the front. Then he collected his few pieces of luggage from the Lotus and walked towards the entrance.

At the top of the steps the columned entrance was guarded by a pair of Regency gilt and gesso *torchéres*. He entered the wood-panelled hall and looked around. As he had remembered, the reception desk was on the left with a door marked 'Office' behind, beyond which was another door marked 'Lake Room'. At the back of the hall a wide oak staircase curved upwards, besides which, according to a sign, a passageway led towards the dining room. On the right of the hall was a door marked 'Poets' Room'. He imagined the Lake Room and the Poets' Room would be lounges.

The light in the hall came from an arched window on either side of the entrance and from a large nineteenth century gilt blackamoor electric chandelier which completely filled a corner. Against one wall was an early Victorian three-piece walnut suite on cabriole legs and against another stood a nineteenth century giltwood credenza with a marble top, which contained a fine collection of Victorian glass. On the walls were an excellent oil painting of Derwentwater by a local artist and an aerial photograph of Surprise View, both in good frames. Oliver decided he was going to enjoy describing the rooms.

He noticed a magnificent longcase clock standing near the bottom of the stairs and went across to examine it. He decided to mention it in his article and thought of a suitable description: *The brass dial had a moonphase in the arch and a flowing ebbing dial in the centre, and was signed Taylor King Street WtHaven. Its case had a swan neck pediment with gilt glass inlay and an arched door flanked by fluted quartered pillars.* In the eighteenth century some of the leading clockmakers were to be found in the major ports like Whitehaven, from where their clocks were sent all over the world. He wondered if the Prime Minister would recognise this one as being the same as the one which stands just inside the entrance of number ten Downing Street.

He went to the reception desk just as a man appeared from the office behind. He was slightly older than Oliver and wore a dark suit. He greeted Oliver with a friendly smile and outstretched hand"Good afternoon, Mr. Mills. We've been expecting you. Did you have a good journey?." His lapel badge said his name was Thomas and he was the manager.

"Very good, thanks," replied Oliver. "I took delivery of a new car this morning and had a clear road most of the way, so I managed to make good time."

"You were lucky. There aren't too many tourists about this weekend. I'll show you your room and make sure you have everything, then perhaps you'd like to meet the owners." He picked up Oliver's suitcase and Oliver followed with the briefcase and photographic case.

As they climbed the stairs Thomas explained "You're in The Langdales, on the second floor. It has one of the best views of Derwentwater."

"The Langdales?," Oliver looked surprised.

Thomas smiled. "We have a tradition at Surprise View that was started by Bunny and Ginger. The bedrooms on the second floor are named after Lake District mountains and the corresponding rooms on the first floor are named after the nearest lake. Your room is The Langdales, so the room below you is Grasmere, which is overlooked by The Langdales."

Oliver laughed. "That must be unique. How do the guests like it?"

"It's very popular," replied the manager. "It's always a great ice-breaker when they arrive. In the Lake Room before dinner you can hear them discussing which room they're in, then discovering that Helvellyn is above Thirlmere, Scafell above Wastwater, High Street above Ullswater, Kirkstone above Windermere and so on. Bunny wanted to put the Prime Minister and his wife in The Old Man, which, as you probably know, is above Coniston Water, but Ginger said that while he would probably appreciate the joke, the newspapers might misinterpret it. So we're putting them in High Stile instead, which is next door but one to you."

Oliver was still amused. "High Stile also seems appropriate for a prime minister. I expect there'll be a fuss about the visit – security and so on?."

"Yes. The Special Branch had a look round when it was first arranged, then came back last week to discuss everything in more detail. They searched the place from top to bottom and took the names of the staff and the guests who will be here at the same time. The publicity will be good for business, but a visit like this can be very disruptive."

Oliver paused to admire a tall, beautifully decorated turquoise vase standing in a niche on the first floor landing. He identified it as an eighteenth century Japanese *Arita-Imari* high shouldered jar.

"Yes, it is a nice piece. I believe it's quite valuable," said Thomas, as they continued up the stairs. "I'm sure you'll like the owners. They're a popular couple. They like everybody to call them Bunny and Ginger, by the way, because they say it encourages a relaxed and friendly atmosphere. As you probably know, their names are Bernard Liddle and Celia Rutherford, but guests, staff and even our trade suppliers always end up calling them Bunny and Ginger. And while we're on the subject, everyone calls me Thomas."

"I'll remember that, Thomas – and I hope everyone will call me Oliver."

They had reached the second floor. As Oliver had guessed, a central corridor ran to a fire exit at the far end. There were five bedrooms on each side, all named after Lake District mountains or fells. He recalled that a mountain has to be over a thousand feet high, otherwise it is a fell. He read the names on the doors on the left as he passed them, hand-painted in chocolate brown on white porcelain discs: Helvellyn, Skiddaw, High Stile, Scafell, then his room, The Langdales.

The Langdales was a beautiful room, brightly lit by the sunlight which poured in through its tall arched window. It contained a magnificent nineteenth century carved rosewood four-poster bed covered by a beautifully embroidered gold bedcover. The velvet curtains and window pelmet were the same royal blue as the drape on the wall behind the bed and the gold of their tassels matched the bedcover. Oliver recognised the wall covering as a silk *moiré* from *Colefax & Fowler*, decorated with a rose border.

As well as the bed the room contained several other good antiques. He identified a highly decorated Edwardian satinwood veneered three-fold screen, a Queen Anne oak gate-leg table and two Louis XV period carved giltwood Bergére chairs. In a corner near the window stood a Victorian ladies' vanity unit on which was displayed a collection of cut-glass scent bottles. The four Victorian watercolours of Lake District scenes on the walls were originals. There was no television, but a selection of books and games had been provided. A vase of freshly-cut flowers stood on the gate-leg table.

Oliver decided to summarise his description of The Langdales with: *The general mixture of fabrics and collections combined to give the room a charming nineteenth century atmosphere*. He went to the window and looked out at Derwentwater. "What a lovely room – with a lovely view," he said.

Thomas put his suitcase on the luggage stand. "Yes, it is a nice room. The rooms on this side are more popular because of the lake view. The ones on the east side overlook the Poets Garden. All the rooms have different decors and furnishings, but we don't rate one better than another. The view is even more spectacular from the Lake Room."

He opened the door of the bathroom and Oliver went in. Unlike the bedroom it was modern and fitted out with the latest in luxury bathroomwares. The towels and toiletries were all of the finest quality.

Thomas said "If you need anything, just pick up the phone."

"Thanks, I will," replied Oliver. "I'd like to freshen up before I start. I told Bunny my plans on the phone. Do you happen to know if he's made any arrangements for the interviews and photographs?"

"Yes, we discussed it. When you're ready, I'll take you round the hotel and introduce you to our key staff. They're all quite agreeable for you to photograph them. Then at 4.30 pm Bunny and Ginger will meet you in the Lake Room. It's usually quiet in there at that time of day, so you shouldn't be disturbed and you'll be able to appreciate the view."

"That sounds fine, Thomas. I'd like to freshen up first, then I'll be down," said Oliver, as the manager went out. He unpacked his things then showered and changed into fresh clothes. When he was ready he picked up his camera and briefcase and went dowstairs.

Photography was another of Oliver's hobbies and he had become quite an expert. The normal practice on an assignment like this would be for the magazine's photographer to accompany the journalist, but at the last moment one of *Venues* two photographers was sent to Wales and the other went off sick, so Oliver decided to take the photographs himself. If they were not good enough one of the professionals would have to come and re-take them later.

Thomas was waiting for him in the hall and they began their tour of the hotel. In the office Thomas introduced him to a young woman. "This is Mia, our secretary and receptionist." In her business suit and large glasses, Mia looked the efficient secretary. As they shook hands she reminded Oliver that they had already spoken on the phone. He asked her if he could take her photograph standing at the reception desk and she readily agreed.

In the dining room the staff had finished clearing up from lunch and were preparing for dinner. A tall, good looking man of Afro-Caribbean appearance wearing an open-necked white shirt and black trousers came over. Thomas introduced him. "This is Callum, our restaurant manager. Later you will see how attractive he makes the dining room for dinner." Another man, shorter and with a neat moustache, arrived from the kitchen carrying a tray of glasses. "This is Hugo, our sommelier. Thanks to Hugo's expertise, Surprise View has one of the finest wine cellars in the world." Oliver shook hands and said he would like to return and take their photographs when everything was ready for dinner.

He followed Thomas to the kitchen, which was bigger and brighter than he had expected. Two men in spotless chefs' uniforms and three women were busy preparing dinner. Thomas beckoned to one of the men and he came over. He was perhaps a year or two younger than Oliver with short, light brown hair. Thomas introduced them. "This is Alexandre, our head chef. He's the person mainly responsible for the cuisine for which Surprise View is so famous. He's one of only four chefs in the country to have been awarded three Michelin stars."

Oliver shook hands. "I'm delighted to meet you, Alexandre. There must be a lot of work involved in preparing dinner for such a famous restaurant. How many of you are there?."

Alexandre looked pleased. "Yes, there is a lot to do. Usually there are eleven of us. Five in the main kitchen, three on preparation and three in the pastry kitchen."

Oliver asked him some more questions about his work, then got him to pose in his chef's hat while holding a butcher's knife over a large joint of meat on a stainless steel worktop, against a backdrop of copper pans.

When they had completed their tour of the kitchens Thomas led Oliver through a glass door and along a corridor towards the back door at the north end of the extension. Just before they reached it a staircase led up to the left. As they began to climb Thomas explained "This leads up to the bedroom floors, but it's for staff and emergency use only."

On the first floor a buxom, middle-aged woman emerged from a bedroom named Grasmere. Oliver realised that it was directly below The Langdales. "This is Mrs. Kemp, our housekeeper. She's doing her afternoon checks of the rooms. Her husband is our groundsman and handyman and they live in the lodge at the end of the drive." Mrs. Kemp smiled as she shook hands with Oliver. "Perhaps Mrs. Kemp will show us High Stile, the Prime Minister's room?," suggested Thomas. Mrs. Kemp seemed happy with the suggestion and the two men followed her up to the second floor.

High Stile was next door but one to The Langdales. Although it was the same size, the decor, fabrics and furnishings were different. Near the window stood a highly-polished Georgian mahogany pie-crust table, on which was a selection of magazines and newspapers. Oliver recognised a *Cumbria Scene*, *Venues* and the latest *Cumbria Star.* He also identified two Edwardian ebonised armchairs on short cabriole legs and a Georgian mahogany serpentine front dressing chest on which was arranged a Victorian collection of North American shell boxes. The white lace drapes and canopy on the Victorian brass double bed contrasted well against the dark furniture.

Although he did not consider High Stile to be any better than The Langdales, he decided to conclude his description with: *The painted effects on the wall, especially the painted cherubs, gave the room a romantic, feminine feel, accentuated by a heart-shaped chair back and echoed by a dried flower wreath above the bed. A very sentimental Victorian room.* He expressed his admiration then took a photograph of Mrs. Kemp turning down the embroidered bed cover. Thomas looked at his watch and reminded Oliver that it was time to meet the partners.

When they entered the Lake Room it was deserted. Oliver looked round and realised that its main feature was the bay window, which was even bigger than it had appeared in the brochure. Beside it a door led out onto the veranda. The view from the window was breathtaking. Not only could he see Derwentwater and its four islands spread out 800 feet below, but the full length of Bassenthwaite Lake as well. The Armathwaite Hall Hotel in its spacious grounds was clearly visible at the far end, ten miles away. The sun was reflecting off the blue surfaces of the lakes and enhancing the greens and browns and mauves of the surrounding fells. He looked down as one of the graceful, old wooden launches of the Keswick Launch Company was dropping off some passengers at the Lodore pier.

"Wow!" he exclaimed. "The view from The Langdales is good, but this is superb. The trees on either side seem to frame the picture. Now I can see why this room is so popular. May I take a photograph of you in the window, Thomas?."

When he had taken the photograph, Thomas said "There's a tradition at Surprise View that guests come into the Lake Room for an aperitif before dinner, which is why there are so many seats. They usually start arriving at seven o'clock, when one of the partners and I chat with them and bring drinks from the bar. Bunny and Ginger usually take turns. In summer the view is the main attraction, but the log fire is almost as popular in winter. Between the two and the unusual names of the bedrooms, there's no shortage of something to talk about, so they soon get to know each other."

"I'll look forward to that," said Oliver. This explained why the room had seemed so cluttered when he came in. In its centre sofas had appeared to be fighting for space with antique chairs and occasional tables, while around the walls were more chairs and sofas and several good pieces of antique furniture. A pair of George II wing arm chairs stood on either side of a large English marble fireplace, around which, on the wall and on small shelves, were numerous ornaments and collectables. A superb porcelain mounted ebony cabinet with Meissen plaques depicting romantic scenes stood against one wall and a Hepplewhite bookcase with crossbanded and panelled doors against another. Numerous pictures and mirrors hung on the Chinese wallpaper which covered the walls.

He began to work on a description of the Lake Room: *A carefully coordinated*

Victorian interior turned the wide bay window of this room into a focal point with its extravagant use of chintz and thick tasselled fringing. The Victorians had never heard of the dictum 'less is more'. No surface was left uncovered. A massing of watercolours, oils and miniatures, all in good frames, proved that the whole is greater than the parts.

His thoughts were interrupted by voices approaching from the hall and he looked round as the owners of Surprise View came in.

Six

For a moment Oliver stared, then quickly pulled himself together and smiled politely. Thomas was about to make the introductions when the man interrupted him. "It's alright, Thomas, Oliver and I have already spoken on the telephone." He turned to Oliver. "I'm Bunny Liddle and this is my dear friend and partner Ginger Rutherford."

Oliver remembered the clipped, cultured voice. Although taken aback, he managed to reply "I'm delighted to meet you," as he shook hands with them in turn.

Bunny Liddle was an imposing figure of a man for his years, standing six and a half feet tall, slim and ramrod straight. But it was his face that came as a shock to Oliver, because it looked as though at some time it had been badly burned and subjected to extensive plastic surgery, when his lips, nose, chin and right ear had been skilfully rebuilt. His right eye was almost an inch lower than his left and set deeper in its socket, being red and watery and without proper eyelid, eyelashes or eyebrows. Above it was a bald area of scalp where the silver hair was missing. When he spoke his damaged lips were pursed and he did so without smiling. As they shook hands Oliver noticed that his right hand felt smooth like a child's and deformed.

Despite his disfigurement, it was clear that Bunny Liddle paid meticulous attention to his appearance. He was wearing a double-breasted navy blazer with gold crested buttons, an expensive hand-made shirt with gold cuff-links, beige trousers with razor-sharp creases and highly polished brown leather brogues. He sported a gold tie-pin in a regimental tie and a yellow carnation in his buttonhole. What remained of his long, silver hair was immaculately coiffured and when they shook hands Oliver detected the smell of an expensive hair oil.

He turned to Ginger Rutherford. She was a fine looking woman who had somehow managed to retain some of the looks of the beautiful 1940s girl she had undoubtedly once been. She was fashionably dressed, her auburn hair showed little sign of greying, and when she smiled her eyes sparkled. Everything about her – the hairstyle, makeup, scarlet lipstick, the silk shirt fastened at the neck by a butterfly brooch, the slacks, shoes, jewellery and perfume – reminded Oliver of the 1940s.

"Bunny and I were excited to hear about the feature, Oliver. We never imagined for a moment that a magazine like *Venues* would want to give us such a splash. Of course, we've seen your articles before, so we felt tremendously privileged that you'd agreed to take it on." She had a refined accent and her voice had a deepness and huskiness that Oliver found endearing.

On meeting the owners of Surprise View for the first time, he realised that their appearances confirmed what he already knew about them – that they were products of the Second World War. However, what came as a shock was Bunny's disfigurement and he guessed that he had been wounded in action. He replied politely "I was delighted to. Surprise View has done so well and as a Cumbrian I've always followed its progress with interest and a little pride."

Bunny's damaged lips curved briefly. "Kind of you to say so, dear boy. Now, why don't we go out onto the veranda? It's such a glorious afternoon and the view and fresh air might give us some inspiration." Thomas said that he had something to attend to in the office, so Oliver thanked him for showing him round, then followed Bunny and Ginger outside.

The veranda turned out to be an ornate affair in an excellent state of repair. As he followed the partners along he thought of a suitable description: *An elaborate veranda with balusters and Classical-style columns and capitals*. Bunny selected one of the wooden tables and they sat down. Oliver put the tape recorder on the spare chair as a waitress arrived and spread a cloth on the table. Ginger explained to Oliver. "We always take tea at this time. Will you join us?."

"Tea will be fine," replied Oliver. He looked across Derwentwater and remarked "It's wonderful to be outdoors on a day like this with such a spectacular view."

They chatted about the view until the waitress returned with a serving trolley. As well as a pot of tea she had brought a selection of sandwiches, scones and home-made cakes. As she set them down the tea service caught Oliver's eye. He recognised it as a rare and valuable Minton with hand-painted botanical decoration. He wondered if he would have the opportunity to look at the markings and serial number underneath one of the pieces.

Ginger poured the tea and Bunny offered a plate of sandwiches to Oliver. "The ones at that end are Gentleman's Relish," he indicated with his deformed right hand. Oliver noticed that the fingers appeared to have been surgically created, being not much more than stubs without joints or fingernails.

He politely held up his own hand. "No thanks. It all looks delicious but I'm looking forward to my dinner tonight and I don't want to spoil it."

"Ginger and I have to attend to the guests later, so we always have something at this time," said Bunny. He helped himself to a sandwich as Ginger began to spread clotted cream and strawberry jam on a scone.

As the partners ate, Oliver looked at the view and sipped his tea. When they had finished Ginger took a jewelled cigarette case from her handbag and inserted a cigarette into a long gold holder, as Bunny produced a lighter from his blazer pocket. When she had inhaled some smoke she turned to Oliver with an apologetic smile "I've never been able to give up this disgusting habit, but I do try not to smoke in the public rooms. I hope you don't mind."

Oliver wondered if a lifetime of smoking was responsible for the deepness and huskiness in her voice, which he found so attractive. He smiled and said. "I don't mind at all. Now, if you've no objection, I'd like to save time by recording the interview, then I can write it up when I get home."

"Excellent idea. Where would you like us to start?," replied Bunny.

"At the beginning. How you met, why you bought Surprise View and opened it as a hotel, how you built up the business, the foods and wines you serve, the guests who come, the awards you've won and so on. Perhaps you could establish a dialogue by taking it in turns to speak. I may interrupt with the odd question." Oliver put the tape recorder on the table with the microphone between them and switched it on.

Bunny smiled at Ginger. "Isn't this fun, darling. You go first," he said, touching her affectionately on the knee.

Holding her cigarette at a safe distance, Ginger leaned towards the microphone and began to speak. "Bunny and I met just before the war ended. He was in a tank regiment which saw a lot of action after D-Day. He was badly wounded near Hamburg and got flown back to a military hospital in Middlesex where I was nursing, which specialised in burns."

Bunny interrupted her. "Ginger was a wonderful nurse. She speeded my recovery by devoting a lot of time to me and keeping up my spirits. When I was eventually discharged I didn't think I would see her again. I managed to get a temporary job helping to run a hotel not far away which was owned by an army friend. It was a wonderful surprise when Ginger came in one evening with a party of friends from the hospital. We agreed to meet the following evening to catch up on what we had been doing and soon we were seeing a lot of each other."'

Ginger: "It was wonderful to be together again, but after a few months we began to tire of London. We were both considering new careers, so we formed the idea of running a business together. We decided we would like to have a small, high-class hotel somewhere in the country, where we could provide our guests with the best of everything. We had heard of a couple of such places that had recently opened and were doing well, calling themselves country house hotels."

Bunny: "We thought that after the austerity of the war years, there would be people who would appreciate such places and be prepared to pay the prices. Ginger had excelled in cookery at her finishing school so we decided that if she did the cooking and I looked after the front of house, we could get it up and running without many staff. By that time we both had some savings, so we began to look around for somewhere. We contacted estate agents all over the country and kept an eye on the property advertisements. Although we looked at several places, they were either too big, too small, too dilapidated, in the wrong location or too expensive."

Ginger: "After a year without finding anywhere we were becoming frightfully despondent. Then we heard about a place called Surprise View, near Keswick in Cumberland. Bunny had gone to a boarding school nearby, so he knew the area and thought it sounded promising. We made an appointment and drove up and were shown round by the agent. We immediately fell in love with the location and the view, but the house was terribly dilapidated. It hadn't been lived in since 1939 and had been used by the army during the war. Goodness knows what they had been up to, because there was some frightful damage.

Bunny: "We made the vendors an offer, which they eventually accepted. Then we applied for planning permission to build an extension and obtained builders' estimates. When everything seemed feasible we took the plunge and bought it."

Ginger: "We were so excited that we immediately gave notice to our employers and landlady. We couldn't wait to get away from London, but it was another three months before we were heading north in our little M.G. with all our belongings packed into the back. We found some temporary employment at a hotel in Windermere which was looking for seasonal workers, so we had somewhere to live until we were ready to move into Surprise View and were able to gain some experience of the hotel business at the same time.

Bunny: "Of course, everything took much longer than we had expected. It was six months before the builders started and another twelve before they had finished. Fortunately, our employer in Windermere said we could stay on as long as we wanted, having discovered Gingers' talents in the kitchen and mine as the restaurant manager. We finally took up residence in the summer of 1949, although the builders were still working on the extension."

Ginger: "We moved into the two floors above the house, where we still live today. Once we were here we were on hand to keep an eye on things, so progress became faster. We spent a lot of money on the interior decor and furnishings, because we wanted everything to be of a very high standard. By Easter 1950 the place was looking splendid and we were ready for our first guests. At first we had only ten guest bedrooms, as we had decided not to use the rooms on the second floor until they were needed. We had brochures printed which we sent to a lot of people we had got to know in London. We also placed advertisements in three society magazines. Soon we began to get enquiries, then our first bookings."

Bunny: "Our first guests included some lively and well-connected people who thoroughly enjoyed themselves. Ginger and I pulled out all the stops and gave them first class attention. Ginger excelled in the kitchen and we served them some very fine wines. When they went home they spread the word about Surprise View and soon we began to get enquiries from other wealthy and well-to-do people."

Ginger: "It was Bunny's wit and charm that attracted them more than anything else. The dear boy puts everyone at ease, whoever they are. Among our first guests were an earl and countess with a reputation for being difficult, whom neither of us had met before. After dinner on their first night, Bunny had them in pleats of laughter with his stories about the war, then he played the piano and they sang along with everyone else. They enjoyed their stay so much that they booked for the following year and pursuaded some of their friends to come too."

Bunny: "We decided that every year we would close after Christmas and reopen for Easter, to enable us to have maintainance work done and take a holiday.

During our first year we managed to run things ourselves, with the help of two part-time staff. But the bookings for the following year were coming in so fast that we decided to open the second floor bedrooms and advertise for a chef, housekeeper and several other full-time and part-time staff. Dear Ginger had done a magnificent job with the cooking, but it was clear that we now needed a professional chef. We received an enquiry from the second chef at a Park Lane hotel who was fed up with London and wanted to move to the country, so we took him on."

Ginger: "Gaston turned out to be a superb chef. It was thanks to him that we won the Restaurant of the Year Award in 1959. I had managed the cooking when we had only a handful of guests, but I lacked the experience to provide a full cordon bleu menu for a busy restaurant every day. By now our reputation was growing in the Lake District and we were having to provide meals for local people and casual visitors, as well as for our resident guests. At first we had no proper wine cellar, so we converted the old cellar under the house and stocked it with some very fine wines. Then we were fortunate to find a sommelier with an international reputation, who also wanted to get away from London."

Bunny: "We went from strength to strength. By 1965 we had eight full-time and ten part-time staff and we needed more. Of course, having so many staff presented administrative problems so we advertised for a manager and once again we made a good choice. Most of the original staff have now gone, but we've managed to replace them with others equally good."

Ginger: "People come to Surprise View from all over the world. They include royalty, politicians, actors, supermodels, rock stars and business tycoons. But whether they be duchess or dustman, Bunny treats them all alike. Of course, we often have to be terribly discreet, because the newspapers sometimes snoop around when they get wind of a celebrity. I see there have already been reports about the Prime Minister's visit next month"

Bunny: "Celebrity seems to be replacing religion as the opiate of the masses, if the television programmes are anything to go by."

Oliver smiled at Bunny's observation. As the flow of the dialogue seemed to have faltered he asked "Have you won many awards?."

"People have been wonderfully kind to us," replied Bunny. "We won the Restaurant of the Year Award seven times, the Hotel of the Year Award four times, the

Restaurant Laureate Gold Award three times, a Cuisine Connoisseur Rosette five times, the Lake Distict Hotel of the Year twelve times and a Taste of Britain Blue Ribbon Award eight times. Of course, we would never have won them without our wonderful staff."

"I suppose the setting of Surprise View is a big attraction?," prompted Oliver.

"The guests adore it," replied Ginger. "The view is a big attraction of course, but all of the Lake District is popular, provided the weather isn't too bad. Most like to do some walking while they're here, partly to work off their meals. The most popular walk is to Ashness Bridge, a mile down the road, but the more energetic ones go up to Watendlath, a delightful collection of cottages and farm buildings beside a little tarn, two miles in the other direction."

"Unfortunately, there are too many people driving cars in the Lake District nowadays," said Bunny. "Narrow roads like these were never intended for motor cars. Although there are passing places, the amount of traffic in the summer makes it almost impossible for local people to go about their business. I can see no alternative to a complete ban on cars, except for the local residents."

"Finally, have you any regrets about opening Surprise View all those years ago?," asked Oliver.

Bunny took Ginger's hand and smiled lovingly at her. Turning to Oliver she said "I know I'm speaking for both of us when I say that the years Ginger and I have spent here have been blissfully happy and we hope to have many more."

"Thank you very much," said Oliver. As he switched off the tape recorder he thought how happy they looked and how well matched they were. "I think you've given me all the information I need, but if there is anything else I hope I can ask you. Now, before you go, may I take a photograph of you standing outside the entrance?"

Ginger stood up. "Yes, we'd love you to, Oliver. We're so looking forward to seeing ourselves in *Venues*, aren't we darling?."

As he followed the partners through the hall, Oliver realised that he had taken a genuine liking to them. He got them to pose on the steps and as he looked through the viewfinder he decided they made a very handsome couple in spite of Bunny's disfigurement.

Before leaving Oliver to return to their private quarters, Bunny and Ginger invited him to join the other guests in the Lake Room before dinner. Oliver assured them that he would be there, adding that he first wanted to take some photographs in the hotel grounds.

He hung his camera round his neck and walked towards the west side of the hotel, but discovered that he was prevented from reaching the clifftop by a low hedge which ran from the corner of the building. In it was a locked gate marked 'private', which he imagined would give access to the west side of the building for maintenance work. As he still had an unobstructed view over the gate he took a photograph of Derwentwater with Bassenthwaite Lake in the distance.

He went in search of the Poets' Garden and discovered it through an opening in the tall hedge which he had passed as he arrived. It turned out to be an immaculate, formal garden, extending along the east side of the hotel, enclosed on its other three sides by the tall hedge. When he looked up at the hotel he realised that guests would get a good view of the garden both from the bedrooms and the Poets' Room.

Two gravel paths crossed the garden at right angles, dividing it into quarters, each with a different theme. He went into the first area on the left which faced the Poets' Room and realised how both the garden and the room had got their names.

A circular gravel path ran round a raised flower bed and around its outside perimeter were six bronze busts resting on pedestals of Borrowdale slate. The carved faces were almost level with his own and as he walked round them he read the names on the plaques:

William Wordsworth | **Dorothy Wordsworth**

Samuel Taylor Coleridge | **Hartley Coleridge**

Thomas de Quincey | **Robert Southey**

The central flower bed was a mass of miniature daffodils which were now dying back and he imagined how beautiful they must have been a few weeks earlier. As he took a photograph of the scene he was reminded of William Wordsworth's most famous poem and thought what a fitting memorial this was to the six Lake Poets.

He strolled through the garden, admiring the neat borders, until he reached the tall hedge at the far end. In it another gate marked 'private' prevented him going any further. He looked through the bars across a driveway into a well-stocked kitchen garden. He realised that this was the secondary driveway he had passed, connecting the main drive to another carpark at the back of the hotel. On the far side of this carpark and twenty yards north of the hotel was a modern building surrounded by trees, which looked as though it might be the staff accommodation.

He walked back through the Poets' Garden, pausing on the way to take more photographs and to chat with some other guests. He intended to take a shot of the front of the hotel but his film was finished, so he returned to the carpark, unlocked the Lotus and got a new film from the glove compartment. He was standing beside the car fitting it into his camera when an Aston Martin arrived along the drive, swung round in front of the hotel and parked.

Oliver was irritated, for two reasons. Not only was the Aston Martin parked in such a position that it was blocking the view for his next photograph, but it was one of the new V8 coupé models in metallic dark green, the sports car he would really have liked, had he been able to afford one.

The driver's door opened and a man got out. He was in his forties, of medium height, somewhat overweight and balding, wearing a business suit which was badly crumpled and had dandruff on the shoulders. Oliver was thinking, rather unkindly, that his appearance did not fit the image of such a car when the passenger door opened and out stepped the most beautiful woman he had ever seen.

She was slim with a superb figure and a pale complexion. Her long black hair was drawn back into a French pleat, making her slender neck seem longer than it was. The shapely legs below her navy skirt were encased in glossy navy stockings and the stilletto shoes on her dainty feet looked expensive, Italian and sexy. When she turned round, her face had a classical beauty, with high cheek bones, a wide mouth and large, expressive blue eyes. Her red woollen jumper, pulled in at the waist by a belt which matched her shoes, complimented her fine figure.

The man lifted two expensive suitcases out of the Aston Martin and locked it, then set off towards the entrance with the woman following. As they passed Oliver standing beside the Lotus with the open camera in his hands the man ignored him, but she returned his friendly nod and smile. Oliver's eyes followed her and as she climbed the steps and disappeard from view, he decided that not only was she very beautiful, but she had a sexy walk as well.

He finished fitting the film, but decided to leave taking the last photograph until the morning, when the Aston Martin might have gone. Instead, he would take the ones of Callum and Hugo, as the dining room would be looking its best by now.

When he entered the hall, the couple were at the reception being greeted by Mia. Oliver paused to examine the aerial photograph of Surprise View on the wall. He decided it must have been taken on a clear day from a few hundred feet, because it showed clearly the hotel in its grounds and a small expanse of Derwentwater as well. He looked along the bedroom windows and found The Langdales on the second floor at the north end.

The longcase clock began to strike six o'clock. When it finished he heard Mia saying "I have your letter here Mrs. McBain. You asked for a lake view this time, so we're putting you in Grasmere on the first floor. You've stayed with us before, so I expect you'll be used to the names. It's just for the one night again, isn't it?."

"That's right. Our wedding anniversary has come round again. Grasmere will be fine. I seem to remember it's at the far end on the left." Mrs. McBain spoke with a soft Scottish accent and her voice had an attractive musical ring.

Mr. McBain looked at Mia for the first time. "Is the bar open?," he asked her abruptly without a smile. Unlike his wife, his Scottish accent was neither soft nor musical.

"It's just opening, Mr. McBain. It opens at six o'clock every day, but if you'd like a drink at any other time one of the waiters will bring you whatever you want," she replied pleasantly.

Oliver continued towards the dining room in search of Callum and Hugo. He was feeling slightly disturbed by all this and wasn't sure why. The McBains seemed too unsuited to be a couple. As well as being very beautiful, she seemed to be educated, sophisticted, and charming. By contrast, not only was he physically rather unattractive, but he seemed to be lacking in the social graces to the point of rudeness. As his wife was speaking to Mia he had leaned against the reception desk yawning and looking bored. When Mia had told them they were to be in Grasmere he had raised his eyebrows, as though contemptuous of such idiocy.

Yes, altogether an unprepossessing sort of man for such a beautiful woman, decided Oliver, as he entered the dining room.

Seven

When Oliver entered the Lake Room shortly after seven o'clock, it was already half full. An elderly man and woman sitting near the door smiled at him. He looked around and saw an assortment of smartly dressed people seated in groups and understood why so many chairs and sofas were needed. All the seats in the bay window were taken and a middle-aged couple were standing there admiring the view. Aware that he was the only one on his own, Oliver found an armchair in the middle of the room and sat down.

Thomas arrived with a tray of drinks, which he distributed among the group in the window and left them a plate of canapés. He turned to the standing couple and chatted with them about the view for a few moments before taking their order for drinks. Oliver suddenly noticed the McBains in the two wing arm chairs beside the fireplace, with drinks and canapés on the table between them. She was half facing Oliver and he thought she looked stunning.

She was wearing a two-tone blue moiré silk dress with a long slit up the left side and held up by shoestring straps. Its deep vee plunging neckline was held together by a gold clasp which complimented her strappy stiletto sandals and evening bag, both of pale gold fine-grained Italian leather. The finishing touches were a necklace of over a hundred diamonds crowned by two huge blue sapphires, a matching diamond bracelet and diamond and sapphire dropper earrings. Her engagement ring was petal-shaped with an enormous solitaire diamond at its centre, surrounded by clusters of smaller ones forming the petals, and her watch an exquisite creation by Cartier with a diamond-studded bracelet. She had changed her hairstyle and it was now piled on top in soft curls and held in place by a gold clasp.

As Oliver stared at Mrs. McBain he realised that it was not her clothes, jewellery and hairstyle that made her so stunningly attractive, but her natural beauty, figure and deportment, which resembled those of a professional model. His eyes moved to her husband. He was still wearing the same suit, shirt and shoes, but had put on a tie and brushed most of the dandruff from his shoulders.

He heard Bunny's voice and turned round. He was now looking even more imposing than before in full evening dress. He went up to the elderly couple near the door and chatted with them for a few minutes, before moving on to another group. Oliver noticed that although his scarred lips were pursed when he spoke and he rarely smiled, he was clearly at ease with everyone and enjoying himself.

Thomas returned with the drinks and canapés for the couple at the window. Then he greeted Oliver and asked him what he would like. Oliver asked for a Campari soda and Thomas went to get it.

Suddenly Bunny was towering over him. "My dear boy, I'm so glad you managed to come. I hope you're finding everything satisfactory. Did you get all the photographs you wanted?" His watery, red right eye seemed to fix Oliver as he spoke.

"Yes, thanks. I got the outside shots, then I took ones of Callum in the dining room and Hugo in the wine cellar," he replied. He did not tell Bunny that he had been unable to take the one of the front of the hotel because of the McBains' Aston Martin.

"I'm so glad. This sort of thing boosts staff morale enormously," said Bunny."

I was very impressed with your wine cellar. I had no idea you had such a big stock. I'm no expert, but Hugo showed me some superb vintages. He had changed for dinner and posed for me in front of his best clarets, holding a bottle of 1945 Chateau Petrus as though it was a new-born baby."

Bunny's lips curved briefly. "Hugo is such a treasure. He had a first-class training and is very highly qualified. He has contacts all over the world, so we're able to get hold of some extremely rare vintages that you won't find elsewhere in this country."

A younger party arrived and managed to find seats, although by now the room was almost full. Callum appeared, resplendent in tails, and began to work his way round the groups, handing out menus and pointing out the special dishes. Bunny announced "Duty calls. I must circulate, as I like to meet everyone before they go into the dining room. I do hope you enjoy your dinner." He moved on to another group.

Callum came and handed Oliver an enormous menu. "Alexandre has asked me to tell you that he particularly recommends the Lomo de Orza this evening. It's one of his summer specialities." He pointed to it and Oliver read. *Lomo is pork loin and the Orza is the terracotta dish in which it is traditionally marinated.* Callum explained

"It's served with salad and a potato rosti. It's popular on warm evenings because its light. I'll come back when you've had time to decide."

No sooner had Callum gone than Hugo arrived with the wine list. After pointing out the different sections he said "I have some half bottles of a 1977 Montrachet Grand Cru and a 1961 Chateau Latour, if you're interested."

"In that case I'll have a half of the Montrachet. I have to make sensible notes this evening and a bottle would be too much." He had already decided what he was going to eat. Hugo moved to the next table and Oliver looked round the room. He realised that not everyone was staying at the hotel when he heard Cumbrian accents from a group behind him and decided they were a local family out celebrating.

A nearby couple began to chat with two young couples who had just arrived. They were laughing about the names of the bedrooms. One couple who were in Ennerdale discovered that another were in Pillar, directly above them. The third couple, who were in Helvellyn, were wondering what the room below them was called. Oliver thought it was probably Thirlmere.

The names reminded him of two reports he had written when he was at the *Cumbria Star*. One was on a fatal accident, when two climbers who were roped together fell to their deaths from Pillar Rock. The other was when the Anglers Hotel had to be pulled down, because of plans to raise the level of Ennerdale Water to provide more water for the Sellafield nuclear plant. After the lovely old lakeside building had gone for ever the Water Board changed its mind. Oliver was incensed, because his parents had often taken him there as a child for Sunday lunch. He remembered the red creeper on the walls, the distant chugging of the generator which supplied it with electricity and the lapping of the water against the stone jetty where the rowing boat was moored.

His nostalgic memories were interrupted by Thomas bringing his Campari and canapés. Oliver swirled the ice and slice of orange around the glass to mix the denser red liquid with the soda water. He liked the dryness of Campari and it sharpened his appetite before a meal. A middle-aged couple who had nodded when he came in were now smiling at him. "Is this your first visit to Surprise View?," Oliver asked them.

"No, we come every year at this time for a few days," replied the man.

"We adore the Lake District. How about you?," asked his wife.

"I used to live nearby, but I've only been here once before, a long time ago," replied Oliver.

They chatted about the hotel and the Lake District. Oliver discovered that he was a merchant banker from Godalming, whose hobby was collecting fine wines. Their conversation was brought to an end when Callum came and handed them menus.

Oliver's attention was drawn back to the McBains. He was trying to attract Bunny's attention by waving. Bunny, his lips pursed tighter than usual, excused himself to the group he was with and went towards the fireplace. McBain handed him his empty whisky glass. Bunny looked enquiringly at Mrs. McBain but she shook her head. As he went to get her husband's whisky Oliver watched as she leaned forward to select a *Venues* from the pile on the table.

He was suddenly aware of Callum standing beside him. "Have you decided, or would you like some more time?"

"I've made up my mind" replied Oliver. "For the starter I'd like the fried scallops with provencale vegetables, a rosette of smoked salmon and Sauterne sauce; then I'll have both the fish and the sorbet courses; for the main course I was tempted to have the fried calf's liver, but Alexandre's Lomo de Orza sounds too good to miss, so I'll have that." Callum thanked him and said he would let him know when his table was ready.

All the seats in the Lake Room were now taken and the hubbub of conversation was growing louder. Oliver counted nearly forty people, as Bunny and Thomas circulated, making sure they all had drinks. Callum went to the McBains for their order and as she leaned forward to put her drink on the table Oliver realized just how revealing her dress was. When they had given their orders he caught another interesting glimpse as she picked it up again. She looked up and smiled at him. Taken aback, he returned it. She glanced quickly at her husband to see if he had noticed anything but he was busy turning the pages of the wine list.

Oliver made an effort not to stare at the McBains. He looked around the room again and for the next ten minutes occupied himself on a suitable description of the scene, until Callum returned to tell him that his table was ready. He put his glass on a tray and Oliver followed him out of the Lake Room and through the hall.

HE HAD ALREADY SEEN THE dining room in daylight, but now, with the light from the big crystal chandelier sparkling in the silver and glass, it looked spectacular. The walls were covered with a silk fabric in crimson and pink stripes, which matched the fabric of the chairs. The plaster mouldings were picked out in gold and each table had its individual lamp with hand-decorated shade in antique gold. Pictures and mirrors hung on three of the walls, while the fourth was taken up by the long window which gave a panoramic view of Derwentwater across the veranda. Oliver remembered that on winter evenings a curtain was drawn across it and logs burned in the big fireplace.

The twenty or so tables were arranged around a central display of elaborately decorated cold foods set on a white linen cloth, the centrepiece of which was an enormous, beautifully decorated, glazed boar's head with an apple lodged in its open mouth. Oliver paused to admire it and remarked to Callum "It's unusual to find displays like this in restaurants nowadays. It must be a dying art."

"Yes, it is, but it's one of Alexandre's many talents. He taught himself in his spare time when he first came to Surprise View," replied Callum.

Oliver followed him to a small table set for one, below an oil portrait of two ladies. He thought it was by Lely, but he wasn't sure, so he made a mental note to come back in the morning for a closer look. Callum put his drink on the table and pulled out the chair. Oliver sat down and looked around the room. The tables were quickly filling up and he guessed that not all the diners had gone into the Lake Room for an aperitif.

A waiter brought him some iced water. He was Asian and his badge gave his name as Rafiq. Ginger, now in a long evening gown, appeared at his side with a basket of different breads. "Bunny and I take turns between the Lake Room and the dining room," she explained. She began to describe the breads as she indicated them with a pair of silver tongues. Oliver chose some olive bread.

When Ginger had moved to the next table, he sat back, sipped his Campari and looked around the room again. He wondered how best to describe the scene and took a small notebook from his pocket. He had noticed some valuable antiques near the entrance and could still see them from where he sat. He thought for a moment then wrote: *This superb dining room could have been furnished by a wealthy Victorian collector. At the entrance an 18th. century marble bust sat happily with an 18th. century French chair alongside a Victorian sideboard and cellaret. The terracotta figures picked up the warm colour of the walls.*

Callum was leading the McBains to a nearby table. Oliver noticed other diners turn their heads to admire her. Callum put McBain's whisky at the setting nearest Oliver and pulled out both chairs. McBain promptly sat down beside his glass, obliging his wife to take the other one, which also faced Oliver. As she leaned forward for Callum to push in her chair Oliver caught another revealing glimpse.

He had always enjoyed good food and wine and although limited to the amount he could drink because of his work, he was looking forward to his dinner immensely. As he finished his Campari he looked round the room again and thrilled at the glittering spectacle. Almost all the tables were now taken and the hubbub of conversation was growing louder as the diners began to relax.

As well as Callum, Hugo and Rafiq, he counted two other waiters and three waitresses, all looking smart as they moved briskly between the tables. Also helping were a teenage boy and girl in white shirts, whom he thought might be catering students gaining work experience. Some of the diners were already being served their starters and Hugo was busy distributing bottles of wine and ice buckets.

Rafiq appeared with his starter as Hugo arrived with the wine. Oliver tried the Montrachet and expressed his approval. Hugo left the half bottle in an ice bucket beside the table. The fried scallops were superb. As he ate them he watched a young waitress serve the McBains their starters, then Hugo arrived at their table with two bottles of house wine, one white and one red, and invited McBain to try them. Oliver could not hear his reply but saw him shake his head. When Hugo had gone McBain picked up the white wine from its cooler and filled both their glasses. He promptly drained his own and refilled it. His wife lifted her glass and as she sipped it her eyes met Oliver's and they exchanged smiles. Once again she glanced quickly at her husband before picking up her knife and fork.

Oliver was becoming aware that Mrs. McBain was distracting him from his work. He told himself that his interest in her was unprofessional and he should pull himself together. She might be a beautiful woman with an unprepossessing husband, but that did not necessarily mean that she would appreciate his (Oliver's) attentions. In any case, the McBains were none of his business and he had work to do. Remembering the purpose of his visit, he began to make notes about the food and wine.

Rafiq brought his fish course, a fillet of halibut served with mariniere sauce and a cheese soufflé. It tasted wonderful and as he ate he tried not to look at the McBains. Hugo came and topped up his wine. There was sudden laughter from the far side of the room. The local family were clearly enjoying their celebration and Oliver thought how happy they looked. As he sipped his Montrachet he wondered if one day he would have a family to take out to a restaurant like this.

His attention was drawn back to the McBains as the waitress served them their fish course. McBain had topped up his white wine and was offering more to his wife, but she was holding her hand over her glass and shaking her head. She said something that must have annoyed him, because Oliver saw the back of his neck redden. For a few moments they exchanged angry words, then sat in silence, looking away from each other. McBain picked up his glass and took a deep swallow, before starting on his fish. Oliver could see the unhappiness in her face as she picked up her own knife and fork.

Rafiq brought Oliver's sorbet. He looked up at him and asked "How long have you been working at Surprise View, Rafiq?."

"Only for six months, sir. I used to work at my uncle's restaurant in Carlisle, but now I prefer it here because everyone is very kind," was his reply.

When he had finished the sorbet Oliver made some more notes. Then he picked up his glass and sipped the Montrachet as he looked round the room again. The waitress was now serving the McBains their sorbets. McBain picked up the bottle of white wine and this time his wife allowed him to top up her glass. He poured what was left into his own and swallowed it in one gulp.

Rafiq took away Oliver's sorbet dish and brought his main course, the Lomo de Orza. The neatly arranged slices of pork were partly covered by the oily marinade. He served the potatoes and left him a side-salad, as Hugo came to top up his half-empty glass.

Oliver took another sip of the Montrachet, then began his main course. It was delicious. The pork, which was meltingly tender, was made wonderfully flavoursome by the marinade, and the salad and potato rosti were perfect accompaniments. He decided to compliment Alexandre on the dish and mention it in his article.

Again his attention was drawn back to the McBains, where the young waitress had just served them their main course. McBain was resting one hand on her waist and using the other to prod his steak with his fork, as he spoke to her in what looked like a patronising manner, as though explaining how steak should be cooked. The girl blushed and smiled nervously. When she had hurried away to the kitchen Mrs. McBain leaned forward and said something to her husband. Oliver saw his neck redden again as they began another heated exchange. In the silence that followed McBain angrily picked up the bottle of house red, filled his glass and swallowed it in one. Then he filled it up again.

The raised voices had caused people at nearby tables to look round. Oliver was furious at McBain's behaviour and was feeling desperately sorry for his wife, who now seemed close to tears. McBain continued to glare across the room in silence as his neck slowly resumed its usual pink colour, but it was clear to Oliver that he was rapidly getting drunk. He tried not to make matters worse for her by staring.

He usually enjoyed the first half of a dinner more than the second. An aperitif sharpened his appetite and the first couple of glasses of wine relaxed him and increased his anticipation of the meal. After the starter and fish courses he would still be looking forward to the main course, but by the end of the main course he would usually be feeling full. Tonight, however, was different. Because he had to describe each course he had deliberately chosen lighter dishes to leave room for a dessert. He had already seen a trolley of delicious cold sweets and now Rafiq brought him a list of desserts and puddings. Oliver ordered the *Surprise View Syllabub.*

He made more notes about the dining room then looked round again. Most of the diners were finishing their main courses and some were being served their desserts. He spotted the merchant banker and his wife at a table near the door and smiled.

A cheer went up from the family celebration. Hugo had uncorked a bottle of champagne and was filling four flutes. The lights were dimmed and a waiter appeared with a birthday cake covered in blazing candles and took it to their table. The young man blew them out and as the lights went up again the family began to sing "Happy birthday to you," as other diners joined in.

A belch from McBain drew his attention back to the couple. He had pushed the remains of his steak away and was now slumped in his chair with his elbows on the table and his glass held in front of his face. He drained it and quickly re-filled it again. Oliver noticed that his posture had deteriorated and more dandruff had appeared on his suit as the meal had progressed. His neck had reddened again, but the cause now, he knew, was the drink. He estimated that he had consumed three quarters of both the white and the red wines, as well as the three large whiskies and perhaps other drinks at the bar before dinner. He was staring into the distance and was clearly the worse for wear.

Oliver's attention was attracted to his wife's legs under the table. She had crossed her right leg over her left and was dangling her stiletto sandal by its strap from her toes. The foot was slim and shapely, with a deep arch and red painted toenails. For some reason Oliver found the sight extremely erotic. He looked up and realised that she was watching him with amusement. The light from the table lamp seemed to be sparkling not only in her diamonds, but in those lovely eyes as well. He smiled and discreetly raised his glass to her, then felt a thrill of excitement as she continued to hold his gaze and run the tip of her tongue around her half open lips.

The spell was broken as Rafiq arrived with Oliver's syllabub and Callum went to the McBains table for their dessert order. When McBain did not reply but continued to stare into the distance his wife looked up at Callum and shook her head. McBain picked up his glass, drained it, then emptied the bottle into it. As Callum was going away he turned and asked him for the wine list, catching his glass with his arm and spilling red wine on the tablecloth. His wife looked furious.

Hugo arrived with the wine list and covered the spill with a napkin. McBain began to slowly turn the pages as his wife and Hugo watched him. Eventually he made up his mind. Hugo looked to where he pointing. "But that's the 1980 Chateau D'Yquem premier Grand Cru. It's a Sauterne, sir," he said in surprise.

His wife suddenly looked anxious. She leaned forward, put a cautionary hand on his arm and whispered something. McBain's neck flushed and his voice became raised "We're celebrating for God's sake. It's only once a year." He looked up at Hugo and said " We'll have a bottle of that."

"Yes, sir." Hugo bowed slightly and went to get it.

The syllabub was delicious. When Oliver had finished it he looked around again and noticed that other diners were already leaving.

Hugo returned to the McBains' table with the Chateau D'Yquem and two clean glasses. He uncorked it and poured some into McBain's glass. He tasted it and immediately screwed up his face in disgust. "Christ almighty, that's bloody sweet. I can't drink that."

"But it's a Sauterne, sir. It's supposed to be sweet. It's usually drunk with a dessert or pudding," explained Hugo.

"I don't care what it is, I'm not having it." McBain's voice was now very loud and his neck had turned crimson.

Heads were turning and his wife looked embarrassed. Suddenly she stood up and took him by the arm. "Come on, you've had enough," she told him in a no-nonsense voice. McBain lurched to his feet without protest and as she led him from the dining room she gave Oliver a look of exasperation which dissolved into a smile.

When the McBains had gone Ginger hurried over with an anxious look. "My dear Oliver, I'm most terribly sorry about that. Clearly, the man had too much to drink. That sort of thing does happen occasionally, but it must have been a frightful bore for you. The poor young waitress was quite upset, so Callum took over the table. They come every year to celebrate their wedding anniversary and he always drinks a lot, but he's never been as bad as this before. His wife's such a darling, too. I really don't know why she puts up with him."

"Don't worry about it, Ginger. I found it quite amusing. It would have taken a lot more than that to spoil such a wonderful dinner."

"That's most sweet of you, Oliver. Now, I hope you'll join the others in the Poets' Room for coffee and liqueurs."

Eight

By the time Oliver reached the Poets' Room it was almost full. It was of similar size to the Lake Room with about the same number of seats, but the decor and furnishings were different. Pale yellow curtains had been pulled across the French window which, as he had already discovered, gave a splendid view of the Poets' Garden in daylight.

He heard piano music and saw Bunny seated at a grand piano in the far corner. Some of the guests had gathered round him and were singing the words of the Cole Porter song he was playing, so Oliver went across and joined in. The piano was an exceptionally fine Erard and as he watched Bunny's hands at work on the keyboard it was evident that having a deformed one did not prevent him from being an expert pianist.

When the song ended Oliver went to examine a bookcase that had caught his eye. He identified it as a Chippendale period mahogany breakfront with a carved cornice and fluted pilasters. Through its locked glass doors he could see a collection of rare works of the Lake Poets, including several manuscripts and first editions.

Oliver had not expected to find the McBains there, imagining that she would have taken him upstairs. He was, therefore, surprised to see them sitting on a sofa. Realising that all the seats had now been taken, she smiled at Oliver and moved along to make room for him on her other side. As he went towards her he was so captivated with her smile that for a moment he did not notice that her husband's chin was resting on his chest and he had fallen asleep.

"I hope I'm not intruding, but all the seats seem to be taken," he said, concious of her closeness as he sat down beside her.

She turned to face him. "Not at all. Did you enjoy your dinner?"

"It was wonderful. How about you?"

"Not as much as previous years," she replied, glancing meaningfully at her inebriated husband.

Callum arrived and they ordered coffee. He asked them if they would like a liqueur. Ignoring her husband, Mrs. McBain asked for a Drambuie. Oliver ordered a Laphroaig malt. Callum asked them which rooms they should be charged to.

"Grasmere." "The Langdales." Their responses came together and they burst out laughing.

After he had gone Oliver said "If my knowledge of the Lake District is correct your room must be directly below mine."

She smiled. "Yes. I believe Grasmere does nestle below The Langdales." He saw the mischief in her eyes and realised she was flirting with him. Her husband began to snore softly. She glanced at him to make sure that he was asleep, then smiled again at Oliver. His hand slipped down between them and brushed against the area of her thigh exposed by the slit in her long dress. Her hand followed his and pressed it against her bare flesh, causing a thrill to run through him which felt like an electric shock.

They quickly removed their hands as Callum returned and began to set the coffee on the table in front of them. When he had gone they leaned forward to pour it and their faces came close together, then as she handed him his cup their fingers touched. As they sat back on the sofa, chatting and enjoying their drinks, their legs touched and remained pressed together. Bunny began to play the piano again as McBain continued to snore quietly and rhythmically.

When the tune ended McBain gave a groan and opened his eyes. His face which, like his neck, had undergone various shades of pink and red during the evening, had now turned grey, and beads of sweat had broken out on his forehead. "Better go to my bed," he muttered.

The pain returned to his wife's face. "Duty calls," she said resignedly, as for the second time that evening she helped her drunken husband to his feet under the curious gazes of other guests. Oliver recognised her embarrassment and, wanting to help, stood up and took hold of McBain's other arm. She said briskly "It's alright thanks, I can manage him. It's been nice to meet you and thanks for the drink." Oliver could only stand and watch with concern as she led him into the hall. As she disappeared from view he realised that they did not even know each others' names.

He continued to sit alone on the sofa, looking round the room and thinking about the beautiful Mrs. McBain. Callum brought him more coffee, but he did not have another Laphroaig. As he sipped his coffee he listened to Bunny's expert playing and thought about her. After a while a hush fell on the room as Ginger, elegant in evening gown and jewellery, joined Bunny at the piano and began to sing 'Lili Marlene' to his accompaniment. Her performance was in the style of Marlene Dietrich and she managed to capture much of the mesmerising and sexually alluring persona of Dietrich as a husky-voiced femme fatale, using her gold cigarette holder to great effect as a stage prop. The audience loved the performance and as the applause died down Oliver guessed that the partners had perfected it over many years.

When the entertainment was finished he took out his notebook and looked around the room. After a few moments thought he wrote: *The grand piano successfully evoked the mood of a light Victorian interior. The walls were painted in distressed drags of buttery yellow and the drapes were made from ivory silk. The generally pale shades and the numerous embroidered cushions added to the femininity of the room.*

No longer able to concentrate for thinking about her, he closed the notebook. He kept wondering how she was coping with her drunken husband in Grasmere. He spotted the merchant banker and his wife and, welcoming the diversion, went across to them. They were ensconsed in comfortable armchairs with drinks between them, looking as though they had had a thoroughly enjoyable evening. "Pull up a pew old chap," invited the banker, gesturing expansively to a nearby chair.

Oliver did so. "Did you enjoy your dinner?," he asked the couple.

"It was simply wonderful," replied his wife.

"It always is here," said the banker. Then he added "How did you like the cabaret just now?"

Oliver laughed. "They seem to have real talent."

"Are you here on business?," asked his wife.

"Yes, I am, as a matter of fact. I'm researching an article on Surprise View which I'm writing for a glossy magazine. I inteviewed Bunny and Ginger this afternoon and they told me the history of the place. It was most interesting."

"I don't suppose they told you about their parties, by any chance?," asked the banker.

His wife suddenly looked embarrassed and put a hand on her husband's arm. "I'm sure our friend doesn't want to hear about those," she said.

"They didn't mention any parties," said Oliver.

Callum arrived and Oliver invited the couple to have another drink. They asked for the same again and Oliver ordered an orange juice, asking Callum to charge them all to The Langdales. When Callum had gone the banker looked round to make sure there was no-one within earshot. He leaned forward and lowered his voice. "As you probably know, Surprise View closes after Christmas and re-opens at Easter. They've done this every year since 1950. Officially, it's to give them a chance to re-decorate and have a holiday, but what most people don't realise is that it also enables them to throw a pretty wild party for their friends every New Year's Eve."

Oliver was intrigued. "I don't suppose they'll want them mentioned if they're private parties, so I won't. Have you been to any?."

Callum came with the drinks and put them on the table. When he had gone the banker's wife leaned towards Oliver and lowered her voice conspiratorially. "We haven't, but a friend has." She was clearly coming round to the idea of discussing the parties and Oliver thought the drink was making them more talkative. He had no intention of mentioning the parties in his article, but was nevertheless curious to hear about them.

The banker glanced round and continued in a low voice. "Their parties are very risqué and have gained world-renown in society circles. People come from far and wide, but mostly from London. The coveted invitations are always obscure: "The Chosen will meet in another part of the wood" or "The Lakers will be re-united," that sort of thing.

"They must be pretty good parties to attract those sort of people to Cumbria in the middle of winter," remarked Oliver.

His wife's eyes lit up. "Bunny and Ginger are party-givers *extraordinaire*. The *torchères* at the entrance are lit and *flambeaux* flare at the foot of the steps. There's music, candlelight and champagne and wonderful food appears as though by magic. All the bedrooms are used," she confided excitedly.

"One doesn't enquire into what for," added her husband. "The early ones in the 1950's were fetish parties, which is how they gained their risque reputation. It's said that men in leather, bondage straps and high-heeled shoes dragged women along by dog-leads and chains. Quite unheard of behaviour in those days, especially in Cumberland."

His wife was warming to the theme. She leaned forward and lowered her voice still further. "Bunny and Ginger wanted special theme parties every year to celebrate the anniversary of when they met. The theme for their ruby was amethyst and for their golden it was flame, when Bunny wore a skin-tight flame-coloured sequinned costume with cloak and a cap of bird-of-paradise feathers, would you believe!." She was almost squealing with delight.

"Two quite senior members of the royal family attended that one, but in an unofficial capacity, of course," added her husband.

"Of course," smiled Oliver. "But how on earth do they manage to get to such a remote place at that time of year?."

"Most come by train to Carlisle. Bunny arranges for them to be met and brought here by car. In the early days he used to ferry them backwards and forwards himself in an old Rolls Royce shooting brake. I understand it was largely due to the goings-on of his guests in the first class sleeper car that the overnight service between London and Glasgow became known as the 'Flying Fornicator'." The banker chuckled and was clearly enjoying himself.

Oliver laughed. "None of this seems to accord with Captain Bernard Liddle, MC, twice mentioned in dispatches."

The banker became more expansive as he continued to indulge a subject close to his heart. "Bunny is a complex character. His legendary parties and outré tastes are but a soufflé. They mask an encyclopaedic mind, nerves of steel, passionate loyalty, a sense of history and deep, profound patriotism. His other great qualities are wit, good taste and an absolute disregard for the opinions of the *bourgeoisie*. "Although a non-smoker himself he always makes a point of smoking a full packet of Ginger's cigarettes on Non-Smoking Day."

Oliver was still amused. "I wonder how he got the name Bunny."

"When he was born his nanny said that he looked like a dear little bunny rabbit and Bunny seemed to be a suitable shortening of Bernard," explained the wife.

Her husband continued. "The dear little bunny rabbit grew into a six-footer with a will of iron. He went to a public school near here, where he developed a reputation for no-nonsense toughness, while excelling both academically and on the sports field. Despite being extremely bright, he didn't go on to university, preferring to get a commission in his fathers' old regiment in time for D-Day.

Oliver continued to chat with the couple. Eventually they announced that they had to go to bed, as they were getting up early to go walking on the fells. By this time many of the other guests had gone upstairs, so Oliver decided to do the same.

When he entered The Langdales a lamp had been switched on, his bedcover turned down and the flowers replaced by fresh ones. He ran a bath, undressed and for twenty minutes lay in the warm water, thinking about Mrs. McBain.

He got into the big four-poster bed and turned off the lights, but found that he was unable to sleep. He kept thinking about the events of the evening and the woman to whom he had suddenly become so attracted, and who had given him the impression that the feeling might be mutual. Although he kept pushing the picture of her from his mind it kept coming back and troubling him. Damn her! Damn both of them! She had already distracted him from his work and made him behave unprofessionally, and now she was preventing him from getting to sleep!

He tried to force his mind back to his work. Who else did he need to interview tomorrow? Apart from the shot of the front of the building, did he need to take any more photographs? Should he get more information from Alexandre about his Lomo de Orza? Did he need to know more about the history of Surprise View? Or the Prime Minister's visit next week? He looked round the room and could just make out some of its features in the moonlight. He decided to make notes about the decor and furnishings in the morning, so he would be able to describe The Langdales in detail.

But try as he might to block it out, the memory of her kept flooding back. Her dazzling beauty in the Lake Room, her unhappiness at her husband's behaviour in the dining room and her embarrassment when people had stared. Their first interested glances towards each other, then the smiles and deliberate eye contact, her closeness on the sofa in the Poets' Room and the almost physical shock when their hands had touched.

Oliver tried to force his mind back to his work, but her face kept reappearing. He wondered what she saw in such a man and whether he behaved as badly towards her at home. Why the hell didn't she leave him? Was it for the sake of their children? Perhaps they didn't have any children. Was it for his money ? He must be pretty rich to have one of the new Aston Martins. Or perhaps she put up with his behaviour because she really loved him?

As he lay there, wide awake, he began to imagine her below him in Grasmere. Had she put her drunken husband to bed and fallen asleep beside him? Had she tackled him about his uncouth behaviour and perhaps had a blazing row? Had she, like Oliver, decided to have a bath? Or was she now lying in bed, thinking of the evening and perhaps of him, too? The thought of her shapely body in some flimsy night attire, or perhaps naked, lying on the bed, made him want her more. He tried to push away the carnal thoughts. Damn the woman, for the effect she was now having on his body, as well as his mind! What was that Commandment? Thou shalt not covet?

Oliver was trying to remember whether it was the seventh or the tenth Commandment that he was in danger of breeching, when he heard what sounded like a tap on the door. He listened, thinking that he might have imagined it, or that it might have been someone walking along the corridor. But then it came again and louder.

Wondering who on earth it could be at that time of night, he switched on the bedside lamp and got out of bed. Remembering that he was wearing only his boxer shorts, he opened the door just wide enough to see who was there. Then he stared in amazement.

Nine

She looked just the same standing there in her long blue dress, jewellery and stiletto heels. When she saw him through the narrow gap she pressed a finger to her lips and pushed the door wider to let herself in. Then she quietly closed it after her and turned the bolt. For a moment they faced each other in the subdued light, her eyes sparkling with excitement as Oliver's registered his delight. Then he put his arms around her, held her to his bare chest and kissed her, as she clasped his neck.

When their mouths parted Oliver whispered "What the hell are you doing here? I was just thinking about you."

Her eyes full of mischief, she glanced down at his boxer shorts and whispered "I thought you must have been."

Oliver laughed with embarrassment. "I didn't think it showed." They held each other and kissed again, then he said "Two questions. What's your first name and where's your husband? I can't call you Mrs. McBain. I'm Oliver by the way."

"I'm Jessica, or Jess for short; and my husband is out for the count and snoring."

"Won't he wake up and come looking for you?"

"He's unlikely to wake for several hours, but if he does happen to miss me he won't think of looking here. It might occur to him that his foul behaviour upset me and I'm spending the night in the car. I was certainly upset, but decided to come to you, instead. You seemed to be a kind man, as well as a handsome one who's on his own, and I was in need of some TLC, so here I am. Don't worry, I came up the emergency stairs and nobody saw me." Her eyes were dancing as she stroked the dark hairs on his chest.

They kissed again, this time more passionately. His hand moved to her breast and felt the nipple through the soft silk of her dress, then continued down to the firmness of her bottom. It found the zip at the back and pulled it down, then he lifted the long dress over her shoulders as she stepped out of it. She draped it over the screen and standing in only her underwear, stockings, stilettos and jewellery she turned to face him.

For a moment he stared at her in wonder, then he took her hand and led her to the bed where they lay down together. He leaned across and kissed her passionately, his tongue exploring hers. When their mouths finally parted he gazed into her eyes and whispered "You're a beautiful woman, Jess." He looked down her voluptuous body and added "I see you go in for expensive underwear, too," his fingers stroking the delicate material of her bra."

No good doing things by halves," she whispered with a smile, half turning onto her side, to allow him to unfasten it. When he had taken it off he stared at her shapely breasts, then gently caressed her nipples with his finger tips and kissed them in turn.

His hand moved down her flat stomach into the front of her knickers. He slipped them down over her feet and added "A matching set, would you believe."

As he kissed and explored her with his fingers she closed her eyes and began to moan softly. When she could wait no longer, her hand reached for the opening in his shorts. "Stop talking and take yours off, too," she whispered.

****

"When he awoke for the second time she was still asleep, with her head resting on his chest, her long black hair spread all around her and her legs intertwined with his. He looked at the bedside alarm clock and saw that it was 3.30 a.m. The movement must have disturbed her, for she opened her eyes.

"What time is it?," she whispered.

"Half past three."

"I suppose I'd better go."

Oliver leaned across and looked into her eyes. "Please stay a little longer." He kissed her breasts, then her mouth. "Does he give you a very bad time?."

"He didn't used to be so bad, but he's been drinking more lately, which is why he's put on so much weight. We've been coming here for five years and he always drinks a lot, but he's never been as bad as this before. When he gets drunk he becomes uncouth and argumentative, as you probably noticed. I nearly walked out on him tonight." Her voice broke with emotion as her eyes filled with tears.

He kissed her forehead. "I wouldn't have blamed you if you had."

She buried her face in his shoulder. "It was awful after I left you. I wished I'd accepted your offer, because I had a terrible struggle getting him upstairs. I suppose it was pride that prevented me. By the time I'd got him to our room he was in an even worse state, so I took him into the bathroom where he collapsed on the floor. He lay there looking like death for half an hour, then was violently sick into the loo. When I thought he'd finished I managed to get him onto the bed, but then he was sick again, all over the embroidered bedcover. I expect we'll have to pay for another one when we leave. He must have brought up everything he ate and drank last night."

"Which was a hell of a lot from what I saw," said Oliver.

She smiled weakly. "Assuming he consumed three quarters of the bill to my one, I value his vomit at two weeks' work at the national minimum wage. But let's not talk about the greedy pig any more." She leaned over and kissed him, then looked into his eyes "What brought you to Surprise View, Oliver?," she whispered.

"I'm here on business, just for one night."

Her smile vanished. "Then in a few hours we'll be going our separate ways again, like ships that pass in the night."

He was about to ask her more about herself when her hand moved down his chest and over his stomach. She examined his face as, for the third time, she felt him harden under her touch

****

They stared up at the bed canopy, holding hands and breathless. After a while Oliver said "This reminds me of an old World War II joke. What's a Fifth Columnist?"

"Go on. Tell me."

"A bridegroom in a four-poster."

Jessica, laughed and looked down his naked body. "You're letting the side down now." This made them both laugh, then they lay still as they thought about their predicament.

Suddenly she sat up and said decisively "It's no good, Oliver. I don't want any trouble. I must get back to him before he misses me." She jumped off the bed and disappeared into the bathroom. When she came out he watched her as she dressed. Once again in her long dress, jewellery and stilettos, Oliver thought she looked just as wonderful as she had at the start of the evening.

She went to the bed, stroked his cheek and kissed him on the lips. He started to get up, but she put a hand on his shoulder and gently pushed him down again. "Go back to sleep, my darling," she whispered. She went to the door and unlocked it. As she quietly opened it she looked back at him and whispered "Same time next year."

Oliver whispered back "See you at breakfast, Jess."She raised a hand in farewell, closed the door and was gone.

****

When he awoke for the third time he looked at the clock and saw that it was 9:25 a.m. He leapt out of bed, cursing himself for not having set the alarm. Apart from the work he still had to do, he wanted to see Jessica again and if possible speak to her alone, before she left with her husband.

He arrived in the dining room ten minutes before the end of the breakfast service. Rafiq greeted him and directed him to the same table. He looked around for the McBains, but could not see them. He noticed that their table had been used and wondered if they had already had theirs. As he ate a simple breakfast he thought about her and their few hours of passion together. He desperately wanted to speak to her again, to make sure that everything had been alright when she had got back to her husband, and to find out more about her.

When he had finished he went into the hall and looked in both lounges, but there was no sign of them. He went to the entrance and looked along the row of cars. His Lotus and the Rolls Royce were there, but the Aston Martin had gone. A police car and a yellow breakdown recovery vehicle were also there and a group of people, including Bunny and a uniformed police officer, were gathered near the Rolls. He recognised the red lettering on the recovery vehicle and realised it was the one he had seen at Barr's Garage the previous day.

Oliver went back into the hall and was greeted by Thomas. "Good morning, Oliver. I hope you've found everything satisfactory."

"Everything's been wonderful, Thomas," he replied. "Isn't it shocking about the damage?."

Oliver looked puzzled. "I saw some people looking at a Rolls Royce outside. What's happened?"

"It belongs to Bunny and Ginger. It's their latest pride and joy. When Mr. Kemp arrived early this morning to hoist the flag, as he does every morning, he noticed that graffiti had been sprayed along both sides, paint stripper poured over the bonnet and the Spirit of Ecstasy stolen from the radiator. When he went into the Poets' Garden the busts of the poets had been pushed off their pedestals and their faces sprayed with the same paint."

Oliver's face registered his shock. "Who on earth would have done a thing like that?"

"I don't know," replied Thomas. "For months we've been having trouble with youths coming up during the night and causing damage. On three occasions guests' cars have been vandalised and a few weeks ago one was stolen. Last month a brick was thrown through the French window of the Poets' Room and some grossly offensive graffiti sprayed on the wall, then a burnt-out car was found down the road at Ashness Bridge. There's a lot of car crime in parts of Cumbria at the moment and young joyriders are driving around all over the place in stolen cars ".

"Things were becoming pretty bad in some of the towns before I left the *Cum bria Star*, but I wouldn't have thought you'd have had any trouble up here."

"Neither did I until all this started," replied Thomas. "We always report incidents to the police, but so far they haven't arrested anyone. They've come to look at the damage, but they don't seem to have any idea who might be responsible. The Rolls is serviced by our local garage and the owner has come up as well, to see what can be done about it."

"I called there for petrol yesterday. It seems to be a well run business and they were very friendly. I remembered the garage from when I was a child and it doesn't appear to have changed much," said Oliver.

"The Barrs are a very nice family. Father, mother and their twin sons all work in the business and live in the bungalow behind. They're expert motor engineers and provide a good, old-fashioned service."

"Well, I hope they manage to repair the damage," said Oliver. He changed the subject. "By the way, I was looking for a couple who were sitting near me at dinner last night. They arrived yesterday afternoon in a green Aston Martin. I've just looked outside, but it seems to have gone."

"I know who you mean," said Thomas. "Mr. and Mrs. McBain. This must be their fifth or sixth visit. They were in Grasmere this time. They had an early breakfast then asked for their bill and left, I'm afraid."

"It was nothing important," said Oliver. "Well, I still have a few things to do, so I'd better get cracking."

Thomas smiled. "I expect I'll see you before you go," he replied.

Oliver returned to the dining room and asked for Alexandre. When the chef appeared Oliver told him how much he had enjoyed the Lomo de Orza and Alexandre gave him more information about it. Before leaving the dining room he confirmed that the portrait on the wall above his table was by Lely.

He went upstairs to The Langdales, packed his things and made some notes about the room. Before he closed the door for the last time he looked around and thought of Jessica. He went to the bed and put his face to the pillow. Her perfume still lingered and made him want her again. He briskly picked up his things, closed the door after him and went downstairs.

With the Aston Martin gone he was able to take the final photograph. Then he went to the reception desk and asked Mia for his bill. Thomas came out of the office and asked him if he had finished.

"Yes, I've got everything I need, thanks, Thomas. I'll start writing as soon as I get home."

"I've made up your bill. Bunny and Ginger have instructed me to charge you only for the bed and breakfast. Last night's dinner is with their compliments. They're looking forward to seeing the feature in *Venues*."

"That's most kind of them. Please convey my thanks," said Oliver writing out a cheque. Then he said goodbye and went outside.

He was curious about the damage and went into the Poets' Garden. The sight of the six busts lying on the path with paint on their faces sickened him and he wondered why the people responsible would have done such a thing.

As he put the Lotus' hood down he watched the Barr twins attending to the Rolls Royce. They had reversed the recovery vehicle into a position where they could winch the magnificent car up the ramp and were about to pull a dust sheet over it. He could see big white letters roughly sprayed along the doors and the damage to the bonnet caused by the paint stripper. The Spirit of Ecstasy was conspicuous by its absence.

Oliver put the Lotus into gear and as he drove slowly past he realised that the white letters were sprayed along both sides of the Rolls and they spelled 'FUCKING SNOBS'.

Ten

The autopilot continued to keep Yanky Mike flying straight and level as Oliver stared down at Surprise View, remembering those events of a year ago.

As soon as he had got back to London he had begun work on the article. It took him less than a week to complete and he was pleased with the result. His photographs had come out well, too, saving *Venues* the cost of sending a photographer. The editor was delighted with everything and it became the main feature in the next issue, which came out just in time for the Prime Minister's visit. It took up the first four pages and included pictures of Alexandre, Thomas, Callum, Hugo, Mia and Mrs. Kemp, as well as a splendid view of Derwentwater with Bassenthwaite Lake in the background.

When he called to see the editor a few days later he counted twenty-four framed covers of *Venue's* on the wall behind her desk. The latest one was his photograph of Bunny and Ginger standing on the steps of Surprise View, which, she told him, had been seen by an estimated eight million people on the news stands. She also added that the feature had boosted the magazine's sales, then offered him a long-term contract as a feature writer, which he gratefully accepted.

The article caused widespread interest and many people got in touch with Oliver to congratulate him. He also received approaches from other publications. But his greatest pleasure was to receive a letter from Bunny and Ginger saying how much they had enjoyed it and how it had resulted in many new bookings.

After the fuss had died down, his thoughts returned to Jessica. He kept seeing her as she had appeared that evening, first in the Lake Room, then in the dining room, the Poets' Lounge and later in The Langdales. He remembered her face, her eyes, her voice, her figure, her hair, even her perfume, and he decided that she was the most wonderful woman he had ever met. Although the weeks and the months went by, the memory of her would not go away. It dominated his waking thoughts and began to interfere with his work. She was affecting him as no other woman had before and it did not take him long to realise that he had fallen in love.

He tried to tell himself that he was being idiotic, that it had simply been a one night stand and that a few hours of passion with a stranger could not possibly make him fall in love. Perhaps she behaved like that with other men and would already have forgotten about him. But then he remembered the look in her eyes as she had clung to him and he refused to believe that. The trouble was he knew very little about her and he kept cursing himself for not having asked her more about herself. But then he would smile as he remembered how her hand had distracted him when he was about to.He remembered his last view of her in the doorway as she was leaving him to go back to her husband. As she raised her hand in farewell she had whispered "same time next year," before quietly closing the door. At the time he had not attached any significance to the words, thinking it was just a flippant remark to lessen the poignancy of the parting. But after a while he began to wonder if the words might have a deeper meaning. Then he remembered how distressed she had been at her husband's uncouth behaviour and could not imagine that she would want to celebrate another anniversary with him at Surprise View.

Oliver's thoughts returned to the present as Yanky Mike reached Derwentwater and Surprise View loomed up closer. He began to study the buildings and grounds, searching for clues why it had not re-opened. His eyes followed the driveway from the lodge to the carpark at the front. There were only two cars there and one of them looked like the Rolls Royce, but he wasn't sure. On the east side of the building the paths and flower beds of the Poets' Garden formed an attractive geometrical pattern, but he couldn't make out whether the busts were back on their pedestals.

His eyes moved along the west side of the building and took in the bay window and the veranda with the long dining room window behind it. They moved up to the first floor and saw the private apartments of Bunny and Ginger then the guests' bedrooms running along the extension. He counted them from right to left: one, two, three, four, five. Yes, the fifth was Grasmere, Jessica's room. They moved up to the second floor. Directly above Grasmere was The Langdales, where it had happened!

He shifted his gaze to the kitchen garden and the smaller modern building which he had taken to be the staff accommodation. Someone was walking across the staff car park towards the hotel. He looked along the bedroom windows again and frowned, then looked at them more closely. The window of The Langdales appeared different to the others. He was trying to work out what was different about it when his view of the hotel disappeared as Yanky Mike passed overhead.

Oliver was curious about the window and why the hotel had not re-opened at Easter. He decided to take an aerial photograph of the building from his present height, then descend and have a closer look.

He took hold of the controls again, switched off the autopilot and looked around for other aircraft. Then he began a wide left turn as he maintained his height of 4500 feet. His right arm reached behind and lifted the photographic case from the back seat onto the seat beside him. He opened it, took out his camera and checked that the telephoto lens was fitted, as he continued the left turn until he was back over Derwentwater. When he could see Surprise View on his left, he increased engine power and steepened the turn until the left wing fell and no longer obstructed his downward view. He opened the perspex flap beside his left cheek and immediately heard the increased wind noise. He pointed the telephoto lens through the opening, put his eye to the viewfinder and as the hotel rushed into the frame he pressed the shutter release.

He quickly put the camera on the seat beside him and closed the flap, then held the controls in both hands and straightened out of the turn. For a few moments he headed east, before reducing power and commencing a wide descending turn to the right.

As the ten mile silver ribbon of Windermere came into view he identified some of the millionaires' residences which overlook the lake. On the surface were the white wakes of boats and water skiers and he imagined the big Sunderland flying boats taking off during World War II, after taxiing out from the lakeside factory where they were built. His eyes moved west to Coniston Water and he thought of Donald Campbell's brave attempt at the world water speed record in 1967 and its tragic outcome.

Now down to 3000 feet he continued the turn around Helvellyn and Thirlmere towards the Borrowdale Valley. He knew this was going to be tricky, because at 1500 feet he would be well below many of the surrounding peaks. When he reached the northern end of Derwentwater he would have two choices if he were to avoid the 3000 foot mass of Skiddaw: either turn east and follow the valley towards Penrith, or slightly west and fly along Bassenthwaite Lake.

Jim had warned him of another danger. The Lake District is used by the RAF for low level training among mountainous terrain. Although the jets would probably be well below him, he would have to keep a sharp lookout for them flying up the Borrowdale Valley and along Derwentwater and Bassenthwaite Lake. As he turned into the valley at 2000 feet and level with the tops of Buttermere Fell and High Seat, he checked that there were none in sight.

Keeping to the east of the Borrowdale valley he looked down and identified the old buildings and tarn of Watendlath at the head of the side valley to his right. Derwentwater now stretched out ahead as the village of Grange passed underneath. At 1500 feet he levelled out, applied flap and trimmed Yanky Mike to fly at 85 knots, keeping as close to the rock face on his right as he dared. When the Lodore Falls came into view his eyes followed them up the cliff until they saw Surprise View again.

He estimated that this time the hotel was 700 feet below and 200 feet to his right. As he flew past, his eyes focussed on the bedroom windows and he realised why The Langdales had appeared so different. It had been bricked up to three-quarters of its height, leaving only a small arched window above. Then he noticed something unusual about the other four windows on the second floor. They had a darker and more reflective appearance than the ones on the first floor, as though tinted double glazing had been fitted. He could not remember that when he had admired the view from the The Langdales and High Stile.

As Surprise View disappeared he continued to fly along Derwentwater, wondering why anyone would have bricked up the window of The Langdales. Perhaps if he took an aerial photograph using the telephoto lens it might provide an answer? He decided to fly to Threlkeld, take the photograph of Ron's house, then return along Derwentwater at a very low height and take one of the windows. He estimated that if he was 800 feet above the lake he would be just about at the same level.

He passed the high ground on the east side of Derwentwater and before reaching Keswick made a right turn. Threlkeld appeared ahead as the Castlerigg Stone Circle passed below. He spotted Ron's house on the edge of the village, with its magnificent view of St. Johns-in-the-Vale, and headed towards it. He checked for other aircraft, knowing that here they might include microlights, hangliders and paragliders launched from the fells. Seeing none, he put Yanky Mike into a steep left turn, opened the flap, pointed the camera out and pressed the shutter release.

He returned to Derwentwater and headed south along its eastern side, now on his left. He descended to 800 feet, trimmed Yanky Mike to fly at 80 knots and as the southern end of the lake approached he edged closer to the cliff. He knew that taking a photograph from the distance he intended, while flying at such a low speed, would require a lot of concentration. He picked up the camera, selected a faster shutter speed, opened the flap and pointed it out. When he saw Surprise View rushing up at the same level and no more than 150 feet away he bent his head to the viewfinder. As the windows flashed into the frame he pressed the release.

There was only time for the one shot. He quickly put down the camera and closed the flap, then concentrated on his flying. He turned away from the cliff, applied full power and went into a steep climb. As he did so a RAF Tornado appeared from the Borrowdale valley, but as it headed for Derwentwater it was well below him and to his right and he was more concerned that he was rapidly approaching 3000 feet peaks while still below 1000 feet.

Keeping his airspeed at 85 knots he watched the altimeter needle slowly climb: 1000, 1500, 2000, 2500. At 3000 feet he levelled out and allowed the speed to build up before trimming. Now he was at the same height as the tops of Scafell, Great Gable, Bowfell and Helvellyn which surrounded him. He made a wide left turn around Helvellyn and when Ullswater came into view he began a gentle descent towards it. Safe in the knowledge that there is no high ground at the northern end of Ullswater, he continued to descend along the long lake. At 1500 feet he levelled out, then watched the boats and the holidaymakers.

With Penrith now lying ahead, Oliver turned north and settled down for the flight back to Carlisle along the flatter ground of the Eden Valley, keeping the grey ribbon of the M6 to his left. His thoughts returned to Surprise View and he wondered why it hadn't reopened. If Ginger had died and Bunny was ill, surely Thomas would be capable of running it? Then there were the windows. The Langdales had been bricked up, leaving only a small window at the top, and the other bedrooms on the second floor appeared to have been fitted with reflective double glazing. He could see no reason for that. Hoping his aerial photographs would throw some light on the mystery, he decided to have the film developed as soon as possible.

His eyes followed the M6 until they came to the urban sprawl of Carlisle. It was time to call the ATC. "Carlisle, Golf Yanky Mike, rejoining from 10 miles south."

"Golf Yanky Mike, Carlisle, report airfield in sight for runway 25 QFE 1009, one Cessna 172 in the circuit," came the reply.

His eyes found the river to the east of Carlisle and the bend where he knew the airport to be. When they spotted the main runway he called "Yanky Mike airfield in sight."

"Golf Yanky Mike, join downwind runway 25 QFE 1009, Cessna 172 left base."

He carried out the pre-landing checks and began to descend towards the main runway. He saw the Cessna 172 which had just landed. At 1000 feet he levelled out and flew parallel to the runway, then called "Yanky Mike downwind."

"Yanky Mike report final."

He continued beyond the runway, then turned left and descended to 500 feet. When he was heading straight for runway 25 he applied flap and called "Yanky Mike final for full stop."

"Yanky Mike cleared to land, wind 250-15."

Oliver continued his approach and made a good landing. As he turned off the runway he got taxi clearance to the apron. When he reached it the Cumbria Police aircraft had already returned and was parked.

His flight had lasted almost two hours. In the flight office Jim greeted him with a smile. "How did it go?," he asked.

"I thoroughly enjoyed it, Jim. I went on my favourite run: Dumfries, Silloth, down the coast to St. Bees Head, then across the Lake District to Penrith. The visibility is excellent and the views magnificent."

Jim was still smiling. "You didn't do any low level flying, by any chance?."

Oliver looked surprised. "Certainly not. I didn't fly below 1500 feet over a built-up area or within 500 feet of any person, vessel, vehicle or structure, except when taking off and landing. Why do you ask?."

"A woman phoned the control tower to complain about a light aircraft flying very low in the Borrowdale area. She didn't have the registration number but said it was blue and white with a single engine. The ATC told them that we don't have any aircraft operating in that area. Of course, I knew it wouldn't be you." There was a twinkle in Jim's eye.

"Certainly not," said Oliver for the second time, hoping that he was sounding sufficiently indignant and convincing. He found a desk and began to fill in his personal log book and the aircraft's log book. Then he wrote out two cheques, one for the hire of Yanky Mike and one for Jim's time.

It was lunchtime and the two men walked to the small terminal building. They bought sandwiches and coffee in the airport bar then chatted as they ate.

When they had finished Jim accompanied Oliver to the Lotus and admired it as he put down the hood. "I hope it won't be another three years before we see you again," he said.

Oliver started the engine. "I'm hoping to come back to Cumbria for good, in which case I'd like to join the group again, if they'll have me back," he called.

As he drove away he looked in his mirror and saw Jim waving. He heard him shout something about low flying. Oliver grinned and waved.

HE DROVE STRAIGHT TO KESWICK and took the film to a photographic shop. He wanted the photographs for later that day, but was told that due to a problem in the laboratory he would have to wait until ten o'clock the next morning. He had nothing planned for the afternoon and Ron and Marjory were not expecting him back until dinner time. He considered driving up to Surprise View to try to discover what was going on, but decided to stick to his original plan, which was to go there the next day, Monday, the anniversary of his visit.

The weather was still glorious and he wanted to get away from the crowds and try out the Lotus on a Lake District pass. He also wanted to visit his parents' grave at Loweswater, as he had not seen it since the funeral. There had been no time to do either of these things on his brief visit to Surprise View' "the previous year. He bought some flowers and put them on the seat beside him, then took the road out of Keswick for Portinscale. When he reached the pretty village at the north end of Derwentwater he took the narrow, twisty road along the western side of the lake towards Grange.

Approaching the southern end of Derwentwater he saw Surprise View on the cliff top on the far side, two miles away. He pulled onto the grass verge and took a small pair of binoculars from the glove compartment. He opened the passenger window and focussed them on the hotel, but found he was too far away to be able to see more than he had already seen from the air. He would need more powerful binoculars, or even a telescope, to make out the detail of the windows from this side of the lake. As he put them back in their case, he hoped the aerial photographs would reveal something.

He sped off again, now looking forward to trying out the Lotus on some of Britain's steepest, narrowest and twistiest roads. As he drove, his thoughts jumped between the Lotus's superb performance and handling, Jessica, his parents whose grave he was about to visit and the magnificent scenery. At Grange he had to slow down to negotiate the tourists in the single, narrow street and to cross the narrow, double hump-back bridge over the River Derwent. At the main road he turned right towards the Borrowdale Valley and away from Keswick and Surprise View.

He had to slow down again at Rosthwaite, where the gap between the houses is only wide enough for one vehicle, before passing the turning to Seathwaite, the tiny hamlet renowned for having the highest rainfall in England. Then he came to Seatoller at the foot of Honister pass, where many of the old buildings are built from slate mined at the summit. He had fun putting the Lotus through its paces on the hairpin bends of Honister Pass. Although not the steepest (nearby Hardknot and Wrynose passes have that distinction), it is steep enough to make driving interesting and the views were magnificent. At the summit he pulled into the carpark of the Honister Slate Mine and parked beside a minibus full of Japanese tourists. He went to the visitor centre and spent twenty minutes reading about the history of the working mine and looking at old mining equipment and early photographs of miners enduring the harsh conditions of by-gone Cumberland winters.

There wasn't time to go on the guided tour and he preferred not to be in cold underground workings on such a glorious day, so he returned to the Lotus and continued down the west side of Honister. The ancient road wound steeply through a desolate landscape of discarded slate waste and huge boulders deposited there by glacial action in the ice age. A few Herdwick sheep, the tough breed native to the fells of Cumbria, had managed to find patches of grass on the stony fellside. It always intrigued Oliver that although the Herdwicks roam freely on these unfenced roads, it is rare to see one lying dead or injured. He wasn't sure whether this was due to the Herdwicks' deftness at avoiding cars or their toughness when struck by one.

He was delighted with the handling of the little roadster on the steep gradients and hairpin bends. Its formidable acceleration enabled him to nip past slow-moving traffic, even on the steepest parts. He doubted if the McBains' Aston Martin could do better on such roads. As his eyes followed the ribbon of road far into the distant green valley he thought about her.

At the end of the valley the road passed between two old stone gateposts standing in front of a solitary house and suddenly he was back among fields and houses. Buttermere appeared on his left and across its calm, blue surface Oliver saw the water cascading down Sour Milk Gill from Bleaberry Tarn, high up on Red Pike. In Buttermere village he had to slow to a walking pace, to avoid hens roaming in the road and visitors buying ice creams from a mobile van. He remembered that Buttermere and Crummock Water were once one lake, until a build-up of silt turned them into two. He followed the road along Crummock Water and after negotiating the dangerous bend at Hause Point, he looked across and saw the sun reflecting off its calm surface and revealing the soft shades of the surrounding fellsides.

When he reached Loweswater village he drove slowly past the house where his parents had lived and where he had been brought up. It did not appear to have changed, but it felt strange that other people were now living there. He continued to the church and parked near the lych gate. As he got out he looked across the road at the Kirkstile Inn and thought that it, too, had changed little since his parents were among its regular customers.

He went to their grave in the far corner of the little churchyard and was pleased to find that the grass had been cut and it looked neat and tidy. He was also pleased with the headstone of Lakeland slate, erected by a local monumental mason on his instructions, but which he had not seen. The inscription included 'tragically killed' and 'at rest among their beloved fells', words he had particularly wanted. He carefully arranged the flowers on the grave and stood beside it for a few minutes. Then he went into the little church and for half an hour sat in his parents' old pew and thought about them and his childhood at Loweswater and the tragic circumstances of their deaths.

As he got back into the Lotus he looked at his watch and realised there was plenty of time to get back to Threlkeld for dinner. He had already decided to return via Whinlatter Pass. The gradients seemed gentle after Honister and as he cruised through the forest he contemplated another pleasant evening with Ron and Marjory. He reached the summit and began the descent towards Keswick. Soon after passing the Forestry Commission's visitor centre he pulled into a layby where other motorists had stopped to admire the view of Bassenthwaite Lake. For a few minutes Oliver sat in the car and thought about the accident, then he got out and began to walk down the road.

The bend and the bridge were less than two hundred yards from where he had parked. He went to the big sycamore tree and felt the scar which was still visible on its trunk. He looked down for the difference in colour in the grass and was not surprised when he could not see it, knowing that features visible from the air often cannot be seen from the ground. He had kept back one of the flowers from the grave and now he placed it at the foot of the tree.

WHEN HE ARRIVED AT THRELKELD Marjory was in the garden to greet him. "Ron and I heard your little aeroplane and came outside. We could see it quite clearly. Did you see us waving?"

"I'm afraid I was too busy holding onto the controls and the camera," replied Oliver. "I think I got a good shot of the house. I've taken the film to be developed. It should be ready at ten o'clock in the morning."

Eleven

When Oliver went to collect the photographs the next morning they were not ready. The assistant apologised and explained that the technical problem was still being rectified and they would be ready at two o'clock. Slightly irritated by this, he decided to drive up to Surprise View and if possible meet Bunny and Thomas. Not only was he concerned about the business and curious to know why the windows had been altered, but he could not stop thinking about his visit and Jessica. He particularly wanted to be there today, the anniversary, just in case.

He returned to the Lotus and took the Borrowdale road out of Keswick. As he approached Barr's Garage he slowed down and was surprised to see a closed sign and a chain across the forecourt. The pumps, kiosk and workshop were locked and it appeared to be deserted. However, the yellow recovery vehicle, with a car on its back covered by a plastic sheet, was parked in the driveway of the bungalow. He wondered if the Barrs were on holiday. He took the left turning to Watendlath and drove up the steep, narrow road, slowing to a walking pace to cross Ashness Bridge. The sight of the little carpark reminded him again of the darker times that he now preferred to forget. Brushing aside the unhappy memories he continued up the hill.

The tall wrought iron gates were closed, so he pulled up in front of them. A sign attached to them said: *The hotel is closed until further notice. Please ring for enquiries.*

He got out and pressed the bell-push on the sandstone gatepost. As he waited he noticed that the gates were held together by a strong chain and padlock. Through them he could see the lodge and the glorious colours of the rhododendrons and azaleas bordering the tarmac driveway, which he had admired the previous year. The door of the lodge opened and a middle-aged man wearing a blue overall came out. He approached Oliver and addressed him through the gates.

"Good morning, sir. Can I help you?."

"Good morning. Are you Mr. Kemp?," Oliver replied.

"That's right, sir. Do I know you?"

"I'm Oliver Mills. I stayed here last June and met your wife. I was writing an article about Surprise View for *Venues* magazine and took some photographs. I heard the sad news about Ginger Rutherford and being in the area I thought I might have a word with Bunny or Thomas."

Kemp made no attempt to open the gates. "My wife told me about your visit, Mr. Mills. We enjoyed your article and kept the magazine. Ginger Rutherford's death came as a terrible shock to us all. Naturally, Bunny was devastated, but he soldiered on until after Christmas, when the hotel closed as usual. He intended to re-open at Easter and carry on without Ginger, but his own health suddenly deteriorated, so he took his doctor's advice and decided to wait until he's better. No extra staff have been taken on and there are just a handful of us left who live here."

"I'm sorry to hear about Bunny. I'd like to speak to him if possible."

"I'm sorry, but his doctor told him that he mustn't have any visitors. Several people have been turned away."

"Perhaps Thomas, then?," asked Oliver, hopefully. "I got to know him quite well and I'd like to meet him again if possible."

"I'm sorry, but Thomas is away today. It's his day off."

It was clear that Kemp was not going to open the gates. "Well thanks anyway. Please tell them I called and was asking after them. I hope Bunny is better soon," he said, getting back into the car.

"I will, sir. Goodbye," said Kemp, continuing to watch Oliver through the gates as he prepared to drive away.

Oliver was annoyed. He had imagined that he would be made welcome by Bunny or Thomas, when he could have given them his condolences. To be refused admission, albeit politely, was quite unexpected. Instead of returning down the hill he continued up it towards Watendlath. He had not been there for years and seeing it from the air had brought back his childhood memories of the farm buildings, the tarn and the pack-horse bridge which crossed the stream, where ducks and geese had waddled about. Not only did he want to visit the little hamlet again, but he wanted to be somewhere quiet where he could think.

As he left the cliff-top behind, he followed the narrow, twisty road into the remote side valley which runs off the main Borrowdale valley. The woodland gave way to more open land on which were areas of rocks and ferns and the occasional Herdwick sheep. After a mile high stone walls on both sides restricted the road to one vehicle, and partially hid his view of the fields containing huge boulders, deposited in the valley in the ice age. Suddenly, on a bend, he came face-to-face with a tractor, when both drivers had to brake hard to avoid a head-on collision. As Oliver reversed into a passing-place to let it go by, he thought how difficult life must be for the local farmers in the tourist season.

He reached Watendlath where the road came to an abrupt end. He got out of the car and stood beside it, looking around at the tiny hamlet and remembering his childhood visits with his parents. Then he set off on foot past the old houses and farm buildings towards the tarn, grateful there were few visitors about. A man painting the windows of his whitewashed cottage watched him approach and they wished each other good morning. When he reached the tarn he stood on the ancient packhorse bridge, enjoying the tranquility of this unique place, immortalised by Hugh Walpole in his *Herries Chronicles*.

Oliver recalled what Thomas Wilkinson had written about Watendlath in 1824: *A native of London or Bath, transported to Watinlath, might sicken for society.* He wondered whether he might sicken for society if he came to live here and decided that he would. Although he was fed up with London and wanted to be back in Cumbria, he could not imagine being happy in such a remote place.

As he walked back towards the Lotus his thoughts returned to Jessica and Surprise View. He kept thinking of her departing words, the closure of the hotel, the bricked-up window and his inability to meet Bunny or Thomas, and the more he thought about it the less sense he could make of it all.

He decided to return to Keswick and as he drove out of Watendlath he began to plan the afternoon ahead. He would have a look at the shops, buy a sandwich for lunch, then at two o'clock pick up the photographs. He was looking forward to seeing how they had come out. If the one of Ron's house was a success he would have it enlarged and framed and give it to them as a 'thank you' and, of course, he was hoping that the ones of Surprise View would throw some light on why the windows had been altered. He had not gone far when he came upon the rusting shell of a burnt-out car, lying on its roof on a grassy area beside the road. The letters 'TWOC' had been roughly sprayed along its side in white paint. He had not noticed it on the way up, because it was on the bend where he had met the tractor and would have been hidden by a mound. Its stark ugliness seemed a blasphemy among the natural beauty and reminded him of his conversations with Thomas and Ron about car crime in Cumbria, and of how his parents had met their untimely and terrible deaths.

When he reached Surprise View he slowed down, but there was no sign of anyone and the gates were still locked. Still annoyed at not being admitted he continued down the hill and pulled into the carpark at Asnesss Bridge. He took out his mobile phone and called the hotel's number. A woman's voice answered pleasantly "Good morning, Surprise View Country House Hotel." He recognised it as Mia's.

"Good morning. This is Oliver Mills. You may remember me from last year, when I was researching the article for *Venues.* I heard the sad news about Ginger Rutherford and as I'm in the area I thought I might call in and have a word with Bunny or Thomas. If it's not convenient, perhaps one of them could come to the phone?"

Mia told Oliver that she remembered him and how much she had enjoyed his article, then gave him the same polite answer, almost word for word, that he had received from Kemp. Oliver thanked her, returned the phone to his pocket, started the engine and headed for Keswick.

This time the photographs were ready. Without opening the packet he hurried through the crowds to the carpark where he had left the Lotus. He got in and began to look through the prints. There were less than a dozen, because he had taken the film out before it was finished. Some were photographs he had taken in connection with his work, before setting off for Cumbria.

He came to the first shot of Surprise View taken from 4500 feet. It was clear, but although he had used a telephoto lens, it included large areas of the surrounding woodland and Derwentwater, and showed insufficient detail of the buildings. Then he came to the one of Ron's house. It had turned out well and he thought they would like it. When he came to the last one he swore aloud. Although he had managed to capture the four bedroom windows at the northern end, everything was blurred and did not reveal the detail of the mysterious new brickwork in The Langdales. He cursed himself for not having used a faster shutter speed.

He was about to put the prints back into the packet when he looked at the last one again. Then he looked at it more closely and frowned. There appeared to be something in the small arched window above the brickwork. He got out and fetched his camera case from the boot. He took out a magnifying glass and held it over the photograph, trying to imagine what it would look like if it was not blurred. The four windows almost filled the picture and the contrast and the colour quality were good. He could even see the differences in the glass, as Scafell, next to The Langdales, appeared darker than Wastwater and Grasmere below.

He looked at The Langdales again, but it was too blurred for him to make out the detail of the brickwork. Then he looked above it and saw what appeared to be a face staring out at him from the small window. He screwed up his eyes, trying to decipher the blurred features. He couldn't be sure, but he thought he could make out the eyes, nose and mouth, and what appeared to be arms raised on either side.

He found the negative and held it up to the light, but it, too, was blurred and added nothing. He looked again at the print, holding it by the corner and moving it backwards and forwards. Eventually he decided it was probably just a reflection. Perhaps double glazing had been fitted to the small window of The Langdales, as well as to the other bedrooms on the second floor, and that it reflected more light than ordinary glass. Anyway, he had not seen anything unusual when he had flown past the first time, when he had first noticed the window was bricked up.

He put the two photographs of Surprise View in his wallet and the packet containing the other prints and the negatives into his camera case. For ten minutes he sat in the car, wondering what to do next. At last he made up his mind. He would go back to Surprise View and have a quiet look round. He knew there were woods to the north and south of the property, so he would use them as cover to reach the boundary fence, then see if he could discover anything that might throw light on the mystery.

When he reached Ashness Bridge he parked at the far end of the little carpark, almost out of sight of the road. He was now too preoccupied to remember that he was at the exact spot where not long ago he had planned something else to happen. He took the binoculars from the glove compartment and hung them round his neck, then put the camera case in the boot and locked the car.

He entered the wood from the carpark and set off for the cliff-top. He knew that if he followed it uphill for about a mile it would bring him to the hotel. But his progress through the trees was slow, because the ground was uneven and he had to negotiate crevices, moss-covered fallen trees and big rocks. When he reached the cliff top he stopped for a moment to look at Derwentwater, but decided that although the view was good, it was not as spectacular as it was from Surprise View.

After half an hour he came to a fence which ran across his path. It was about five feet high and made of stout, plastic-covered wire mesh. A sign attached to it said 'private' and he realised he had reached the grounds of' "Surprise View. He followed the fence to the cliff and discovered that it continued over the edge, making it impossible to get round the end. He returned to the sign and realised that in the other direction the fence met the tall beech hedge which bordered the road to the entrance gates and the lodge.

He went up to the fence and looked into the hotel grounds. He recognised the layout from the previous year, when he had looked through the gate of the Poets' Garden. In front of him was the modern staff building, beyond which part of the hotel itself was visible. Between them he could see part of the staff carpark. To his left was the kitchen garden, enclosed on three sides by the fence, the beech hedge and the tall hedge of the Poets' Garden. The secondary driveway, connecting the main drive to the staff carpark, ran between the two gardens. Immediately in front of him was an overgrown area containing a compost heap, some rusting garden machinery and an old garden shed.

He went back to the cliff top and looked through his binoculars towards the bedroom windows, but the hotel was built so close to the edge that he was unable to see them. He returned along the fence to the 'private' sign, just as an elderly Ford Escort arrived along the drive and disappeared into the staff carpark. He heard the engine stop, car doors being slammed and mens' voices. He caught a glimpse of two coloured men walking towards the hotel who looked like Callum and Rafiq.

Oliver had no wish to have come all this way for nothing, so he decided to enter the grounds and find someone who could throw light on what was going on. If anyone objected to his presence he would somehow bluff his way out of the situation. Where the 'private' sign was attached to the fence seemed to be the best place to enter, because the dense undergrowth would provide some cover. He grasped the wire mesh and found that it took his weight, so he hauled himself over the top and landed on his feet on the other side.

He looked around and seeing nobody began to cautiously make his way towards the hotel. As he crept forward he found himself waist-high in thistles, nettles and brambles and realised that he was in a corner of the kitchen garden that had not been cultivated. Approaching the compost heap his foot caught in some rusty barbed wire, but he quickly regained his balance. As he continued towards the old shed he noticed that most of the glass was missing from its window.

He was about fifteen feet away from the shed as he crept stealthily past it. He glanced through the broken window, but it was dark inside. He had taken another half dozen steps when he felt a sharp sting in the back of his left thigh. He spun round and seeing nobody he put it down to a thistle or more barbed wire. He moved his hand down to rub the area and began to feel light-headed. His hand continued downwards, his knees buckled and he collapsed on the ground.

Twelve

Gradually he became aware of a bright light shining in his face, then he realised that he was feeling dreadful, with a blinding headache and a bad taste in his mouth. He tried to turn his head away from the light, but the effort was too much. A feeling of nausea swept over him, so he closed his eyes and fell asleep again.

Later (was it five minutes or five hours?), he re-opened them. The light was still there. He focussed his eyes and identified the source as an ornate ceiling light with five tasselled shades. He turned his head to the right and found he was looking at a bigger light, which was rectangular with a rounded top. He focussed again and saw an arched window, with long curtains down both sides. Through it white clouds were moving across blue sky.

The light from the window was also too bright, so he turned his head to the left and found that better. As his eyes re-adjusted he began to recognise objects. A table, two chairs, a bookcase, a wardrobe, a dressing table, some ornaments, two doors. The feeling of nausea returned and he closed them again.

When he awoke for the third time he looked around. He realised he was in a bedroom which looked familiar, but he couldn't think why. It wasn't his flat, so where was he?

Slowly, he began to recall recent events. He had bought a new sports car and driven up to Cumbria for a holiday. He had stayed with Ron and Marjory, then gone flying in Yanky Mike and taken some aerial photographs. One of them was blurred and he tried to remember why it was important. Of course! The windows of Surprise View!

He looked to the right again and this time he recognised the window. It brought back the memory of Jessica. He looked around the room again and realised that although it was familiar it wasn't The Langdales, because the decor and furnishings were different. Then he remembered taking the photograph of Mrs. Kemp turning down the bedcover in the Prime Minister's room. What was its name? High Stile! Next door but one to The Langdales. He recognised the Georgian mahogany dressing chest with its collection of North American shell boxes, and the white lace canopy over the bed on which he now lay. He wondered if it was the bed the Prime Minister and his wife had slept in.

He was still feeling ill and his mouth tasted horrible. He saw a glass of water on the bedside table and managed to raise himself sufficiently to drink some, before collapsing back onto the bed. He lay there, trying to work out what had happened, then he felt the need to urinate and wondered if he could get to the bathroom. He looked down the bed and saw that he was still dressed in his jeans, shirt and trainers. The bedside alarm clock showed 6.30 pm and he reckoned he must have been there for over three hours. When the need to go became urgent he managed to get off the bed and stand up. Holding onto chairs and the wardrobe for support, he reached the bathroom and relieved himself, then drank four large glasses of cold water. Feeling weak he sat on the lavatory with his head in his hands, wondering what had happened.

The water hastened his recovery and after a while he went back to the bedroom, collapsed into one of the armchairs and tried to remember what he had been doing. Gradually he pieced together the events of the past two days, up to the point when he had entered the grounds of Surprise View. He remembered passing the old shed, the sharp sting in the back of his left thigh, then nothing. He felt the area with his hand and realised it was still sore, so he struggled to his feet, loosened his jeans and put his hand inside. He could feel a plaster over the spot and wondered how it had got there. Perhaps he had been taken ill and they had carried him upstairs to recover?

He was gazing at the window, trying to work it out, when he noticed something. He remembered that The Langdales and High Stile both had sash windows, because he had admired the view from both bedrooms and had opened the window in the Langdales for fresh air. Now it looked as though the inside of the window had been covered by a sheet of secondary glazing.

He went across to examine it and found that there was indeed a sheet of glass on the inside. He touched it and realised it was much thicker than the usual sort. It had a solid appearance and when he knocked on it there was little sound. It was tinted and looked like security or armoured glass. It was sealed into the plaster all round and when he looked closely it was almost an inch thick. He remembered that one of the reasons he had photographed the bedroom windows was because he couldn't understand why the upper ones had appeared darker than the lower.

As he stood at the window wondering why the extra glazing had been fitted, a military jet approached from the south. From his vantage point Oliver was looking down on it as it flew up the middle of Derwentwater at 200 feet and disappeared along Bassenthwaite Lake. He realised that although it had been in his view for several seconds he had not heard it. He touched the glass again and wondered if it had been fitted to prevent guests from being disturbed by low-flying aircraft. But if so, why hadn't it also been fitted to the first floor windows?

He suddenly noticed a small window in the door which hadn't been there the previous year and went to examine it. It was six inches square and made of the same thick glass as the glazing over the window. Through it he could see the doors of two bedrooms across the corridor and a few yards along it in both directions. As his hands came into contact with the door he realised that instead of wood he was touching cold metal. He examined it and saw that the timber had been covered by a thick sheet of steel which overlapped the frame and had been painted the same cream colour. There was no lock or handle on the inside.

He banged on the door and shouted, then looked through the small window again. Almost immediately two men came into view from the left. They were wearing blue-black uniforms with silver buttons and insignia, and uniform caps. One of them stood back while the other unlocked the door with a key attached to his belt by a chain. When he came in Oliver recognised him as one of the Barr twins from the garage, whom he had last seen loading the Rolls Royce onto the recovery vehicle. But instead of a mechanic's overall, he was now wearing what appeared to be a prison officer's uniform from the 1950s or 1960s. The leather strap of a wooden truncheon and a pair of the old-style police handcuffs showed below the flap of his uniform jacket.

He looked at Oliver without smiling. "Are you feeling better?," he asked.

"A little. What am I doing here? What's happened to me? Why are you wearing a uniform?," replied Oliver.

"Bunny is coming to speak to you soon and will explain everything. Meanwhile, would you like something to eat? It's nearly supper time."

Oliver considered. "I want to speak to Bunny, then get out of here, but if I'm going to be delayed I suppose I'd better eat something. I couldn't manage anything heavy."

"I'll order something," replied the Barr twin. He went out and locked the door. Through the small window Oliver saw the two men disappearing along the corridor. He thought the second one was one of the waiters from the previous year, but he couldn't be sure.

He turned round and spotted the bedside telephone. A card gave the numbers for the hotel services. He dialled 0 for an outside line, but got no dialling tone, so he dialled the number for the reception and recognised Mia's voice. "Can I help you?," she asked politely.

"This is Oliver Mills. I'd like to speak to Bunny Liddle or Thomas, immediately, please."

There was a short delay. "Bunny has asked me to tell you that he will be up to see you very soon," she replied.

"Right, now will you please give me an outside line."

"I'm sorry, Mr. Mills, but we're having problems with the telephones today," replied Mia.

Oliver put down the phone. He suddenly remembered his mobile and reached into his pocket, but it was not there. Realising his situation, he swore aloud. He was under lock and key in a bedroom at Surprise View and out of touch with the rest of the world. Bunny had better come up with a good explanation for this!

He decided to freshen up and went into the bathroom. As well as the usual luxury toilet requisites, there was a gold-plated razor with an amber handle and a matching badgers hair shaving brush, which bore the name of a Paris manufacturer and looked expensive. When he had shaved, showered and dressed again he felt slightly better. He picked up some magazines from the pie-crust table and sat in one of the armchairs, waiting for Bunny to come. One of them was the issue of *Venues* containing his feature. The pictures reminded him of the aerial photographs and he reached into his jacket for his wallet. Everything else was there, but the two photographs were missing.

The sound of a key being inserted in the lock startled him and he quickly returned the wallet to his pocket. Alexandre came in with a tray, which he put down on the table between the armchairs. He was wearing a chef's white jacket. "I don't suppose you're feeling too good, so I've made you a cheese omelette," he said without smiling. Oliver looked at the tray. As well as the omelette, there were some plain biscuits and a glass of water.

"Thanks, Alexandre," said Oliver as he was leaving. Then he added "Now will you please tell me why I've been locked in this bedroom?."

"Bunny will be up soon and will explain everything," said the chef as he went out. Oliver heard the key being turned in the lock and saw the Barr twin watching him through the observation window.

After the simple meal he felt slightly better. He was looking for another magazine when he heard the key in the lock again. The twin held the door open and the tall figure of Bunny strode in. As Oliver stood up the twin removed the tray and went out, leaving the two men facing each other.

Bunny was wearing a tweed sports jacket, grey flannel trousers and was carrying a gold-handled cane. The silk handkerchief in his top pocket matched the pale blue stripe in his old school tie. Although he still stood very straight, Oliver thought he looked older. "What *am* I going to do with you?" asked Bunny reproachfully, when Oliver ignored his outstretched hand. His voice was still cultured and clipped, but it had a harsher tone. His watery, red right eye continued to fix Oliver.

"First you can explain how I was suddenly taken ill on your property, what happened to my leg and why I've been locked in this bedroom. Then you can release me," Oliver replied, abruptly.

Bunny sat down in one of the armchairs and gestured with his cane for Oliver to take the other. When they were facing each other he put the cane on the table and said "My dear Oliver, you should have realised by now that you are not in a position to dictate terms to me. Whether you are released at all depends entirely on what you tell me and whether it is the truth. The fact that you were a guest here and wrote an excellent article about Surprise View will make no difference to my decision." He leaned forward and his voice suddenly became harsh. "Now tell me, why were you trespassing in our grounds this afternoon?"

Astonishment and indignation showed on Oliver's face as the significance of Bunny's words sank in. "There's a perfectly simple explanation. I heard that Ginger had died and the hotel had not re-opened at Easter. I was in the area and decided to pay you a visit, to offer my condolences and perhaps be of some help. I tried to gain admittance in the normal way but Mr. Kemp said you were too ill to see anyone, so I decided to find someone who could tell me what's going on. I realise I might have been trespassing, but I don't expect to be locked up like a common criminal, even though the prison is a luxurious one."

Bunny's damaged eye continued to fix him. "That's the story you told Kemp and Mia. But it doesn't explain why you had these in your wallet." He reached into his pocket and put the two aerial photographs of Surprise View on the table.

"So I was searched. I suppose you took my mobile as well?."

"And your binoculars and car keys. But don't worry, they're perfectly safe." Bunny's voice suddenly became harsh again. "Now who took these photographs and why?"

"I did," replied Oliver. "Flying is my hobby. I have a pilot's licence and went for a pleasure flight in a light aircraft from Carlisle Airport yesterday morning. It was a lovely day and I flew over the Lake District and saw Surprise View. I noticed something unusual about the bedroom windows and decided to have a closer look. I thought the upper one at the northern end had been partly bricked up and couldn't understand why, so I took two aerial photographs. Unfortunately, the one of the windows is blurred and doesn't reveal much."

"We heard a small aeroplane buzzing around yesterday," said Bunny. "It sounded different to the military jets and came closer to the cliff. It was obviously breaking the low-flying rules for civil aircraft so I asked Mia to make a complaint to Carlisle Airport." He examined the photograph of the windows, then looked at Oliver. "I agree, it is rather blurred. But I think it tells a story, don't you?"

Oliver shrugged. "The end window on the second floor looks as though it's been bricked up almost to the top. There appears to be something pale in the small window above the bricks that looks like a face, but is probably just a reflection in the glass. I was curious because it's The Langdales, which was my room last year."

Bunny looked at the photograph again. "I quite agree, it does look like a face. How very strange. But as you say, it's probably just a reflection." He put the two photographs on the table and fixed Oliver with his damaged eye "Now, would you like me to tell you what's been going on at Surprise View since your visit last year?."

"If it includes an explanation for my treatment."

"It does," said Bunny. He paused for a moment before continuing. "I expect you remember the trouble we had here last year, just before you left?."

"You mean the damage to your Rolls Royce and the busts of the Lake Poets?

That was very unfortunate."

Bunny's face flushed. "It was more than unfortunate, it was bloody criminal. As Thomas told you at the time it was just one of a series of similar crimes committed against us," he said angrily.

When Oliver did not reply Bunny continued more calmly. "When Ginger and I opened Surprise View all those years ago, it seemed as though we were leaving the problems of the city behind. For years everything was just as it should be in such an idyllic place. With hard work we built up the business and succeeded in attracting the sort of clientele we had set out to find: discerning people with taste, who would appreciate good service and could afford to stay at a prestigious hotel in a beautiful location and dine in one of the world's top restaurants. We were good employers and our more famous guests helped to put the area on the map, so the local people liked having us on their doorstep and most of them even managed to overlook the fact that we weren't married. Until three years ago we experienced no trouble of any sort."

"Then what happened?," asked Oliver.

"For some time crime and disorder had been on the increase in certain parts of Cumbria. Car crime and burglary were getting out of hand in Carlisle and West Cumbria. We kept hearing about it on the local news, but we were not troubled by it at Surprise View and Cumbria's industrial towns seemed worlds apart from the Lake District. Of course, large numbers of tourists have always caused a few problems in places like Keswick, Ambleside and Windermere, but the troublemakers rarely ventured into these quieter parts.

Then two years ago some local criminals discovered the little road up to Watendlath. The first we knew about it was when three guests' cars were damaged one night, then a few days later one was stolen. A fortnight later a brick was thrown throught the French window of the Poets' Room and some ghastly graffiti painted on the wall. A few nights later someone entered by the same window, defecated on the Chinese rug and stole some valuable porcelain. In the morning a burnt-out car was found at Ashness Bridge, which had been stolen in West Cumbria and driven up here by so-called joyriders. I don't think they were ever caught. The blackened, rusting shell was a blot on our beautiful landscape for three months before the council removed it. Word about the road must have spread quickly, because soon there were other incidents. Then twelve months ago when you were here there was that frightful damage to the poets and our Rolls Royce.

"I hope you managed to have it repaired without too much expense," said Oliver.

"The expense was not the issue, because we were insured. I expect you saw the Barr family from the local garage collecting the Rolls as you were leaving? They managed to remove the paint and obtain a new Spirit of Ecstasy, but the bonnet had to be taken off and re-sprayed. They also cleaned the paint off the poets and replaced them on their pedestals. However, what upset Ginger and me more than anything else was the intrusion and violation of this sacred place. It was clear from what they had done that those responsible were the scum of the earth."

"Oh, come on, Bunny, that's a bit strong. Mindless vandals would be a better description."

Bunny grabbed his cane and struck the top of the table. "Mindless poppycock," he shouted. "Mindless is a word too often used to describe such scum. They're not mindless at all. Even if they had been high on drink or drugs they would have known perfectly well what they were doing and why. They're the scum of our society, with a hatred of beauty, culture and wealth, whose motivation is envy, greed, malice and a desire for wanton destruction."

Oliver was not going to be provoked again. "Was there any more trouble after that?," he asked quietly.

Bunny made an effort to compose himself. He put down his cane and continued more calmly. "Three weeks later your article appeared in *Venues*. Ginger and I wrote to you saying how much we'd enjoyed it and we received your note in reply."

Oliver smiled "I was pleased that it had drummed up more business for you."

Bunny did not smile. "It was a fortnight later that disaster struck. Alexandre had reported that our usual supplier was out of stock of some things that he needed for dinner, so Ginger said she would get them from a cash and carry. She jumped into the Rolls and set off for Workington. When she arrived she parked the Rolls in the cash and carry carpark and went in and bought the items that Alexandre had asked for, plus a few other things that we needed.

"She was loading them into the Rolls when a car appeared in the carpark, driven by two scum. They saw Ginger standing beside the Rolls Royce and weaved towards her with the windows wound down, then began to circle her with screeching tyres, while shouting abuse at her and laughing. For a few moments poor Ginger was frozen to the spot, then she tried to jump out of the car's way, but it caught her leg and knocked her to the ground. Still shouting abuse at her the scum paused only to snatch her handbag and break off the Spirit of Ecstasy from the front of the Rolls, before driving off at high speed."

"Was Ginger badly hurt?," asked Oliver.

"She was still on the ground so someone from the cash & carry called an ambulance and she was taken to the West Cumberland Hospital. I was told about it and Mia gave me a lift to Workington, where I picked up the Rolls and drove to the hospital. Her only physical injuries were bruises to her leg and ribs and grazes to her knees and hands, but she was shocked, so the doctor decided to keep her in overnight for observation. The next day she was discharged and advised to rest for a few days."

"So what caused her death?."

Bunny looked at him. "The scum who knocked her down did, although it can't be proved. The police still don't know who they were. When we got Ginger home she was still very upset, so our own doctor came and examined her and more or less repeated what the hospital had said. So she agreed to rest in our private quarters, out of the way of the guests and staff, until she was fully recovered."

"Didn't that do the trick?"

"No, it didn't. Poor Ginger kept dwelling on what had happened and became convinced that the two scum had deliberately tried to kill her. She became withdrawn and stopped eating, so after a few days when it was clear she was not improving I asked our doctor to take another look at her. He gave her a thorough examination and said that although there was nothing physically wrong she was suffering from depression, which he thought had been brought on by the attack, so he prescribed a course of anti-depressants.

"She took them for a week which, I am told, is not long enough for them to be effective. One night she went to bed at the usual time. When she didn't appear for breakfast in the morning I went into her bedroom, but she wasn't there. I started to look for her and when I couldn't find her in the obvious places, I asked the staff to help.

"It was Mrs. Kemp who eventually found her. We heard her screams from downstairs. She was in the bathroom of an unoccupied bedroom on the second floor. It was The Langdales, the room you were in last year. My poor darling Ginger had hanged herself from the rail of the shower curtain by her dressing-gown cord."

Thirteen

The silence in High Stile was broken by a uniformed warder arriving with a tray. Oliver recognised him as one of the waiters from the previous year.

"Thank you, Lucas," said Bunny, as he put it on the table. "I'll let you know if I need anything else." Bunny was visibly upset and when Lucas had gone he wiped his eyes with his silk handkerchief. When he was more composed he picked up the coffee pot and offered some to Oliver.

"No thanks. I'll stick to water for the moment," said Oliver. He paused and added "I'm very sorry about Ginger. It must have been a terrible shock for you. I know you were very close."

Bunny filled his cup. "We had been together for fifty years and were partners in every sense of the word. She was a kind and gentle lady who never harmed anyone. She was awarded the MBE for her charitable works, as you probably know."

"I believe you met at the military hospital where you were being treated?"

Bunny wiped his eyes again. "I have told few people about how Ginger and I met, but I will tell you. When my tank was hit and caught fire – or 'brewed up' in the army parlance of World War Two – I was the only one to get out. When the medics saw how badly I was burned they immediately flew me back home. I was fortunate to be sent to a military hospital in Middlesex which specialised in burns and was modelled on the well known RAF hospital at East Grinstead where new techniques in plastic surgery had been pioneered on badly burned aircrew. Still only twenty, I almost gave up with the pain, but the surgeon gave me new confidence when he explained what could be done. I then had to endure weeks of painful skin grafts, with twenty-five operations in all. First he saved the sight in my right eye by performing an eyelid graft which prevented the cornea drying out. Then he gave me a new upper lip, lower chin, part of my right cheek and a new nose, when I had to have a pedicle from my left arm."

"What's a pedicle?," asked Oliver.

"It was a piece of skin cut from the inside of my left arm and shaped into a sausage to form my new nose. However, to maintain the blood supply it had to remain attached to my arm, so for months I had to hold my arm close to my face. Although I did not appreciate it at the time, much of what the surgeon did for me was innovative and saved me from a lifetime of blindness and even worse disfigurement, perhaps in an institution. The nurses were wonderful, too. They did everything for me, from giving me saline baths to help the grafting process, to assisting me at the lavatory."

Oliver was staring at Bunny's face and wondering at the skill of the surgeon. "It sounds as though major advances had been made since the First World War."

"They certainly had. When I was considered well enough I was transferred to a nearby convalescent home, where there were a lot of young army types recovering from plastic surgery. Sitting together in the lounge with our bandages and pedicles, we must have looked like a scene from a science fiction film. The treatment was as innovative there as it had been at the hospital, because by then it was recognised that the psychological recovery of young burns victims was as important as the physical. Everything was geared towards raising our spirits and re-introducing us to the outside world. The nurses were attractive as well as highly qualified, and parties were encouraged when a considerable amount of beer was drunk and singing around the upright piano went on late into the night. During the day the nurses took those of us who were fit enough into the town. By then the locals were used to seeing bandaged young men with uniformed nurses, so they paid us little attention. My nurse was a beautiful nineteen year old redhead called Celia Rutherford, known to all as Ginger.

"I had been there just a few days when my fiancee came to see me. We had been childhood sweethearts and the evening before I joined my regiment we had agreed to be married as soon as the war ended. I had not seen her since because she had not been allowed to visit me at the hospital. The staff would have warned her what to expect, but when Ginger brought her into my room and she saw my pedicle and bandages her smile froze. I knew then that it was over, so the 'Dear Bunny' letter that followed a few days later came as no surprise.

"Darling Ginger did a wonderful job keeping me cheerful and preventing me from giving up. We had a lot of fun with the others and she even managed to convince me that she found me attractive. However, a relationship would have been against the rules, so it wasn't until later, when we met at the hotel where I was working, that we started going out together. By then we both knew that I would never be able to have children, because when I was wounded it was not just my face and arm that were badly burned. She assured me that this made no difference, but because I didn't want to deprive her from having children by someone else, I never proposed marriage."

"It's a very romantic story," said Oliver.

Bunny wiped his eyes again. "I'm sorry, but I miss Ginger dreadfully. Of course, there had to be a post-mortem and an inquest. The police had recovered the stolen car but had not traced the two scum. A witness said they had swerved away from Ginger at the last moment but she had jumped in the same direction. Our doctor gave evidence about treating her for depression, but as she hadn't left a suicide note and there was nothing to link the depression to the accident, an open verdict was returned."

"Perhaps the lads in the car were just fooling around and didn't intend to harm her," suggested Oliver.

Bunny leapt to his feet, grabbed his cane and struck the top of the table, startling Oliver. "Stuff and nonsense," he shouted, his face crimson. Making a visible effort to compose himself he sat down and continued in a voice charged with emotion "The two scum in that car murdered Ginger just as surely as if they had put a gun to her head. The only witness came from a nearby housing estate and was clearly more in sympathy with them than with the wealthy owner of a Lake District hotel and a Rolls Royce."

He wiped his eyes and allowed his breathing to return to normal. When he continued his voice was calmer. "The funeral service in Keswick was a frightful ordeal. Afterwards, the mourners returned to Surpise View for the funeral tea which I had laid on in the Poets' Room. When they had finished they left in small groups, paying their respects to me as they went, until only the senior staff and the Barrs remained. I knew they were very cut up about Ginger, so I invited them upstairs to my private lounge. There were Thomas, Mia, Callum, Hugo, Alexandre, the Kemps, Lucas, Rafiq, Barr and the twins. Fortunately, there were enough seats for us all.

"For a while everyone sat in silence. Then I gave them a glass of sherry and we talked about Ginger and the tragic circumstances of her death. I could tell by the conversation that they thought it should be avenged in some way, but it was Barr who actually put it into words. Have you met him, by the way?"

"Yes, I called there for petrol on my way here last year. They struck me as a very pleasant family," replied Oliver.

"They are now a very sad family. One evening, shortly after your visit, a car containing four youths drove onto their forecourt. Mrs. Barr was watching them from the kiosk as they filled up with petrol and when she realised they were going to drive off without paying she ran out to stop them. As the car shot away it caught her arm. She was not badly hurt but was shaken, so her husband took her to the cottage hospital for a check-up. She was detained overnight for observation and discharged the following morning. The doctor told her that apart from a bruise or two there were no physical injuries and advised her to rest for a few days."

"I'm sorry to hear it. She seemed a very decent sort when I paid for my petrol."

"She was an active member of the Womens' Institute and well liked in the Keswick area. The police found the car further up the valley the next morning, abandoned and burnt out. It had been stolen earlier in the day from Whitehaven. They still haven't caught the youths responsible. Three weeks later, just as she seemed to be getting over it, Mrs. Barr had a severe stroke which has left her almost completely paralysed. She now faces a future of being confined to a wheelchair, unable to walk or swallow, with tears running down her cheeks and saliva down her chin as she makes pathetic efforts to speak."

Oliver looked shocked. "What a terrible thing to have happened."

"Yes, it is. The Barrs were a very close and happy family. All four worked in the family business. The twins still live with their parents in the bungalow behind the garage and play rugby for a local club on Saturdays. They and their father are totally devastated by what's happened."

"I'm not surprised."

"Everyone present agreed that we should convene a formal meeting and that I should be the chairman. I was happy to comply. I opened the proceedings by saying that I believed we all had a single common interest, which was to catch and punish the scum whose criminal activities were causing so much misery in the area."

Bunny saw the surprise on Oliver's face. "You think I was putting myself at risk of being charged with conspiracy or incitement? Not so, because I was pretty sure of my ground. I knew that each one of them had a good reason for feeling the same way as I did."

"I can understand you and the Barr family feeling that way, but why should your staff have such a hatred of a few local tearaways?," asked Oliver.

"Call them tearaways if you like, but I will continue to call them scum. They're the scum of the earth. Be that as it may, I will answer your question. I already knew much about their pasts, but I wanted to hear it again from their own mouths. This is what each of them told the meeting:

"Rafiq said that two years earlier he and his cousin had left their native Pakistan to open an Indian takeaway in a former mining village near Whitehaven. They had been told about the vacant premises by an uncle who has an Indian restaurant in Carlisle, so they took the plunge and invested all their savings into the venture. They worked hard and the business began to make a small profit. One Saturday night some local men went in shouting racial abuse and attacked them with iron bars. Rafiq's cousin was so badly injured that he suffered brain damage and will never work again. Rafiq was too frightened to run the business alone, so he went to work for his uncle in Carlisle. However, he was subjected to racial taunts there, so he applied for a job at Surprise View. Ginger and I were pleased to take him on and he has turned out to be one of our best waiters.

"Mia had become a young single mother living alone in Keswick after her partner left her. She was a qualified nurse with a part-time job at the cottage hospital. One day she took her only child, a two year old boy, out in his pushchair, when a car went out of control across the footpath. Mia was unhurt, but the child, still strapped in his pushchair, was crushed under the car. Two youths ran off, leaving Mia screaming hysterically. They had stolen the car earlier in the day in Cockermouth, but so far the police have not traced them. After the accident she decided to give up nursing and applied to become a receptionist here.

"Hugo's knowledge of wines and his many contacts took him all over the world. When in Africa he had worked for a group of wealthy American conservationists, who appreciated good food and wine. While they were benefitting from Hugo's expertise in fine wines, Hugo became interested in their work. When he returned to this country he became the sommelier at a top London restaurant, but soon found that after Africa he did not like the city life. One evening he was mugged by a gang of youths and badly beaten up. He had seen our advertisement for a sommelier at Surprise View, so when he had recovered sufficiently he applied and got the job.

"Thomas brought his wife and two children from Gloucestershire to live in Cockermouth when he became the manager of the Workington branch of his firm of estate agents. When the disorder in West Cumbria escalated his office became a target. Thomas was subjected to verbal attacks in the streets, his car was vandalised and finally stolen. The window of his office was broken no less than nine times and then the building was set on fire. That was the last straw for his employers and they closed their Workington branch. However, shortly before Thomas was made redundant, his wife left him and took their children back to Gloucestershire, because they did not like living in Cumbria. Although Thomas is now estranged from his family, he has turned out to be the best manager we have had.

"The Kemps are our longest-serving members of staff. When he left school he served his time with a firm of builders, then after his National Service he joined the prison service. A few years ago they moved to Penrith to look after her elderly parents, where he set himself up as a jobbing builder while she got a job as the housekeeper at a local hotel. Unfortunately, his business did not do well and he was struggling to pay the bills. One night his premises were broken into and his van, tools and equipment were stolen. He made an insurance claim but was promptly reminded that he had not paid his premium. He was declared bankrupt and they lost everything, including their home. Although the police had found an abandoned car containing the same fingerprints as those at the scene, no arrests were made. Ginger and I heard of their plight and offered them jobs and the lodge to live in.

"Callum moved from Manchester to Carlisle, to become the manager of a new nightclub there. He had imagined that as there are so few coloured people in Carlisle he would be accepted by the local community, but he soon found himself the victim of racial taunts and abuse, both at work and on the streets. After locking the nightclub one night he was badly beaten up by some local youths. A friend told him that Surprise View were advertising for a restaurant manager, so he applied and we were pleased to take him on.

"Lucas was a young waiter working at a hotel in Maryport. Word got around that he was in a gay relationship with another employee and he was subjected to some very unpleasant homophobic attacks. He saw our advertisement for a waiter in the *Cumbria Star*, so he applied and got the job.

"Alexandre admitted that he was the only one present not to have suffered directly at the hands of the scum, although he hates them just as much as the rest of us. We took him on as a trainee chef five years ago and he has done extremely well, having worked his way up from chef de partie to sous chef and finally to head chef. His speciality pork dish has won him several awards and helped win him his third Michelin Star. He's always trying to improve it, even though everyone tells him it's already perfect."

Oliver smiled. "It's called Lomo de Orza. It was on the menu last year and was absolutely delicious. Because you were attending to the Rolls Royce as I was leaving I didn't have the opportunity to tell you how much I'd enjoyed it, but I mentioned it in my article. I always thought Alexandre was a French name?."

"He's really Alexander, or Alex after his father, but he prefers to be called Alexandre. There's still a belief that the French make the best chefs, although it's not always so nowadays." Bunny paused to pour the remains of the coffee into his cup, before continuing.

"Quite apart from the personal grief they were all still feeling, they were appalled by the escalation of crime at Surprise View. When they came here it was a peaceful place in a beautiful setting, with a wealthy clientele who appreciated the finer things in life and valued good service. But after the scum discovered the little road up to Watendlath things were never the same again. There was always some reminder of their nocturnal visits, such as a burnt-out car, criminal damage or graffiti. The staff had been upset by the damage to the Rolls and the busts, but after that things got steadily worse. Several guests told us they would not be coming back because of all the crime. In some cases their cars had been damaged or stolen while they were here.

"I told the meeting that I thought we should punish the scum whose criminal behaviour was causing so much misery. There was unanimous agreement. Thomas asked me if I had any ideas how this could be done. I said that I had, but I was not prepared to say any more until everyone had taken a vow of secrecy. They all agreed to this and one by one stood up and solemnly repeated some suitable words that I had prepared.

"When they had all taken the vow I began to explain my idea. We would set out to capture car thieves from the local towns and bring them back to Surprise View for appropriate punishment. I looked round and could see this had gone down well. I told them that I was prepared to close the hotel for as long as was necessary to achieve this, but I would need their assistance. If they agreed I would continue to employ them at the same salaries.

"When everyone did agree I continued. I said that I had heard of police using specially adapted cars to trap car thieves. When a thief breaks into the car he finds that the engine will not start and when he tries to get out the doors will not open. The police, who have had the car under observation, then move in and arrest him. I suggested that we use this method to capture the scum and convert some of the rooms here into prison cells to hold them. We would then subject them to appropriate punishments and attempt to train them to become civilised human beings."

Oliver's face, which had first registered shock, now registered a sudden dawning. "Does this explain the disappearance of the nine youths from Cumbria?."

Bunny regarded him patiently. "All will be revealed to you in the fullness of time, Oliver. My idea was greeted with enthusiasm, so I asked them for their own suggestions. Barr immediately said that he and the twins could adapt a car for the purpose. It would have to be a model popular with car thieves and strengthened to make it escape-proof. He thought that Saturday evenings would be the best time to deploy it, when towns are busy and cars are often stolen.

"Kemp then reminded everyone of his experience in the prison service. He suggested converting the second floor bedrooms overlooking the lake into prison cells to hold the scum, as the windows would be out of sight. He could make them secure by fitting armoured glass over the windows and reinforcing the doors. Thomas suggested installing CCTV cameras in the cells area and in the grounds. Electronics are his hobby, so he had the necessary expertise.

"Hugo surprised everyone by suggesting that we use an animal tranquiliser to capture the scum. When in Africa he had helped his employers to trap large animals, using a new fast-acting tranquiliser. He knew where to get hold of some and had a good idea about the dosage. If we could make a devise to inject it into the scum when they got into the car, they would be unconcious within seconds.

"One of the Barr twins said he could make a spring-loaded mechanism to fit into the seats. The weight of a body would trigger it and inject a dart containing the drug into the scum's backside. He thought they should be fitted into all the seats, in case there were more than one of them."

"Now I understand how you managed to capture me. I suppose I was shot from behind by a dart. My left thigh still feels sore," complained Oliver indignantly.

Bunny's lips curved briefly. "You'll soon get over it. It takes a few hours. It's a bit like recovering from a bad hangover. The other twin then suggested using their breakdown recovery vehicle to deliver the trap car to the location and bring it back afterwards with the scum inside, as it should attract little attention. When he and his brother had got the car into position they would park some distance away and keep it under observation. When a scum had broken in and was tranquilised, they would pull a sheet over the car, winch it up and bring it back to Surprise View. As each put forward his suggestion it was greeted with applause from the others."

"You were fortunate to have such talented helpers," said Oliver. "How did you intend to punish the thieves when you got them back here?."

Bunny picked up his cane and went to the window, then there was a long silence as he gazed at the view. Eventually he turned to face Oliver. He fixed him with his watery, red right eye and said "That's what they all wanted to know. I suggested that as soon as a scum was brought back to Surprise View he should be locked in a secure cell where he could do little damage. When he had come round he would be told that he was going to be birched for stealing the car, with additional strokes for other bad behaviour, such as foul language, threats or violence after his capture. The birching would be carried out by our warders in full view of other scum who might be in the cells. When he had recovered sufficiently he would be given two choices: either agree to a course of training, designed to turn him into a civilised human being, whereupon he would be transferred to a comfortable cell like this one."

"And if he didn't agree?."

A rare smile appeared on Bunny's scarred lips. "He would be executed."

Fourteen

Oliver continued to stare at Bunny, aghast. Eventually he said "You didn't actually go ahead with all this?."

"My dear boy, please save your questions for later and don't be naive. The word execution brought a spontaneous cheer and I used the opportunity to refill their glasses. When they had settled down again Kemp asked me what method we should use. I said I hadn't given the matter much thought. He then looked at me eagerly and put forward his own suggestion.

"When he was a prison officer he had seen the execution suites at several British prisons, before they were dismantled following the abolition of capital punishment in 1965. At one prison he became friendly with the prison engineer, who showed him the old Home Office plans for the execution chamber and scaffold, which had become a standard design. Kemp was fascinated by them and managed to make copies.

"He had always wanted the opportunity to build a working replica from the plans. He thought this could now be done by using two of the guests' bedrooms, one on the second floor and the one immediately below it on the first. Each room would be divided into two by building a partition wall, when half the upper room would be the condemned cell and the other half the execution chamber. The space below the execution chamber would be the pit into which the condemned prisoner would fall. Doors would lead into the execution chamber from the corridor and from the condemned cell.

"Kemp's suggestion was received with loud applause. I then proposed that we should adopt all the suggestions and when this was agreed I closed the meeting. They were all excited, so before we went our separate ways I reminded them about the need for strict secrecy."

"Unfortunately, we were obliged to run the hotel for another month, before we could close for the winter break. It wasn't easy to entertain the guests to our usual high standard and keep up the Christmas spirit, when our thoughts were with Ginger and our plans for avenging her murder. Those of us involved had to be very discreet and we made it a rule not to discuss it except at pre-arranged meetings.

"It was a huge relief when we finally closed and the last guests and the part-time staff left. In January Mia wrote to people with reservations for this year, informing them that due to Ginger's death and my sudden illness the hotel would remain closed until further notice. She also cancelled our orders with the catering suppliers and wine merchants, and our advertisements for seasonal staff.

"Even before Surprise View closed the Barrs had stopped taking in cars for repair and had made a start converting the one that was to be our trap car. They had chosen a sporty saloon model which is popular with young people and frequently stolen. They fitted steel sheets and special locks into the doors and replaced the windows and windscreen with toughened glass. To make it more appealing to the greedy scum, they fitted several attractive and expensive accessories. They also installed a miniature radio transmitter which can be picked on the recovery vehicle's radio, to let our team hear what the scum was up to when he got inside."

"All that must have cost the Barrs a lot of money," observed Oliver.

"I had already agreed to pay for the car and compensate them for their loss of profits. Ginger died a rich woman and left everything to me. I knew the operation was going to be expensive, but if it avenged her cruel murder it would be well worthwhile.

"As soon as the guests and part-time staff had gone, Kemp, with the help of Callum, Rafiq and Lucas, began work on the bedrooms. We had decided to use The Langdales and Grasmere for our execution suite, because we wanted it to be at the far end of the corridor and it seemed poetic justice that the scum should be hanged at the very spot where Ginger died. I remember you were in The Langdales last year, Oliver."

"That's right. Now I understand why the window is bricked up."

"Kemp wanted to follow the Home Office plans exactly. In the 1950s the windows of prison cells were high up in the wall, with bars on the inside, so they bricked it up to the same height. To make the execution suite as authentic as possible, they chipped the plaster off the walls and exposed the bricks. They removed the partition walls of the bathrooms and built new ones across the middle, then painted the walls in the same two shades of green that were used in prisons in those days.

"Next they started fitting out the execution chamber. They inserted two hooks into a heavy beam, which they lifted into the loft so the hooks would be directly above the scaffold. Then they cut two rectangular holes in the wooden floor – one in the centre for the trapdoors, the other against the north wall for the staircase down to the pit. Kemp made the trapdoors and the Barrs the operating mechanism. When everything was installed they tested it with a sandbag weighing twelve stone. We had fitted two hooks in the beam to enable us to have double executions and from these they suspended heavy chains.

"We had decided to carry out the executions in accordance with the Home Office rules and established practices of the 1950s. A few days before an execution the prison received a wooden box from Pentonville Prison, which was the training prison for executioners and the distribution centre for the necessary equipment. Kemp had obtained a list of the contents and began to assemble everything we would need to do the job properly.

"His next job was to convert the other four bedrooms into cells. He fitted armoured glass over the windows and covered the insides of the doors with steel sheet, having first cut observation windows. Scafell, next to The Langdales, would be our secure cell where we would put the scum on arrival. The bathroom was stripped out, the bricks exposed and it was fitted with two bunk beds, a lavatory and a handbasin, all securely fastened down. Helvellyn, Skiddaw and High Stile were to be our comfortable cells where we would put scum on the training course. Apart from the additional security to the windows and doors, they would remain as luxurious, en-suite bedrooms.

"We already had a CCTV system, but Thomas installed more sophisticated equipment in the cells area and the grounds. Each cell has two cameras and everything can be recorded. You may not have noticed it, but there's a camera pointing at us now, so if you were to attack me the warders would come in immediately.

"Kemp made a portable bench with adjustable straps, for when we birch the scum. It's a beautiful piece of craftsmanship made from polished English oak, on wheels so that it can be moved to different positions. There are plenty of young birch trees in the woods so he was able to make several birches of different sizes. To keep the long twigs supple, they have to be kept in water. We discovered that the Japanese *Arita-Imari* jar, which you admired last year in its alcove on the stairs, makes an ideal receptacle. One of Kemp's former colleagues knew where there was a store of obsolete prison equipment, so we were able to obtain uniforms, caps, insignia, whistles, handcuffs and truncheons, of the types used in the 1950s and 1960s."

Bunny stood up and went to the window. "By the middle of February everything was ready. The Barrs had completed the modifications to the trap car and tested them. Hugo had got hold of some of the tranquiliser and we tested the dart mechanisms by dropping a pig's carcass onto the seats. The cells and execution suite were finished and the gallows tested by hanging a dummy. I called a final meeting in the Lake Room, which everyone attended. They all reaffirmed their allegiance and repeated their vow of secrecy. Then I asked for volunteers for the different jobs.

"I was selected the commander and Kemp the chief warder and my second-in-command. The Barrs wanted to use their vehicles to capture the scum and Hugo thought he should go with them in case there was a problem with the tranquiliser, in which case he would have a dart gun with him.

"Rafiq, Lucas, Callum, Thomas and the Barr twins would be the warders and draw up a rota so there would always be two of them on duty. One of their jobs would be to birch the scum, with assistance from other staff if necessary. Alexandre would be responsible for the catering and help out elsewhere if required. Mia would be our medical officer and my personal assistant and Mrs. Kemp would see to the household matters. Barr said that although they had closed their garage to the public, he still had to be at the bungalow most of the time to look after his wife. However, he would accompany his sons on Saturday nights and help out at Surprise View whenever possible.

"Although we had agreed to be a democratic organisation, I told them that when it came to deciding the fate of the scum I was to be the interrogator, judge and executioner. They agreed to this and appointed Thomas the assistant executioner, or the 'Number Two' as he used to be known.

"That meeting was held on a Monday in late February and before it closed we decided to put our plan into operation on the Saturday night. We didn't want to travel far for our first capture so we decided on Keswick, where several cars had been stolen from a poorly-lit carpark on the edge of the town where there are no CCTV cameras.

"The Barrs and Hugo arrived in the recovery vehicle at nine o'clock. There was nobody about and only a few cars parked there. They went to the darkest corner and unloaded the trap car, then drove the recovery to the opposite corner and kept the car under observation through night vision binoculars from the rear cab. They could tell by the static noise from the radio that the transmitter was working.

"They waited for almost two hours, then a teenage scum in a hooded jacket appeared from the direction of the town and started looking at the cars. He spotted the trap car, approached it, then looked around to see if the coast was clear. He paid no attention to the recovery vehicle parked thirty yards away. He used a torch to examine the car inside and out, then took a screwdriver from his jacket, pushed it into the lock of the driver's door and gave it a twist. The lock, being the standard one, broke easily, so he opened the door and got in.

"They heard the various sounds on their radio: the approaching footsteps, the lock breaking, the door opening, the rapid breathing of the excited, greedy scum as he got in and slammed it; then a sharp intake of breath and a curse, followed by a fumbling noise, then just regular steady breathing.

"They waited for several minutes and when there was no change in the breathing they started up the recovery and drove across to the car. In the headlights they saw the scum slumped in the driver's seat, still clutching the screwdriver in his grubby hand. His gasp and curse must have been caused by the sting in his backside as he sat on the seat, but he would not have been able to see what caused it. The tranquiliser must have acted very quickly, because he didn't even have time to use his screwdriver on the ignition lock before losing consciousness. The team winched the trap car onto the recovery with him locked inside, covered it over with a plastic sheet and set off for Surprise View.

"They phoned us with the good news, so Mrs. Kemp had the gates open and we formed a reception party at the back door. The Barrs used a tool to open the door of the trap car, because the special locks they had fitted had activated when the scum got in. He was still unconscious, so Rafiq and Lucas, the duty warders, carried him up to Scafell on a stretcher. They searched him and confiscated certain contraband before locking the door.

"The following morning I went up to meet him. Rafiq and Lucas were still on duty and they showed me the items which were laid out on their desk. Apart from the screwdriver and torch, there was a flick-knife, some illegal drugs and a wallet containing a credit card and driving licence which were in a woman's name and had clearly been stolen.

"The scum had started to come round an hour earlier, having slept soundly since his arrival and was now demanding to know where he was and why he'd been locked up. He had assumed he was in a police cell, until he noticed the uniforms were different."

"I should imagine he was feeling pretty ill. I still haven't fully recovered," said Oliver.

Again Bunny's lips curved slightly. "As I have already told you, it takes a few hours. You'll have got over it by the morning. I saw the scum through the observation window, sitting on a bunk with his head in his hands. He was about eighteen, average height, slim, with cropped hair and sores round his nose and mouth from sniffing solvents. In his hooded jacket he looked like many of the delinquents who hang around our streets.

"When Rafiq unlocked the door and we went in, he gave us a sullen look When he realised we were not police officers he began shouting threats at us for detaining him, using the foul language that is, sadly, so common nowadays. Rafiq's right foot promptly lashed out and caught him squarely in a very sensitive area, causing him to scream in pain and collapse on the floor.

"After he had quietened down Rafiq and Lucas held him while I gave him a few strokes with my cane. Then I informed him that we are a private organisation, dedicated to capturing and punishing people like him who cause distress to others by stealing their cars. I explained that he was in a secure cell at a secret location where he would not be found, and that he was completely at my mercy. Finally, I sentenced him to twelve strokes of the birch for stealing the car, plus a further six strokes for his threats and bad language. As I spoke I had the satisfaction of seeing his expression change from sullen and resentful to fearful and respectful. To allow what I had said to sink in, I decided to leave him for a while before we administered the punishment.

"I am too old to participate in such strenuous activity and dislike the sight of blood, so it was Chief Warder Kemp who took charge of the proceedings two hours later. Needless to say, he'd been looking forward to the moment. Thomas and Rafiq were the duty warders and Callum, Hugo and Alexandre went along to assist. The punishment bench was wheeled into position outside Scafell.

"It was fortunate that the extra helpers were there, because the scum put up quite a fight. They eventually managed to strip him and strap him face down onto the bench, but during the struggle he made an unfortunate remark about Callum's skin colour. Kemp decided that he, Thomas and Hugo would each give him six strokes. When they had finished, Kemp told the scum that he was to be given another twelve strokes – six for the further foul language to be administered by Alexandre, and six for the racial abuse to be administered by Callum. When the birching was finished the scum's entire back, from his shoulders to his thighs, was a mass of bloody welts. The warders carried him back into Scafell and dumped him on his bunk.

"Later that day I went up to see him. He was still naked and lying face-down on his bunk. When I entered I had the satisfaction of seeing the fear return to his eyes. His back was raw, so I sent word for Mia to bring her medical box. When she came she said the wounds would have to be treated with iodine to prevent infection, so she produced a bottle of the stuff from her box and poured some onto a cloth. Before leaving the treatment in her capable hands I instructed the duty warders to give her whatever assistance she required. I understand they were both needed to hold the patient down, as she carefully and methodically worked her way down his back, all the time thinking about her little boy crushed in his pushchair under the stolen car.

"I didn't visit the scum again for a few days, but Kemp kept me informed of his progress. He remained locked in Scafell, fed on a typical 1950s prison diet provided by Alexandre. He was still naked, because his back had been too raw for clothes and his own were inappropriate for our 1950s image. I was delighted when Kemp told me that since the birching he had begun to show respect to the staff and had not been heard to swear once. It confirmed my view that corporal punishment, if sufficiently painful, is effective even with psychopaths.

"Five days after the birching Kemp told me that his back was beginning to heal, so I considered it time to have a chat with him about his future. When I went into Scafell he was sitting on his bunk and when he saw me the fear returned to his face. I stood over him and explained that he now had two choices.

He could agree to participate in our rigorous training course which was intended to turn him into a civilised human being, whereupon he would be transferred to a comfortable cell. I warned him that the course would be arduous and require his full co-operation. If he didn't agree, or if he subsequently failed the course, he would be sentenced to death and executed. I went on to explain that our new execution suite was next door to Scafell and we were very keen to try it out. I told him he had an hour to make up his mind.

"When I mentioned execution the scum went pale. As I stood up to leave he blurted out "Please sir, I agree to be trained. I'll do anything you want."

"The next morning the warders escorted him, still naked, along the corridor to Helvellyn. He had probably never seen such a luxurious room, because he stopped in his tracks and gawped idiotically at everything. Mrs. Kemp had obtained some new clothes for him from my gentleman's outfitters in Penrith and laid them out on the bed, but before the warders allowed him to touch anything they took him to the bathroom and stood over him as he shaved, showered and brushed his teeth.

"When Kemp went up to Helvellyn the scum was looking remarkably smart in the tweed sports jacket, grey flannel trousers, white shirt, sober tie and brown leather brogues that his wife had carefully selected. Kemp began to explain the training course. He told him that Helvellyn was one of our guest bedrooms and he was responsible for it and would be punished for any damage. If accidental he would be birched, but if deliberate he would be hanged. Alexandre would bring his meals, dishes selected at random from our à la carte menu. Before going out Kemp left him a book on English china and told him to learn the names of the Royal Doulton figures displayed in the Queen Anne corner cupboard in Helvellyn, adding that he would be tested on them the following day.

"We drew up a list of instructors for the course. Callum would teach table manners; Alexandre haute cuisine and the arts; Hugo fine wines and current affairs; Thomas conversational and interpersonal skills, and the Queen's English; Mia literacy, numeracy and personal hygiene; Kemp physical training, fitness and deportment. The course started well and for the first few days the scum made good progress.

"Kemp interviewed him and obtained a considerable amount of useful information, including details of the crimes he had committed and his accomplices. It was our intention to capture and punish as many scum as possible in the hope that the information they gave us would lead us to the ones who had attacked Ginger and my staff. We decided not to use the scums' names but to refer to them by number. Our first scum, therefore, became known as Scum One."

The telephone rang, interrupting Bunny's narrative. With tightly pursed lips he went to the bedside table to answer it. "I'll be down right away," he said tersely. Turning back to Oliver he said "It seems we have another intruder, so we'll have to continue our conversation later." Picking up his cane he strode out of the room, then Oliver heard the door being locked.

Alone again, he wondered who the intruder could be. Then he thought about what Bunny had told him and wondered how much of the plan they had already put into practice. So far nine youths had gone missing from local towns in three months. Were they alive or dead? He looked at his watch. It was almost seven o'clock and he thought about Ron and Marjory. They were expecting him for dinner again and he was already late. He wondered what they would think when he didn't turn up without letting them know, and what they would do when he had not appeared by the morning. And what about his appointment with the MD? If he didn't keep that he could say goodbye to the editor's job. He suddenly became very aware that he was a prisoner and out of touch with the outside world.

He began to wonder how he was going to get out of his predicament. Bunny had told him so much about what was going on at Surprise View that it seemed unlikely he would let him go. He picked up the phone and dialled the number for an outside line, but there was still no dialling tone. He went to the window and touched the thick armoured glass, then to the door and touched the cold steel. He looked around the room and spotted a small black perspex dome on the ceiling near the window. He went into the bathroom and saw another one in the corner above the bath. He wondered if the warders had noticed his curiosity on their CCTV monitor.

Still feeling under the weather, he sat down again and closed his eyes. He contemplated his chances of escaping or contacting the police. The cells seemed to be secure and well guarded, so perhaps his chances would be better if he was allowed out for exercise or for some other reason. He would just have to wait and see what tomorrow would bring.

His thoughts returned to what Bunny had told him and he wondered if any of the youths had been hanged. The whole thing seemed so indescribably evil that he could not decide whether Bunny and his gang were bad or mad. Were they all equally dedicated to the cause, or would one of them eventually talk?

He had been deep in thought for twenty minutes when the rattle of the key made him jump. The door opened and the duty warders came in carrying a stretcher, on which lay a young woman dressed in a white sweater, jeans and trainers. Her long, black hair hid her face, but Oliver could see that she was attractive with a good figure. The warders lowered the stretcher to the floor and lifted the limp body onto the bed. Before they went out one of them pushed a pillow under her head as the other put her shoulder bag on the bedside table.

Oliver went to the bed, knelt down and gently moved the hair from the pretty face. Then his heart missed a beat and he gasped as he realised that he was looking at Jessica.

Fifteen

It was almost two o'clock in the morning before the tranquiliser began to wear off. Oliver had left the bedside lamp on and had lain beside her on the bed, holding her hand and watching her as she slept. He may have dozed off himself, but the change in her breathing made him open his eyes. She had not moved and was still lying on her back where the warders had left her, but now her eyes were open and were staring blankly at the ceiling. He squeezed her hand, then leaned over so that she could see his face.

"Hello, Jess," he said.

At first she showed no sign of recognition, then a faint smile came to her lips and she whispered his name once, before closing her eyes again. She slept for two more hours, when her only movement was the rise and fall of her shapely breasts.

When she awoke for the second time she turned her head towards him, squeezed his hand slightly and whispered "Hello Oliver."

He leaned over and kissed her on the forehead, then lightly on the lips. "Hello darling. I'm going to look after you," he said.

She sighed. "I feel awful. Can I have a drink of water?"

He was prepared for this. He gently raised her head and held the glass to her lips. "You've been drugged. You'll feel pretty lousy for a few hours. It's how they caught me earlier in the afternoon, but I've almost recovered now."

Suddenly she looked apprehensive. "Where are we?," she whispered.

"We're in one of the bedrooms at Surprise View. It's High Stile on the second floor, the one the Prime Minister was in last year – next door but one to The Langdales, which was my room." He smiled and added "You remember The Langdales, don't you?"

The faint smile returned. "I'll never forget it," she whispered, before closing her eyes again.

The next time she woke she wanted to go to the bathroom. He helped her there and afterwards encouraged her to drink several glasses of cold water. Soon she felt well enough to sit in one of the armchairs. He sat in the other and held her hand.

"What's going on?," she asked.

"I was just going to ask you the same question. What the hell are you doing here?."

She smiled. "I came looking for you and now I've found you. But first you must tell me what's happening, then I'll tell you about me."

"It's an incredible story and I'm afraid we could be in serious danger. Do you feel up to hearing it?."

"Not really, but I'll do my best."

Oliver told her everything he knew: his article for *Venues*; his conversations with Ron about the editor's job, the closure of Surprise View and the nine missing youths; his flight in *Yanky Mike* and the blurred photograph of the bricked-up window and the ghostly face; his attempts to visit the hotel and his capture. Finally, he repeated everything Bunny had told him. Jessica listened, wide-eyed, and when he described the punishments and the conversion of The Langdales and Grasmere into an execution suite, her hand went to her mouth and real fear showed in her face.

"What do you think they'll they do to us?," she asked.

"I've been wondering that myself. Bunny is no fool. He's put us in here together and will assume that I'll tell you everything I know. He's unlikely to allow us to tell the police what's going on, so he may decide to keep us here." Oliver did not want to alarm her more than necessary by mentioning Bunny's other option.

She rested her head against the back of her chair and closed her eyes. "So we're in one hell of a mess. Do you think we could escape?"

"This room might look like one of the bedrooms, but in fact it's a prison cell. Try not to look at the security measures as I point them out, because the warders are probably watching us on their monitor. The black dome on the ceiling near the window conceals the camera. The window is covered by a thick sheet of armoured glass and the door by a steel sheet on the inside and locked from the outside. They're too tough to be smashed with a piece of furniture and if we tried to signal from the window the warders would see us on their monitor. They all seem pretty fit and have truncheons and handcuffs. We'll have to be careful when we use the bathroom, because there's a camera in there, too."

"Charming."

He leaned forward and squeezed her hand. "Don't worry too much, Jess. I expect Bunny will come and talk to us, so we may be able to pursuade him to release us. If not, they're bound to let us out sometime, for exercise or something, so we might get a chance to escape." He was sounding more cheerful than he was feeling. "Now it's your turn to tell me what you're doing here. I haven't stopped thinking about you for the past twelve months. I didn't think we'd ever see each other again."

"Neither did I, and I've been wanting you so much, Oliver. When I left you and returned to my pig of a husband, he was still asleep on his vomit-covered bed, so I changed into my nightie and sat in a chair. I tried to doze, but I couldn't stop thinking about you. I could still smell you on me and didn't want to wash you away.

"He woke at his usual time of half past six, fresh as a daisy would you believe, and announced that he had to be at a meeting in Carlisle at nine o'clock. He must have slept like a log after spewing up his anniversary dinner, because he hadn't noticed that I'd gone AWOL. We had an early breakfast, then packed and put our luggage in the car. When we went to pay the bill I was feeling guilty about the bedcover, but he told me not to say anything. I kept hoping you would appear before we left and I would at least have the opportunity to give you my name and phone number, but you didn't and my ex was in a hurry. As we were driving away I noticed your sports car was still there. The staff all seemed to be pre-occupied with the Rolls Royce and nobody mentioned the bedcover."

Oliver was staring at her. "Did you say ex?."

"I did. I left him three months later. As we were driving to Carlisle I couldn't stop thinking about you and I knew then that you meant far more to me than just a one-night stand. But I couldn't be sure that you were unattached and would feel the same way about me. I suddenly realised we had told each other practically nothing about ourselves and had no means of getting in touch."

He was now smiling. "I am unattached and it was just the same for me, Jess. Even if I had known how to get in touch with you, I wasn't sure that you would have wanted me. I kept thinking that perhaps you really loved your husband and had only come to my room to get back at him for the way he had treated you. By the way, why did you say 'same time next year' as you left?"

She thought for a moment. "I don't know, really. I was unhappy and insecure, but although I was fed up with my husband I hadn't decided to leave him then. I might have said it as a light-hearted remark to make the parting easier, as I thought we would probably never see each other again, but it could also have been my way of telling you that I was hoping that one day we would."

"Well, it succeeded in bringing us both back to Surprise View yesterday, even if it has resulted in our present predicament. What finally made you decide to leave him?."

"His drinking became worse and he became cold and remote towards me. Then I found out that for several months he'd been having an affair with one of the women from his factory. Fortunately, my job at the bank gives me financial independence and as we had no children to consider I decided to leave him there and then. I went to stay with my sister and the next morning after he'd gone to work I returned to the house, collected some things and left him a note telling him that I was divorcing him. Then I instructed a solicitor to commence the proceedings. I suppose it's my own fault for marrying him for his money in the first place, although he wasn't too bad looking then.

"After I'd made the break I began to think about you all the time, but I had no means of getting in touch and didn't even know you surname. I wondered if you'd remembered my parting words and decided to come here yesterday, just in case."

"It's Mills. But how did you get caught?."

"It was early evening when I arrived. I was thrilled when I saw your yellow Lotus parked at Ashness Bridge on my way up the hill. It was wonderful to know that you were nearby and we would probably be seeing each other again. I didn't know about the hotel being closed until I read the sign on the gate. I rang the bell and a woman came out of the lodge and explained about Ginger and Bunny and the closure."

"That would be Mrs. Kemp. I had to contend with her husband earlier."

"Without mentioning you, I told her that I'd stayed at Surprise View several times, but when it was clear that she wasn't going to open the gates I said goodbye and drove down to Ashness Bridge and parked next to you. I used my mobile to phone the hotel and got the same story that Mrs. Kemp had told me. I think I spoke to Mia."

Oliver smiled. "Great minds think alike. You did exactly what I'd done earlier."

"I sat in the car trying to work out where you could be. I thought you must either be at the hotel or trying to get there. As you'd left your car at Ashness Bridge it seemed possible that you'd been turned away too and decided to make your way up through the woods. So I locked the car and set off to walk."

He laughed. "That's exactly what I did. What happened next?."

"I eventually reached a fence with a 'private' sign on it, from where I could see the hotel. The fence didn't seem too high and there was nobody about, so I climbed over. I walked through some long grass and weeds and came to an old shed. I had just passed it when I felt a sharp pain in my bum. I remember thinking that I must have been stung by something and reached down to rub it, then nothing else until I woke up beside you."

He did not laugh this time. "That's exactly what happened to me, except that I was alone when I woke up. There must have been someone in that shed who fired tranquiliser darts at us. When I came round the back of my leg was still quite painful and someone had put a plaster on the spot."

Jessica struggled to her feet, loosened her belt and reached inside her jeans. She blushed and exclaimed weakly "The cheeky sods have put one on me! It still feels tender." She collapsed back into the chair.

"They also confiscated my mobile and car keys," said Oliver, getting up to fetch her shoulder bag from the bedside table.

She opened it and looked inside, then said resignedly "They've both gone, but everything else seems to be here." She rested her head against the chair and closed her eyes. "God, what a mess! I still feel pretty rough. Can we have some more sleep?"

He looked at his watch. "Good idea. It's been a rough night."

He went to the window. Dawn was breaking and the sun was beginning to bring the colours of the fells to life, but the lake was still an inky calm. He closed the curtains and went back to Jessica. Taking her hand he helped her from the chair and led her back to the bed, where they lay down together and fell asleep.

****

It was nine o'clock when Oliver awoke. She was still asleep and he tried not to disturb her as he crept to the bathroom. By the time he had shaved, showered and dressed, she was awake.

He went to the bed and kissed her. "Do you feel better?," he asked.

She gazed up at him and smiled. "Better for being with you again, Oliver. I think I'll get up now."

"Don't forget about the camera in the bathroom. I ignored it, because there doesn't seem to be much we can do about it. If we cover it over the warders will come in to see what we're up to."

"I suppose you're right, but I'm a woman and they're men," she said, heading weakly for the bathroom.

When she re-appeared some of the colour had returned to her cheeks and she was looking more like her old self. He took her in his arms and kissed her. She looked up into his eyes and said "Please look after me Oliver. When we get out of this mess can we always be together?"

"We'll get out of it somehow, Jess, then I'll never let you go. I think of you all the time and love you with all my heart," he replied.

"I love you, too, my darling. I've thought of no-one else since last year."

They kissed long and passionately, then hurriedly separated as the door was unlocked. One of the twins came in with a tray, which he put down on the table without speaking.

Oliver waited for the door to be closed again. "Dead on cue. They must have been watching us and seen that we were up and about."

"I hope they enjoyed the view in the bathroom," remarked Jessica drily.

Their breakfast was a bowl of cornflakes, a slice of bread with margarine and marmalade, and a mug of tea. They sat in the armchairs and ate without enthusiasm. When they had finished they pushed the tray away, then held hands and talked of their love for each other, their happiness at being together again, and the danger they found themselves in.

Soon Alexandre appeared and without looking at them or speaking picked up the breakfast tray. Oliver said pleasantly "Thanks, Alexandre. Will Bunny be coming to see us?."

The chef frowned. "He doesn't tell me his plans," he replied, as he was going out.

When the door was locked again Oliver looked at Jessica. "They're not as friendly as yesterday. Something must have upset them."

"My unannounced arrival, I expect." As she was still under the weather, they spent the rest of the morning sitting in the chairs, holding hands and talking.

Lunch was no better than breakfast, but afterwards Jessica seemed more cheerful. She smiled at Oliver and said "I've been in these clothes for nearly two days, so I'm going to have a bath. I see we've got one of those Jacuzzi baths. I haven't been in one before."

"Good idea. I think I'll do the same. Mind if I join you?," he asked with a grin.

She giggled seductively. "Come on then. Save water – share a bath with a friend. We've got some catching up to do."

****

Their bath, which lasted an hour and a half, seemed to transform the couple. Although they were still in the same clothes, Jessica had done her hair and was looking quite radiant.

"You must have worked wonders on me in there, because I feel a different woman," she said.

Oliver took her in his arms and kissed her. He smiled into her eyes and said "You're looking more like your old self, Jess. If you were wearing the jewellery you had on last year I'd say you looked like a million dollars."

Suddenly she became serious. "Half a million, actually. My ex bought them for me after a particularly good year at his factory. He insisted on locking them in the safe in the bedroom and would only let me have them when we went somewhere special. When I walked out on him that night he must have changed the combination number, because when I went back for my things I couldn't open it, so I didn't get them back."

"That sounds a bit mean," said Oliver.

"He was in some ways. He'll probably give them to his next woman, or allow her to wear them occasionally if she toes the line. I'm not really bothered because I don't usually go in for expensive things and they weren't really me." She smiled again and added mischievously "But wearing all those diamonds as you made love to me for the first time in The Langdales did make me feel deliciously decadent."

"I seem to remember you doing me a painful injury with your bracelet. I thought for a moment you'd made me impotent."

"And I seem to remember you were soon back in action, my darling."

Their laughter was cut short by the sound of a key in the lock. They turned round and saw Bunny standing in the doorway. He was holding a silver tray on which stood three champagne flutes and an ice bucket containing a magnum bottle. They thought he looked extremely dignified as he succeeded in putting it down on the table without dropping his cane.

Sixteen

"What *am* I going to do with you two?." Bunny fixed the couple with his damaged right eye as he towered over them.

When they did not reply to his clearly rhetorical question, he took the chair with the heart-shaped back from the dressing table and sat down facing them. As he lifted the magnum from the ice bucket Oliver recognised the famous Louis Roederer Cristal label. When he had filled the three flutes Bunny raised his own to the couple. "This is certainly no time for celebration, but as I have always told our guests, champage is a drink that can be enjoyed at any time – so bottoms up!." A brief twinkle appeared in his undamaged eye.

They sipped the wonderful cold champagne, then put their glasses down on the table. Bunny looked at Oliver. The twinkle had vanished and when he spoke his voice was cold. "Yesterday I asked you why you had come here and you gave me an explanation that I was inclined to believe. However, you made no mention of this young lady who, I recall, was staying here last year at the same time as you. Yesterday, within a few hours of each other, you both made enquiries with the Kemps at the lodge, then phoned our reception. Each time you were told that the hotel is closed until further notice. Shortly afterwards you were both captured at the same spot, while trespassing in our grounds. Later, we discovered your cars parked together at Ashness Bridge. I find all this too much of a coincidence to believe that you are not involved in some sort of a conspiracy against us."

Oliver was wondering if Bunny was giving them the champagne to make them more talkative. Jessica was staring wide-eyed at his scarred face and he hoped she would not divulge too much. He decided to reply first and chose his words carefully. "I met Jessica for the first time when she was staying here with her husband last year. After dinner they invited me to join them for coffee and we chatted for half an hour before they went to bed. I didn't meet her again until last night, when your warders carried her in on a stretcher."

Bunny's damaged lips curved briefly. "Oliver, I am not a fool. I happen to know that afterwards she went to your bedroom and you spent most of the night together, before she returned to her drunken husband in the early hours."

Jessica managed to look shocked. "What utter nonsense," she exclaimed indignantly. Oliver simply looked at the floor and shook his head.

Bunny was looking at the couple patiently. "My dear young things, hotel staff have a nose for such things and Mrs. Kemp has a nose like a bloodhound's. After you had gone she reported to Thomas that someone had been sick over the bedcover in Grasmere and had ruined it. When she went to make the bed in The Langdales she found copious amounts of evidence that it had recently been occupied by two very active people – she did not say 'slept in'. Callum said that he had seen Oliver stroking Mrs. McBain's leg on the sofa in the Poets' Room as her drunken husband snored beside her.

"Thomas played back the video recording from the camera on the second floor. It showed Mrs. McBain appearing furtively from the staff staircase and knocking on the door of The Langdales, before being admitted. Five hours later she is seen leaving The Langdales and returning the same way. The recording from the first floor camera showed her leaving Grasmere and returning five hours later."

The couple said nothing. The twinkle returned to Bunny's good eye as he continued. "Should further evidence of your relationship be required, we have a video recording of your remarkable activities in the bath this afternoon. I thought my toast to you just now was rather appropriate, didn't you?."

Oliver did not reply. He glanced at Jessica and saw that she was blushing. Bunny paused before continuing. "Mrs. Kemp guessed what had taken place between the three of you." He looked at Jessica. "Are you still married to that drunken boor, Mrs. McBain?."

"I've just divorced him, so I'd rather you call me Jessica if you don't mind," she replied.

"As you wish. So it seems that you two have become an item, as they say." The twinkle returned briefly as for the second time Bunny picked up his glass and raised it to them. "Jolly good luck to you both."

"Thanks, Bunny," said Jessica.

Bunny put his glass on the table and walked to the window. For a few moments he looked at the view, then turned to face them. "This does not alter the fact that you present a danger to our organisation and your presence here is most inconvenient. Yesterday, Oliver, I told you a considerable amount about our activities before being interrupted by the totally unexpected arrival of Jessica. I expect you have already passed the information to her?."

"Jessica simply came to look for me, thinking that I might be here. I haven't had time to tell her anything yet, so you can safely let her go."

"Very chivalrous, I'm sure. However, you must realise that I daren't do that. No, I'm afraid you'll both have to remain locked up in here until I decide what to do with you. Alexandre will bring you your meals. He's very versatile and can produce 1950s prison food just as readily as haute cuisine."

The couple stared at Bunny, stunned. After a long silence he asked them amiably "Would you like me to finish telling you about our activities?."

"I think we'd both be interested to hear them," replied Oliver.

"As you probably realise, we have so far captured nine scum. Scum One is still in Helvellyn, progressing on his training course. Exactly two weeks after he arrived we captured Scums Two and Three in a carpark in Workington. We put them in Scafell and when they came round we discovered they were brothers, aged nineteen and twenty-one. They turned out to be a couple of extremely unpleasant psychopaths totally lacking any feelings or remorse. When we came to birch them it took eight of us to strip them and deal with them one at a time. Afterwards they went berserk in Scafell and managed to wrench the handbasin from the wall, so when I went to see them, instead of telling them about the training course I simply condemned them to death.

"They had been so violent that we decided it would be safer to hang them seperately. We transferred Scum Two to the condemned cell, leaving Scum Three in Scafell. Fortunately, they were less violent after they were separated. Two warders remained on condemned cell duty with Scum Two until we hanged him at nine o'clock the following morning. The gallows worked perfectly and everything went without a hitch. After the body had been taken down we transferred Scum Three to the condemned cell and hanged him twenty-four hours later."

The colour had drained from Oliver's face as Bunny was relating this. Jessica, too, had turned pale. He jumped up and advanced on Bunny with clenched fists.

"You must be mad if you think you can get away with this, you murdering bastard," he shouted.

Bunny grasped his cane like a sword and pointed it at Oliver's chest. His voice came like a whipcrack. "Sit down and behave yourself or you will both find yourselves back in The Langdales, not as illicit lovers but as condemned prisoners." In an instant he had changed from being Bunny the successful, urbane hotelier to Captain Bernard Liddle MC, twice mentioned in dispatches.

However, it was not the change in the old man's demeanor that prevented Oliver from grabbing the cane from his deformed hand and attacking him with it, but Jessica's warning shout that made him hesitate and look round. Callum and one of the twins had rushed into the room and were advancing on him with their truncheons in their hands.

He unclenched his fists and backed away from Bunny, then sat down and allowed his breathing to return to normal. Jessica reached for his hand and squeezed it. Bunny lowered his cane. "That's better. You won't get another warning," he said, his voice and complexion returning to normal. He dismissed the warders with a gesture of his hand and when they saw that the situation was under control they went out, but Oliver noticed the twin continue to watch them through the observation window.

Bunny continued his narrative as though nothing had happened. "It was quite a coincidence that the first ones to be executed at Surprise View should be from Workington, when the last executions in this country, which took place simultaneously at prisons in Manchester and Liverpool at 9 a.m. on the 13th. August 1964, were of two men who had committed murder in Workington. Then everyone was so confident of reprieves that when the one in Liverpool was told by the prison governor that the Home Secretary had refused them, he went berserk and bent the bars on the window of the condemned cell."

When the couple said nothing Bunny continued. "Of course we're not mad at Surprise View. Each of us knows exactly what we're doing and why, and we all have our personal reasons. We know we won't get away with it for ever and that sooner or later the police will arrive. But before that happens we hope to have attracted sufficient attention to our cause to result in changes to our ludicrous criminal justice system."

"What's wrong with the system?, asked Jessica.

Bunny jabbed a finger at her. "I'll tell you what's wrong with it, young lady. Every day in this country the lives of decent, ordinary citizens are made hell by the activities of a minority of our young people. The present laws tie the hands of the police when dealing with them, and prevent the courts from handing out proper sentences. Citizens daren't take appropriate action, fearful of the consequences of taking the law into their own hands. As a result, an underclass of untouchables has grown up, whom I prefer to call the scum of our society."

Bunny went to the Georgian pie-crust table near the window and picked up three issues of the *Cumbria Star.* He returned to his seat and began to turn the pages. "These are typical of the reports that appear every week in our local papers: *Violence in Cumbria on the increase; church destroyed by fire after burglary; car crime 'out of control' in county; man dies during rioting after addict's funeral; anti-social family evicted after a thousand incidents; weekend madness – major disorder outside nightclub & fifteen windows smashed in town centre; Cumbria tops league in binge drinking.* Would you like me to go on?."

"Those sort of things happen everywhere nowadays, Bunny. It's the way society has gone in the past few years. Cumbria is not unique," said Oliver.

Bunny leapt to his feet and hurled the newspapers to the floor, startling the couple. "Poppycock and balderdash," he shouted furiously. "They certainly do not happen everywhere. Most Cumbrians are respectable, law-abiding citizens. If the criminal scum would stay in their filthy industrial towns and villages, as they used to, it wouldn't be so bad. But when they bring their despicable activities to these beautiful places they must be caught and punished. Those wonderful comrades I saw killed in Normandy would turn in their graves if they could see the society that has emerged from their noble sacrifices. Furthermore, I have a duty to avenge Ginger's cruel murder."

When the couple did not reply Bunny sat down again and wiped his eyes. After a long silence Oliver said quietly "Bunny, I think you should know that eighteen months ago my parents were killed in a car crash in the Lake District, not far from here. The other car, which had been stolen, was being driven recklessly. Two youths, who have not yet been caught, drove away from the scene, leaving my parents to die in their burning car, then they set fire to the stolen car to destroy the evidence. I desperately want to see justice done, but I want to see the youths arrested and dealt with by the criminal justice system, not lynched by vigilantes."

Bunny snorted. "The British criminal justice system is useless. Even if the police do catch them the courts will be unable to hand out adequate sentences. Anyway, we're not vigilantes at Surprise View and we don't lynch people. We're simply doing what the state should be doing, as our punishments are the approved ones handed out by the courts in this country before the abolition of corporal and capital punishments. They contain the necessary four elements of an effective punishment, which are retribution, deterrence, incapacitation and rehabilitation."

"They're certainly strong in retribution, but if nobody outside Surprise View knows what's going on here, birching and hanging these lads is hardly a deterrent to others, and someone who has been hanged can't be rehabilitated into society," said Oliver. When Bunny did not reply he continued his argument "Offenders still received a fair trial in the 1950s and weren't hanged for stealing cars."

"We treat them perfectly fairly at Surprise View," replied Bunny impatiently. "As an alternative to being hanged they have the chance to undergo a training course intended to turn them into civilised human beings. Only if they choose not to take it, or they demonstrate that they are incapable of being trained, do we execute them."

"No civilised society birches people for such minor offences," said Jessica.

"That's where you're wrong, Jessica," said Bunny, using her name for the first time. "Singapore is a civilised, modern society that is virtually crime-free because of the firm stance it has taken against anti-social behaviour. Punishments meted out by the courts include between four and ten strokes of the cane for writing graffiti. As a result, there is no graffiti in Singapore."

"I believe they still have a mandatory death sentence for drugs trafficking," said Oliver.

"Quite right. Hangings take place on Fridays in the Singapore prison. We don't have a special day for them at Surprise View."

"Drugs trafficking is one thing, but writing graffiti on walls is another. Surely nobody in this country would find that sufficiently offensive to want offenders caned for it?," said Jessica.

"Don't underestimate the strength of public feeling against anti-social behaviour. Some people find it so offensive and intimidating that their lives are affected by it. For example, the elderly lady who daren't visit her church on Sunday evenings for fear of intimidation in the streets; the person who is put off using public toilets because they are so filthy; the motorist who is forced to take another route because of roaming gangs; the owner of the nice home whose outlook is ruined by litter and graffiti; the pedestrian who collects chewing-gum on his shoes from the pavements, then finds more of the revolting stuff stuck on the seats of trains, buses and restaurants, having been discarded by the demented ruminants who chew it."

Jessica was smiling at Bunny's vehemence. "Don't these things ever happen in Singapore?," she asked.

"Very rarely. Singapore is an incredibly clean country, which can be attributed to its penalties for these so-called minor misdemeanors. There are fines for jay-walking, spitting, importing chewing-gum and not flushing a public toilet. The fine for smoking in a prohibited area is one thousand dollars. Because of its strict anti-littering laws, which include a two thousand dollar fine and a Corrective Work Order to clean a public place for a repeat offence, Singapore has become known as the Garden City."

"The people must live in fear of such draconian laws," she said.

"Not at all. Ask any Singaporean and he will tell you that it's the only sensible way to run a society. When Singapore broke away from Malaysia in 1965 it was faced with the problem of how to have four million people of many different ethnic groups living harmoniously on a tropical island, and it came up with this formula. Consequently it now has a vibrant, multicultural, law-abiding population of Chinese, Malays, Indians and other races, who respect each others' religions and customs and help celebrate each others' festivals, which include Chinese New Year, Hari Raya Haji, Deepavali and Christmas. The ethnic groups are fully integrated and don't lead parallel lifestyles, eyeing each other's cultures and customs with deep suspicion, as they do in this country."

Oliver was shaking his head. "The British people have lived under the threat of invasion for thousands of years, which has made us slightly xenephobic. Also, we have a tradition of Christianity, human rights, tolerance, equality, democracy and opposition government, not authoritarian rule."

Bunny snorted. "Opposition government means broken promises. I couldn't count the number of times an opposition government in this country has promised to crack down on crime and anti-social behaviour in its manifesto, then failed to keep it when elected."

"Singapore has only four million people to control. There are nearly sixty million of us in Britain," said Oliver.

"Which means we have fifteen times as many burly policemen with strong right arms, able and willing to give young offenders a sound caning in our police stations. It's simply a matter of scale. I was caned several times at school and it certainly didn't do me any harm."

Oliver caught Jessica's eye and they exchanged smiles. Jessica said "You're wrong about corporal punishment, Bunny, because violence only breeds violence."

"From which I infer that non-violence breeds non-violence. If so, why has today's young generation, most of whom have never received corporal punishment, turned out to be the most violent this country has ever known?"

The ensuing silence encouraged Bunny to continue. "Singapore has compulsory national service, which gives young men skills for other trades, low unemployment and because of its policy of good cheap housing at low interest rates for all, there is very little homelessness. As a result, it has become the business core at the heart of south-east Asia's thriving economy, with the world's best airport.

"You're beginning to sound like a travel brochure now," said Oliver. "Do you imagine that when all this comes out, public opinion will be on your side?."

"Yes, I believe it will. On the rare occasions that victims have stood up to scum in this country they have received a considerable amount of public backing and have even become national heroes."

Oliver was beginning to tire of the argument. "What happened to the others?," he asked.

"The following Saturday evening our team went to Maryport. They left the trap car on some waste ground and kept it under observation from a side street. Sure enough they soon made another capture. Scum Four turned out to be a seventeen year old who already had a long criminal record. At first we thought he was going to be co-operative, because when we offered him the chance of the training course he jumped at it. However, on the second day he swore at Thomas as he was trying to teach him how to speak the Queen's English, so I condemned him to death and we executed him the following morning."

Jessica was now staring at Bunny in horror and contempt. "You're a snob and a reactionary, as well as a murderer!," she exclaimed, her voice choking with emotion.

"My dear Jessica, don't upset yourself so. Everyone is a snob of one sort or another. Sir John Betjeman summed it up very neatly when he wrote of 'that topic all-absorbing, as it was, is now and ever shall be, to us – CLASS."

"Rubbish," snapped Jessica.

Seeing her face still flushed and not wanting her to provoke Bunny further, Oliver quickly intervened. "All that sort of thing went out a long time ago, Bunny. We live in a classless society now."

"Have it your own way," replied Bunny patiently, clearly reluctant to be side-tracked into a puerile argument about snobbery and class. "The following Saturday they went to Carlisle and made another capture. Scum Five was twenty-three, our oldest so far. After we had birched him he agreed to be trained, but he lost his temper as Callum was teaching him how to hold a knife and fork properly, so we executed him the following morning."

Oliver shot Jessica a warning glance. She bit her lip and continued to glower at Bunny in silence.

"Unfortunately, when they went to Ambleside the following Saturday they were unsuccessful. However, a week later they captured a fifteen year old in Whitehaven. Despite his young age, Scum Six was a hardened little criminal and a drug addict. When he had recovered sufficiently from his birching I went up to Scafell to explain the options to him and he boldly told me to fuck off. I'm pleased to say that by nine o'clock the next morning his cockiness had left him, because he cried and pleaded for his mam, as he called her, as the warders restrained him sufficiently for me to pinion his arms, before carrying him, screaming, to the scaffold."

"For God's sake, stop it! I don't want to hear any more of this," sobbed Jessica covering her ears.

Bunny ignored her. "Scum Six was our youngest so far and when he was reported missing the police began to take things more seriously. We had been following the reports in the *Cumbria Star* and up to then the disappearances had not attracted much attention, but when the fifteen year old went missing it made the local headlines and the Head of CID took over all the cases."

"So things are hotting up for you," said Oliver.

"I have no doubt we will be caught eventually, but I am an old man and no longer fear the consequences. I will be satisfied if our achievements result in changes to the system." He paused. "The following Saturday they were successful again in Carlisle. Scum Seven was a sixteen year old local delinquent. He agreed to be trained and we transferred him to Skiddaw, where he co-operated for three days. The following afternoon he was supposed to be reading a book on Renaissance art when he went berserk. Before the warders could overpower him, he had smashed a valuable French side cabinet, together with Ginger's fine collection of Staffordshire figures displayed inside. Somehow he composed himself during the night, because at nine o'clock he managed to stand unaided and look me in the face, as I pulled the hood over his head and adjusted the noose round his neck."

Anticipating another outburst, Oliver gave Jessica's hand a cautionary squeeze. Bunny noticed the movement and said "You asked me what happened to them so I'm telling you. The team had to miss the next Saturday because of a mechanical problem with the trap car. However, the following week they were successful in Cleator Moor. Scum Eight was an eighteen year old who already had several convictions for drug offences and dishonesty. Apart from being illiterate and innumerate he was extremely fat. He agreed to be trained, but after a couple of days when this proved impossible I simply condemned him to death. The following morning he was calm enough until he felt the noose being pulled over the hood, when his knees began to sag. The warders on the cross-planks had to support his very considerable weight as I rushed to the lever."

Oliver glanced at Jessica and was relieved that she was keeping quiet.

"Scum Nine was brought in from Whitehaven ten days ago and is our latest capture. He's an unemployed nineteen year old with a long criminal record from a council estate. He agreed to be trained and so far is making satisfactory progress in Skiddaw, next door to you. Unfortunately, they were unsuccessful in Wigton last Saturday.

"Of course, not all the captures have gone without a hitch. Scums Two and Three tried to kick their way out of the car when they felt the darts and managed to do some damage before losing conciousness. The dart failed to tranquilise Scum Five, so they had to unlock the door to let Hugo fire one into his neck.. Last week as they were returning from Whitehaven with Scum Nine they were followed by a police car, which had them worried until it turned off for Workington."

"So out of the nine you have so far murdered seven. I don't suppose you can train more than two at a time because you don't have enough cells," observed Oliver.

"Executed, please, not murdered. Yes, we are short of cells, which is why it's inconvenient having you here. We will shortly be converting the five bedrooms on the other side into cells for trainees."

"Have you any plans for this Saturday ?" asked Oliver.

"Of course. Our policy is to capture scum every Saturday, whenever possible. We're going to try in Appleby shortly, when the horse fair starts."

Jessica was still looking shocked. Oliver had buried his face in his hands. "This is ghastly. It seems incredible that such terrible things should be happening in such a beautiful place. I implore you not to kill any more, Bunny."

Bunny picked up his glass and walked to the window. For a few moments he stared at the view in silence, as he finished his champagne. Still facing the window he said "Yes, I quite agree with you Oliver, Surprise View is a very beautiful place, which makes the scums' criminal activities seem worse, don't you think?."

Suddenly, he threw his head back and began to roar with laughter. Oliver and Jessica were startled, not just because of its sheer unexpectedness, but because they had not seen him laugh before.

"Surprise View!" Bunny exclaimed as he continued to roar with laughter. He turned and faced them. "Surprise View, oh yes, that's very appropriate. I hadn't thought of it before. Ginger would have loved that. Surprise View, indeed!." The couple were staring at him in astonishment as he continued to laugh until his scarred face was crimson and tears were rolling down his cheeks.

Eventually, his laughter subsided. He wiped his eyes with his silk handkerchief and put his empty champagne flute on the table. Still chuckling to himself, he picked up his cane and went to the door. As he was going out he turned to the couple and burst out laughing again.

When he had recovered sufficiently he said "Surprise View! Oh yes. That's very funny. You two have certainly been surprised at my view."

Seventeen

The couple stared at each other as the sound of Bunny's laughter receded down the corridor. Oliver saw the dejection on Jessica's face and gave her hand an encouraging squeeze. "Cheer up," he said.

"I just wish he wouldn't keep calling them scum. It's a horrible word," she replied, still looking miserable.

"I suppose calling them that instead of using their names shows the utter contempt they have for them." When she continued to look miserable he smiled and raised his champagne flute to her in a mock toast. "Bottoms up, darling!."

It had the desired effect. She smiled wanly as she raised her own glass. "Bottoms up, Oliver. I hope the video makes them go blind." This made them both laugh.

They drained their glasses, then Oliver held her and kissed her and felt her body relax in his arms. "We'll just have to make sure we're under the bedclothes in future," he said, giving her bottom a queeze.

She giggled and wriggled away from him. "Not now, darling, its broad daylight and they can see what we're up to. Perhaps they're peeping toms."

"It will just have to keep till later then." He glanced at the magnum of champagne, still two-thirds full. "We'll keep that for later too and make an evening of it. It should stay cold in the ice bucket."

For the next hour they sat in the armchairs and chatted. At seven o'clock the door was unlocked and Alexandre appeared with their supper, which he put on the table without speaking. When he had gone they looked at the unappetising meal. It comprised two thin slices of some unidentifiable fatty meat curled up at the edges with greyish mashed potato and overcooked cabbage, swimming in a pool of half-congealed gravy, followed by a square of pale sponge in congealed custard.

When she had eaten as much as she could, Jessica grimaced and put down her knife and fork. "I wonder which Alexandre finds the most difficult – preparing Cordon Bleu meals for the guests or 1950s prison food for the prisoners?"

They pushed away the uneaten remains and continued to chat until the door was unlocked again and Callum appeared. They were getting used to the sight of the uniforms by now. He picked up the tray and as he was leaving Oliver asked him "As we may be locked in here for some time, do you think we could have a television?"

"I don't see why not, but I'll have to ask," was the reply.

He was soon back, accompanied by Rafiq carrying a television set. They put it on the pie-crust table beside the pile of magazines and plugged it in. As they went out Oliver thanked them.

The ITV national news had ended and the Border regional news was just starting. They heard the newsreader announce "Cumbria police have still not traced the nine youths reported missing from local towns in the past four months. Cumbria's Head of CID will not say whether the disappearances might be connected, but the police are making nationwide enquiries and will welcome any information from the public."

"Things are hotting up for Bunny. It won't be long before it's on the national news," he said.

"I'm praying that the police arrive here soon. Surely someone noticed the Barrs' breakdown vehicle at the times of the disappearances, or saw it afterwards on CCTV recordings, and put two and two together?"

"Not necessarily," replied Oliver. "Their choice of vehicle was clever. Cars are always breaking down or being in accidents and local garages like Barr's are contracted by the motoring organisations to provide a twenty-four hour service to turn out and recover them, together with the passengers and luggage. It's unlikely that anyone would pay much attention to Barr's recovery vehicle late at night anywhere in Cumbria, with or without a car on its ramp. Of course, the police were not looking for the trap car because it was never reported stolen."

"Well, they can't get away with it for ever. I hope to God they get caught before they can hang anyone else," said Jessica.

When the news ended Oliver took the magnum from the ice bucket and filled their glasses. Jessica joined him in his armchair with her arm around his neck, as they sipped the cold champagne and watched a film. By the time it had finished the bottle was empty. Oliver drew her face towards his and stroked her cheek. "I love you, my bonny wee Scottish lassie. Och aye, I do. When we get out of here we're going to spend the rest of our lives together."

She giggled. "I might be Scottish but I never say och aye. That's funny, because that's just what I was going to say. About the rest of our lives, I mean." She giggled again. "Oh dear, I think I'm getting tight. Let's go to bed."

He laughed. "Wanton woman! That's just what I was going to say." He pulled her to her feet and began to turn off the lights.

"What on earth are you doing?," she giggled."We don't want to be the stars of another of Bunny's peep-shows, so we'll have to manage in the dark."

****

Tuesday morning was bright and sunny. After breakfast she asked him "Do you think they might let us out under supervision, to get some exercise?."

"It's worth asking. It won't be much fun being locked up in here all day with nothing to do, even if it is a beautiful room," he replied.

"Nothing to do?." She was looking at him mischievously. "We found plenty to do last night and managed to get some exercise at the same time. But seriously, we do need to get some proper exercise if we're not going to turn into couch potatoes. You never know, we might have to make a run for it."

"Apart from being wonderfully slim, you look pretty fit. Do you exercise much?."

"I used to play tennis and hockey at school. Before I was married I took up judo at a local club and did quite well at it, but had to give it up because my ex disapproved. After we were married I joined a gym, where I used to work out regularly. It got me out of the house and with working at the bank all day I needed the exercise. Since I went to live with my sister the gym has been paying me to take keep-fit classes three evenings a week."

"Good for you. I play golf occasionally and try to keep reasonably fit by swimming."

He put the question to one of the twins when he came for their breakfast tray. "I'll see what Bunny says, but I wouldn't be too hopeful," was the reply.

When they were alone again they went to the window and stood with their arms around each other gazing at the view. It was a beautiful, cloudless day and they could see the full ten miles to the north end of Bassenthwaite Lake. On the far side of Derwentwater a party of walkers was setting off for the top of Catbells. There were dozens of yachts and rowing boats on the lake and one of the old passenger launches was heading gracefully towards them leaving a white wake behind it.

"Isn't this view simply magnificent," sighed Jesica. "The Victorians called Derwentwater the Queen of the Lakes."

Oliver nodded. "It's easy to see why. Now, close your eyes and tell me how many islands there are," he instructed her.

"Four."

"Sometimes there's a fifth, when a mass of weed is brought to the surface by methane gas. Did you know that the level of Derwentwater falls by several inches every year? Nobody's quite sure why, but there's said to be a leak"

"I wonder where it leaks to. Now I'll ask you one. Do you know why the Aurora Borealis are sometimes called Lord Derwentwater's Lights?"

"I haven't a clue," replied Oliver.

"Because they flashed very brightly on the night the Third Earl of Derwentwater was executed for his part in the Jacobite Rebellion."

"Where on earth did you learn that?"

"Ginger told me three years ago."

"Poor old Ginger. She was quite a character." Oliver pointed towards Keswick. "Friar's Crag is just along there, from where Ruskin got what he described as the finest view in Europe. The island nearest Keswick is the largest of the four and the only one that's inhabited. It's called Derwent Island. There's an eighteenth century Georgian mansion on it that was built by an eccentric, which is now owned by the National Trust. They're always looking for new tenants."

"I'm not surprised. They must get fed up with having to get into a boat every time they need some milk or a newsaper," she said.

Oliver laughed. "The last ones had to make thirty-five boat trips to move all their belongings across and were once iced in for ten days. The terms of the lease require someone to live there all the time and the National Trust has to be informed whenever they're going to be more than half an hour's drive away. Furthermore, the house has to be opened to the public five days a year."

She giggled. "It sounds just the place for us, darling. I've always wanted a stately home and you could keep fit by swimming backwards and forwards with the shopping."

They kissed, then continued to look at the view in silence. After a while she sighed and said "William Wordsworth once said that the Lake District belongs to the people who have an eye to perceive and a heart to enjoy."

"Poor old Wordsworth probably couldn't see it very well because he had very poor eyesight," said Oliver.

"Was he shortsighted?"

"No. As a result of an unfortunate choice of lady friend while on a visit to France at the time of the revolution, he developed chlamydia which spread into his eyes. His vision became so poor that he had to have extra candles on his pew at his church at Grasmere. The holders can still be seen today."

"He should have stuck to admiring daffodils. Was he at Grasmere when he saw the famous golden host?"

"Wrong on two counts. It was on the shores of Ullswater and it wasn't William but his sister Dorothy. She mentioned them in her diary and her vivid description inspired William to compose his immortal poem," replied Oliver.

"Perhaps his inspiration was helped by drugs and a touch of madness. I read somewhere that Coleridge and Ruskin were both depressives who took laudanum. When Coleridge was in the Lake District he used to take a potent mixture of opium and spices called Kendal Blackdrop," said Jessica.

"Many people in those days took what are now illegal drugs. They would have been useful in the absence of proper medicines. Queen Victoria took cannabis for her period pains."

A disturbance in the corridor brought their conversation to an abrupt end. Oliver rushed to the door and looked out. Hugo and Lucas, the duty warders, were pushing the punishment bench into position outside High Stile. Callum appeared from the right holding a large object in his arms. Oliver recognised it as the *Arita-Imari* high shouldered jar which he had stopped to admire on the staircase the previous year. As he carefully lowered it onto the carpet the handles of three birches protruded obscenely from its broad neck. He saw Oliver watching and grinned broadly.

As the three men disappeared from view, Oliver was engulfed by a feeling of dread. Soon he heard noises from the next room. First bangs and shouts, then a scream followed by cries. A young male voice began to plead "Please don't birch me again. I'm sorry, I couldn't help it, it was an accident. I'll pay for the damage, but for God's sake don't birch me again." Oliver recognised the broad accent of West Cumbria and remembered that the last capture, the nineteen year old from Whitehaven, had been put in Skiddaw for his training course.

The two warders came back into view holding the youth by his ankles, followed by Callum and Kemp grasping his wrists. Apart from a single earring, the pale, slim body suspended between them was naked. He was struggling and sobbing and Oliver could see the terrified look on his face as they carried him to the bench. Despite his frantic pleas they turned him over and dropped him face-down on the polished oak. They attached the straps to his wrists and ankles and tightened them so that his arms and legs were stretched outwards and downwards, making further movement impossible. The youth's bullish, cropped head was turned towards Oliver, enabling him to see the terror on his spotty face, as well as the welts from his previous birching, which still covered his back.

Kemp looked into the *Arita-Imari* jar and selected one of the birches. As he lifted it out drops of water fell onto the carpet. He stood in front of the youth, playfully waving the supple twigs in his anguished face and splashing it with water. He took a coin from his pocket and looked at Lucas and Hugo. He spun it and when the four men saw how it landed on the carpet they gave ironic cheers. Kemp handed the birch to Hugo.

Oliver became aware of Jessica at his side. "What's happening?," she asked anxiously, trying to see through the small window.

"They're about to birch the youth from Skiddaw for breaking something. I don't think you'll want to watch."

"Oh God, they're sadists. Whatever he's done, he doesn't deserve this. I'll lock myself in the bathroom until it's over."

Oliver continued to watch in fascination as Hugo removed his cap and tunic, tucked his black tie into his blue uniform shirt and went to the far side of the bench. Determination appeared on his face as he raised the birch high above his head, then there was a swish and a crack as he brought it down with all his strength across the bare shoulders of his victim. The youth gasped, his fists clenched and his face contorted with pain.

Hugo's arm went up again and Oliver realised that he was putting his all into the punishment. He began to count the strokes: one, two, three, four, five. With each one the gasps grew louder and the face registered greater pain. The sixth stroke landed on the same spot as the first and produced a loud scream. Hugo was now breathing heavily and his face was flushed, both from the effort and the satisfaction of a job well done.

The youth was opening and closing his eyes and sobbing with the pain of the welts which were beginning to bleed. Suddenly he noticed Oliver watching him and for a brief moment there was eye contact between the two prisoners, when the youth's pleaded for mercy and compassion, as Oliver's conveyed his sympathy and encouragement.

Hugo handed the birch to Lucas. When the youth saw it in the hands of the younger man and realised his punishment was not yet over he began to panic "Please, no more. I'll pay for the damage for God's sake, but I can't take any more."

With an eager look on his young face, Lucas grasped the birch and went to the far side of the bench. He raised his arm high above his head and brought it down with tremendous force across the victim's buttocks. Oliver saw that he was targetting the lower part of his back. After the sixth stroke he realised that he must be at least as strong as Hugo, as the bloody welts now extended evenly from his shoulders to his thighs.

Lucas replaced the birch in the *Arita-Imari* jar and the four men unstrapped the moaning victim and carried him back to Skiddaw. There was a thump as they dropped him onto the wooden floor, then a bang as the door was slammed. They reappeared and removed the bench and the *Arita-Imari* jar. Kemp was the last one to disappear from Oliver's view and as he did so he gave him a cheerful wave.

Shocked and sickened, he turned away from the scene. He knew that it had not been morbid curiosity that had made him watch the punishment, because he had already made his mind up that somehow or other he would give evidence against Bunny and his gang in court. He remembered Jessica and opened the bathroom door. She was sitting fully clothed on the edge of the bath, with the taps running and the jets on. Her face was pale and when she saw Oliver she ran to him and flung her arms round his neck.

"It's alright, darling. It's over now," he said, stroking her head.

"I thought the noise of the water would block out the sound, but I still heard the poor boy's screams. They're bloody sadists."

"I know. It was terrible. I hope I never have to watch anything like that again. But it's over now, so let's try to think of something else. I wonder what's on television."

They settled down to their daily routine. At lunchtime Callum made no mention of the birching, or their request to be allowed out to exercise. After lunch they watched an old film. When it ended Jessica stood up and said. "This is no good, Oliver. We're turning into couch potatoes. Come on, strip off, we're going to do some exercises."

Oliver raised his eyebrows as she began to undress, but followed her instructions. "This is one way of getting a man's trousers off him, but you're not having everything," he laughed.

In only her bra and pants, Jessica turned on the radio and found Radio One. She turned up the volume until the loud rhythm filled the room, then they went to the window and lifted the pie-crust table with the television on it out of the way. When they had cleared enough space she told Oliver to stand facing her and follow her instructions, then they began their work-out in time to the music.

It lasted for half an hour and when it was over Oliver was exhausted. Jessica turned off the radio and laughed at his breathlessness. "That's how I run my classes at the gym. If you were one of them I'd tell you that you're not in bad shape, but you could benefit from more regular vigorous exercise. We should keep this up twice a day for as long as we're in here, because it might come in useful."

The sweat was glistening on Oliver's face. "I'm surprised you don't give them all heart attacks. I've discovered muscles I didn't know I had," he said breathlessly, eyeing her up and down. Suddenly he took her in his arms and kissed her.

"What's come over you, all of a sudden?," she laughed when he released her.

Oliver noticed a movement at the observation window. Callum was watching them and grinning broadly. He ignored him. "It must have been the sight of you leaping around in you bra and knickers. Fancy a shower?."

She giggled seductively. "That sounds like a good idea. I can massage your aching muscles and anything else you have in mind, my darling. The shower curtain should block the camera's view."

Eighteen

When the couple looked out of the window on Wednesday morning the mountain tops were hidden in cloud, and although it had stopped raining, the trees and the ground below were still wet. As soon as they had finished dressing, the door was unlocked and Lucas appeared with their breakfast. When they had eaten they sat in the armchairs. Jessica turned the pages of a *Cumbria Scene* magazine and Oliver tried to read a novel from the small selection he had found on a shelf. But despite their outward calmness, each had an inner dread of what the day ahead might bring.

He suddenly glimpsed a warder going past, followed by Kemp and Mia, then they heard the door of the adjoining cell being opened. He jumped up and went to the door in time to see Mia disappearing from view, holding a green plastic box by its handle. He turned back to Jessica. "The angel of mercy has just gone into Skiddaw with her medical box. I think she's going treat the poor devil's back with iodine."

"Oh God, I couldn't bear to hear him scream again. Let's do our keep-fit now. It's a bit soon after breakfast, but it will take our minds off what's happening next door and the music will block out the sounds."

She found Radio One and turned up the volume, then they stripped off to their underwear and began their workout. When it was finished they left the radio on and disappeared into the bathroom. An hour later they reappeared and turned it off. At first they heard nothing, but when Oliver pressed his ear to the wall he heard groans. He continued to listen and heard the youth mutter "I'll kill the fucking bastards" and repeat this several times.

He turned to Jessica. "They must have given him the iodine treatment and left him to recover, because he's muttering threats. I hope for his sake they don't hear him."

They settled down to their routine. As they had heard nothing about their request to be allowed out for exercise, they reminded Callum about it at lunchtime. "Bunny hasn't made up his mind yet," was all he would say. In the afternoon they did another work-out. When it was finished she told him "You're improving. I think we'll make it a longer session tomorrow."

"You're wearing me out, you Scottish slavedriver!," he replied breathlessly, taking her by the hand and leading her to the bathroom. "Shower or Jacuzzi?"

"You choose this time, you sexy Sassenach!"

****

Thursday was a glorious day. After breakfast they went to the window. There was hardly a cloud in the sky and the sun was picking out the greens, browns and mauves of the fells around Derwentwater. Already there were several boats on the lake and on the far side a group of people had parked their minibus and were walking along the narrow road towards the big house where Hugh Walpole had lived. Suddenly, the tranquility was shattered by two military jets flying up the lake at very low height. The combined noises of their engines was just audible through the armoured glass.

"Aren't there a lot of complaints about low flying in the Lake District?," asked Jessica.

"Quite a lot. When I was at the *Star* we were always publishing letters from irate local residents. The RAF have a liaison officer in the area who handles their public relations. They have to practice low flying in mountainous terrain, because in the Falklands..."

He had stopped in mid-sentence and was staring at the door. "What's the matter?," she asked anxiously.

He went to the door and looked to the right. "I just saw Bunny go past with a warder. I think they've gone into Skiddaw." He went to the wall and for several minutes kept his ear pressed against it as she watched him anxiously. When he turned back to her his face was pale. They heard a door being slammed then saw Bunny returning in the opposite direction.

Jessica saw the shock on Oliver's face. "What's happened?," she asked in alarm.

He swallowed. "It was awful. I heard Bunny condemn the poor lad to death. Apparently the warders heard him making the threats. He began to cry and plead for his life."

Jessica put her arms round him and held him tight. "Oh God, I'm frightened,

Oliver. We've got to get out of here."

"I know, darling. We might just get a chance if they let us out for exercise." They held each other for several minutes, until they saw Kemp and the twins walk past heading for Skiddaw.

This time there was no need to press their ears to the wall, because they could hear the youth shouting and pleading for his life. "For Christ's sake don't hang me. I didn't mean it, I didn't think you could hear me. Please don't hang me."

"Get your arms behind you," shouted Kemp.

"Christ, mind my fucking back," screamed the youth.

"Keep still while I put these on. It's not your back you need to worry about now."

"I'll bring his clothes later," called out one of the twins. The three men emerged from Skiddaw with the naked youth suspended between them, his wrists held behind his back in old-style police handcuffs. As they passed High Stile Oliver saw the terrified look on his face and heard his anguished pleas. The iodine had changed the colour of his wounds from vivid red to yellowish-brown. The sounds receded down the corridor as the party disappeared towards The Langdales. For a few moments there was silence, then the sound of a heavy steel door being slammed.

When Oliver looked round Jessica had disappeared. He found her in the bathroom, pale and trembling. She looked up at him fearfully as he put his arms around her. "That poor boy. I just caught a glimpse of him. He looked terrified and his back looked awful. Will they really hang him?" she asked.

"I expect so. According to Bunny, all the others were executed at nine o'clock in the morning the day after they were condemned."

"We can't just let it happen. We've got to do something to stop it."

"I suppose we could plead for his life and explain that he hadn't intended to be overheard. After all, it was a pretty natural thing to do, after what they'd done to him."

Jessica was looking puzzled. "You said he was just muttering. I wonder how they heard him?."

Oliver frowned, then exclaimed "Christ! I should have thought of it before." He put a finger to his lips. She watched him in surprise as he went to the bath and turned on the taps and jets. He held her in his arms and whispered in her ear "The cells must be bugged for sound, as well as having cameras. I don't know where the microphones are, but they can probably hear everything we say when we're talking normally. If we don't want to be overheard we'll have to come in here and run the bath and whisper. I just hope they didn't pick up on what we were saying earlier about escaping."

Jessica moved her mouth to his ear "We could stay in the bedroom and turn on the radio or TV and whisper. But won't they be suspicious if they see us whispering?."

"Probably, but if we're under the duvet they won't know," he whispered, giving her bottom a squeeze.

Some of the tension disappeared from her face and she managed a smile. "Come on then, my priapic man, let's give it a try."

****

After lunch they sat in the armchairs and began to read. Suddenly, she put down her 'Cumbria Scene" and said "It's no good, Oliver, I can't stop thinking about that poor boy. We can't just let them murder him tomorrow morning without trying to prevent it. The least we can do is protest."

"I agree. Perhaps we should demand to speak to Bunny," he replied.

When she nodded he picked up the phone. She heard him say that they needed to speak to Bunny urgently. He put it down and turned to her. "Mia says she'll pass the message on, so we'll just have to wait and see what happens."

After their afternoon work-out they showered and changed, then waited for Bunny to come. They discussed what they would to say to him, in mitigation of what the youth had been heard to say and as a plea for clemency. When Bunny had not appeared by supper time, they reminded Callum.

"I'll pass the message on," was his reply, as he went out.

After supper they thought about the youth in the condemned cell as they waited for Bunny. At eight o'clock they turned on the radio and found Radio Cumbria. There was a report about the missing youths on the local news which was similar to the one they had heard on the Border TV news, but there was no mention of it on the national news.

When Bunny had not come by eleven o'clock, Jessica picked up the phone and dialled the number for the reception, but got no answer. She dialled the number for room service and again there was no answer. She dialled the number for an outside line, but there was no dialling tone. "It looks as though they're ignoring us," she said morosely, putting it down. They went to the door and looked left and right, but there was no sign of anyone. For several minutes they hammered on it with their fists, but the thick steel deadened the sound and nobody came.

When nobody had come by midnight they went to bed, in dread of the morning. For the first time they did not make love, but spent most of the night under the duvet, whispering about their plight and ways of saving the condemned youth. Eventually, just before dawn, they dozed off.

The bedside alarm startled them into full wakefulness. Its display said 8:30 am on Friday. "Half an hour to go," he said. He jumped out of bed, went to the door and looked left and right. "I can't see or hear anything."

"I'm going to keep trying." She sat up in bed and picked up the phone, then began to dial repeatedly. After several minutes she banged it down in disgust and complained bitterly "I still can't get anyone."

"They must have heard us planning to protest and decided to hold us incommunicado until it's over," he said. He switched on the television and pressed the mute button as a breakfast show came on the screen. "At this time of morning they show the time, so if Bunny is as punctual as I believe him to be, we should see some activity in about twenty minutes."

"We can't simply do nothing. Let's try banging on the door again," she said. They pulled on their clothes, then hammered on the door and shouted for several minutes, before finally giving up. He glanced at the screen. "It's no good. Either they can't hear us or they don't want to. The poor kid's got fifteen minutes left."

She sat on the edge of the bed holding her head in her hands. "If they do hang him, I hope it's quick, because he's suffered enough already."

"According to Bunny, they observe the same strict procedures that were followed before the abolition of capital punishment. If that's the case, his death should be quick and painless." He went back to the door and looked in both directions, then turned back to her. "Still nothing happening." He went to the bed and put his arm round her.

Suddenly she stood up and said "We've got to stop them if we can. I'll try phoning again." Oliver went to the window, as she picked up the phone and began to dial again. Eventually she screamed "bastards!" into it and slammed it down. He went to her and held her as she sobbed on his shoulder. "Don't get too upset, darling. We've done all we can." He took her hand. "Come and look at the view."

They stood at the window and held each other. When her sobs had subsided she gazed at Derwentwater and sighed. "It's said that beauty is in the eye of the beholder. Most people would consider this to be one of the most beautiful views in the world, but to some, including the poor boy they're about to hang, it would mean nothing."

"It's understandable if children aren't taught to appreciate beauty and never get taken anywhere nice," he said.

"Which explains why the young tearaways who've been making life hell for everyone at Surprise View see the road to Watendlath merely as a convenient place for their criminal activities."

He nodded. "Bunny and his gang certainly had grounds for complaint, but who would have thought they would have gone to these lengths to seek their retribution?."

Jessica sighed. "In another hour the holidaymakers will be out on the lake. Some will look up and admire this attractive building. If only they knew what was going on here, or if only we had some means of telling them."

He glanced at the muted screen. The presenters of the breakfast show were laughing silently as they introduced another guest. "Ten minutes to go. It'll be too late for the poor lad in the condemned cell, I'm afraid."

She suddenly looked fearful. "Will we hear anything?."

"I'm not sure. The condemned cell is next door but one and the execution chamber is on the other side. We might hear something if he starts to shout or fight when they go in for him. To be on the safe side you could cover yourself with the duvet."

"Couldn't we turn up the television?"

He looked at her and said earnestly "Look darling, I'm a journalist. I hope one day to give evidence against these murderers, so I'm going to watch, listen and remember what happens here today." He went into the bathroom and she followed, then she watched him as he stepped into the empty bath, picked up a tumbler, and held it against the tiled wall. After a few moments he turned to her and said "It was very faint but I thought I heard a deep voice reciting something, then male voices singing. It sounded like the hymn *The day Thou gavest, Lord, is ended*, but I may have been mistaken. I'll have another look along the corridor."

They returned to the bedroom. The screen said 8:55 a.m. Jessica continued to watch it as Oliver went to the door and looked out.

"Shouldn't something be happening by now?," she asked nervously.

He looked left and right, then turned back to her. "In the 1950s the executioner and his assistant, the prison governor and various officials assembled outside the doors of the condemned cell and the execution chamber at two minutes to nine, so something should be happening very soon. If they come up the staff stairs we won't see them, but if they use the main staircase they'll walk past."

"It's 8:57. I'm shaking like a leaf."

"So am I, so I dread to think how the poor lad's feeling." He was looking to the right. "Hang on, I think they're coming."

"I don't want to see or hear anything, so I'm going to hide in the bed," said Jessica.

Oliver watched the approaching procession. In the lead was Hugo in his warder's uniform, then Bunny and Thomas, both in dark suits, white shirts, dark ties and polished black shoes, each holding a leather strap, followed by Kemp in his Chief Warder's uniform and braided cap. The handkerchief in Bunny's top pocket was not the usual floppy, brightly-coloured silk, but a stiffer, white fabric. They all looked solemn. As they passed High Stile Oliver banged on the door and shouted Bunny's name, but they gave no sign of having heard. They passed the empty Scafell and proceeded to The Langdales, where they gathered outside the condemned cell in silence. He could just see Kemp's back.

He was beginning to wonder if there would be anyone else, when the second party filed past. It consisted of Alexandre, Mia and Mrs. Kemp as the witnesses, followed by Callum and Rafiq in uniform. The witnesses were dressed in sober suits and reminded him of respectable mourners at a funeral, except that Mia was holding the green medical box by its handle. They passed the first party standing outside the condemned cell and proceeded out of view towards the execution chamber.

He turned away from the scene. Jessica had disappeared and the screen now showed 8.59 a.m. The presenters and their guest were still laughing silently. He looked out again and could still see Kemp's back. Suddenly he heard the rattle of keys in locks and steel doors being swung open, then Kemp's back disappeared.

He dashed to the bathroom, grabbed the tumbler and pressed it to the wall. He reckoned it was fifteen seconds to nine. For a moment he heard the same deep voice, then something heavy being moved, followed by Bunny's voice. He thought he heard the youth's voice, but he wasn't sure. The voices became fainter, then a short silence, followed by a crash that reverberated through the building.

The noise was so loud and unexpected that Oliver, whose nerves were already at breaking point, almost dropped the tumbler. With thumping heart he jumped out of the bath and went into the bedroom. He saw the curled-up shape under the duvet and sat on the bed, allowing his breathing and pulse to slow. His hand found her shoulder and squeezed it. "It's over now, darling," he said gently.

She emerged like a frightened rabbit, her eyes wide with fear. "What was that noise, for Christ's sake?"

"It must have been the trapdoors falling. I didn't expect anything like that," he replied.

"Thank God it's over. I hope it was quick and he didn't feel anything."

"If they did their calculations correctly, death would have been instantaneous."

"It's horrible to think of him hanging on the end of a rope."

"The 1950s rules required the medical officer to certify death. I expect that's Mia's job here."

"I hope she enjoys it."

"Then the body had to hang for an hour before it could be taken down. The executioner and his number two always did that. They attached a pulley to the chain, put a rope under the armpits, hoisted it up, removed the noose and hood, then lowered it to the floor of the pit and put it in a coffin."

Jessica was still looking shocked. "I can't imagine Bunny doing that," she said with a shudder.

Their conversation was interrupted by the door being unlocked. Alexandre came in with their breakfast. "I'm afraid things are running a little late this morning," he said pleasantly, putting the tray down on the table.

He went out and as the door was being locked again Oliver yelled after him "Murdering bastards!"

Nineteen

Later that morning Kemp paid them a visit. Jessica's hackles rose when he appeared in the doorway in his Chief Warder's uniform and braided cap. Fearing she might give him a tongue-lashing, Oliver gave her a warning glance, because he did not want her to wreck their chances of being allowed out for exercise and was already regretting his outburst to Alexandre.

Kemp had anticipated the cold reception. He raised a hand and said. "I know what you're going to say, but I haven't come here to be lectured. Bunny and I have discussed your request and have no objections, provided you don't go down to the ground floor. You'll be supervised by the duty warders."

Jessica looked surprised. "Is there a gym at Surprise View?."

"I'm afraid not. Our guests would never expect such a thing. If they want exercise they go for healthy walks on the fells. All we can offer you are the corridors and staircases of the bedroom floors for jogging. There's nowhere else, so if you're not interested you'll have to remain locked up in here."

"I suppose it's better than nothing," she said without enthusiasm.

"When can we start?," asked Oliver.

"This afternoon. The duty warders will come for you every afternoon at three o'clock, for a half hour session. They'll be watching you, so don't try anything, or the consequences will be severe," Kemp replied, turning smartly on his heel.

When he had gone Oliver said "The corridors are about forty yards long. If we keep up a good pace for half an hour, we should get quite a lot of exercise."

"Not as good as a gym, but better than our work-outs in here. Anyway, we can still do those in the mornings as well. It's a pity we haven't got a change of clothes. These will get sweaty, but I suppose we can rinse them through. I don't mind exercising in my undies in here, but not outside."

They were waiting eagerly when Rafiq came for them at three o'clock. "Follow me and do exactly what I say," he instructed.

For the first time since their capture they stepped out of High Stile. They followed Rafiq to the warders' station, which was at the end of the corridor near the staff staircase. It comprised a large desk with a chair on either side and some shelves fixed to the wall beside it. On the desk were a telephone, a radio handset, a CCTV control panel and recording equipment, a TV monitor and some office files. As he got closer, Oliver identified the desk as a beautifully veneered mahogany Victorian partners' pedestal desk. He imagined Bunny and Ginger facing each other across it as they worked on their accounts in their upstairs office.

Callum was sitting in one of the chairs with an open file in front of him, watching the monitor. He nodded to the couple as they approached. Oliver noticed that the TV screen was showing a corridor with the caption 'first floor' and the time and date.

Jessica was staring wide-eyed at something behind Oliver. He looked round and where, the year before, there had been the door of The Langdales, there were now two steel doors, twelve feet apart, each with a swivel flap at eye level. He suddenly remembered they were outside the execution suite where, less than six hours earlier, the youth had been hanged.

Rafiq began to give them instructions. "Your route is along this corridor, down the main staircase to the first floor, back along the first floor corridor, up the staff staircase and back to this station. We will be watching you on the monitor so don't try anything or you'll regret it. I'll come with you on your first circuit." He removed his cap and tunic and tucked his black tie into his shirt. "Right, let's go," he ordered briskly.

They followed Rafiq along the second floor corridor at a fast jog. Oliver read the names on the doors: Scafell, High Seat, High Stile, Kirkstone, Skiddaw, High Street, Pillar, The Old Man. When they got to Helvellyn he thought of the first youth in there on his training course. They ran down the main stairs to the first floor landing, where he saw the *Arita-Imari* jar standing in its alcove with the handles of several birches visible at its neck.

The first floor corridor was deserted, but the lights were on and the black dome on the ceiling reminded him that they were being watched. As they ran along he read the names: Derwentwater, Windermere, Ullswater, Coniston, Ennerdale, Thirlmere, Bassenthwaite, Buttermere, Wastwater. They passed a valuable marquetry side cabinet then came to the last room on the left, Grasmere. As they ran past he imagined the youth's body on the rope and wondered if it had been taken down.

Then they were running through the open emergency door, up the staff staircase and back to the warders' station.

"Right, keep that up for half an hour," instructed Rafiq breathlessly, sitting down opposite Callum.

The couple continued their run without an escort. Each time they passed the warders' station Rafiq and Callum were at the desk, watching their progress. Oliver noticed that the monitor still showed the first floor corridor. However, after a dozen laps their interest in them began to wane, as Callum became absorbed in his file and Rafiq gave them only a cursory glance as they ran past, panting and perspiring.

When their half hour was up Rafiq escorted them back to High Stile, where they collapsed into the armchairs. When they had recovered they went into the bathroom, stripped off and turned on the shower. They held each other under the powerful jet and began to whisper.

"Any ideas?," asked Jessica.

Oliver moved his mouth to her ear. "It won't be easy. The warders can see us on the second floor corridor and the camera covers the first floor corridor. But I didn't see any cameras on the stairs. The trouble is, the main staircase can be seen from the reception and the staff staircase from the kitchens."

She moved her mouth to his ear. "Where do you think they've put our cars?"

"I don't know. They'll want to keep them out of sight. There could be a garage at the back, or they might be on the staff carpark. But even if we could get to them, we wouldn't know where to find the keys."

"Couldn't we make a run for it if we can reach one of the entrances?."

"Possibly. But we'd need a good head start. When we don't reappear the warders will raise the alarm and everyone will start searching. Remember, they have tranquiliser guns and perhaps other firearms as well. The Kemps will guard the gates, other staff will search the grounds and they'll telephone the Barrs for them to come up and help. There's no point in us going up to Watendlath because the road ends there and if we go down to the main road we're likely to run into the Barrs."

"So we'll need a car"

"Either ours or one of theirs. I want to take a look at the staff carpark. If Rafiq and Callum are on duty again tomorrow and they drop their guard as they did today, I'll make a detour down the staff stairs and have a quick look around."

"For goodness sake be careful, darling," replied Jessica, as they continued to hold each other under the warm water.

"Don't worry, I'm a big boy now."

Her wet hand reached down between them and her slim fingers found his hardness.

"I know. What are we going to do about it?."

****

The rest of Friday was uneventful. They watched a lot of television as they tried to put the horrors of the execution out of their minds. By supper they had regained their appetites and managed to eat everything. Afterwards, they kissed and cuddled in one of the armchairs, then went to bed and made passionate love for an hour under the duvet, before collapsing, exhausted, into each others' arms.

On Saturday morning they awoke feeling refreshed, but still thinking about the events of the previous day. After breakfast they did their morning work-out.

Once again they were ready in good time for their afternoon run and gave inaudible sighs of relief when it was Rafiq who came for them at three o'clock. They followed him to the warders' station, where Callum was reading a file and did not bother to look up. As they began their run the warders paid them little attention, but the monitor still showed the first floor corridor. After half a dozen circuits Rafiq began to read a paperback as Callum continued to be engrossed in the file. Oliver noticed that the monitor was now showing the inside of a bedroom, with a youth sitting at a desk on which was a pile of books, and Thomas standing over him. The caption read 'Helvellyn'.

They began the next circuit and when they reached the main staircase he whispered "They're not paying us much attention. When we're out of sight of the camera on the staff staircase I'll nip down for a quick look. It should only take half a minute, so they're not likely to miss us."

As they ran along the first floor corridor they were concious of the black dome on the ceiling behind them. When reached the staff staircase and were out of its line of vision they stopped, looked up and down and listened. Satisfied there was nobody about, he left her keeping watch and crept cautiously down.

"Be careful, darling," she whispered after him.

The stairs ended in the corridor near the back door. The door was of solid wood with no handle or lock, but a sign above said 'Emergency Exit – push bar to open'. Beside it was a window which overlooked the carpark. He looked towards the glass door of the kitchen and seeing nobody he went to the window and looked out. There were eight cars in the carpark, including his yellow Lotus Elise, an elderly red Mini which fitted the description of Jessica's, Bunny's Rolls Royce and an old Ford Escort which looked like the one Callum and Hugo had arrived in. On the far side of the carpark stood the staff building, but there was no sign of life.

He turned away from the window and glanced towards the kitchen, but it was still deserted. He was about to run back up the stairs when he noticed a small wooden cabinet on the wall. Through its glass front he could see rows of keys on hooks. He looked along them and recognised his car keys by the Lotus badge on the fob.

The detour had taken him just over half a minute. As he ran back upstairs Jessica was looking down anxiously and beckoning him to hurry. He gave her a thumbs-up sign and they continued their run up to the second floor. As they passed the warders' station, Rafiq and Callum were still reading and the screen was still showing Helvellyn. Confident that the detour had not been noticed they began the next lap. When their half hour was up, Rafiq signalled them to stop, then escorted them back to High Stile.

"I don't think they suspected anything," whispered Jessica when they were under the shower. "What did you see?."

Oliver held her from behind and began to whisper in her ear, telling her what he had seen, both inside and outside the building.

"Yes, that's my Mini," she whispered, when he described it.

He pressed his mouth closer to her ear. "If Rafiq and Callum are on duty again tomorrow and we get the chance, I think we should make a break for it."

"O.K. But I'll be so nervous I won't be able to sleep tonight for thinking about it."

He kissed the side of her neck and began to fondle her breasts as the warm jet continued to beat down on their bodies. She turned her head and whispered "You're becoming a big boy again. Perhaps you're turning into a frotteur."

His hands travelled down over her flat tummy and through her pubic hair, then he felt her body jerk as his fingers began to explore her. He knew she was ready for him when she leaned forward with her hands against the tiles.

As he entered her he kissed her ear and whispered "I can assure you that my intentions are strictly honourable."

****

They were lying naked under the duvet when the telephone startled them into wakefulness at 6:30 p.m. Oliver recognised Alexandre's voice. "Bunny likes me to prepare something special for dinner on Saturdays and doesn't want you to be left out. Tonight it's my pork dish, Lomo de Orza, which I remember you had last year. There will also be a starter, dessert and suitable wines. Callum and Hugo will serve it to you at eight o'clock."

Oliver thanked him and told Jessica the news. She looked surprised, then worried. "I wonder what they're up to? We'd better have it, I suppose. I'll smarten myself up."

They had just finished getting ready when, twenty minutes sooner than expected, the door was unlocked. Hugo appeared in tails, with a silver tray on which were two cocktail glasses. "Surprise View champagne cocktails," he announced with a smile, placing the tray on the table.

When he had gone the couple eyed the frosted glasses with suspicion. Oliver picked one up, examined it closely, sniffed it, then cautiously tasted it. "Seems the genuine article," he said approvingly, handing the other to Jessica. Then he winked and added "To our future, darling."

She glanced at the black dome as she raised her glass to him. "To our future," she replied, her eyes conveying what she dared not say aloud.

At eight o'clock the door was opened and Callum and Hugo, both in tails, wheeled in a large serving trolley. Oliver was surprised, because he knew they would have had to carry it up two flights of stairs. On the top shelf were three bottles of wine. The two whites were in coolers and the red, which had been uncorked, was lying in a basket wrapped in a white napkin which hid the label.

The couple watched with a mixture of suspicion and fascination as Callum spread a cloth on the table and laid two place settings. Oliver wondered if it was Bunny's natural hospitality that made him include them in the weekly treat. He recognised the dinner service as a rare and valuable Coalport, decorated with a bold Japanese pattern in underglaze blue and gilt, with red, yellow and brown flowerheads and trailing honeysuckle. Callum held the lid of the soup tureen by its gilt lions' head handles and removed it. "Smoked trout and avocado soup garnished with caviar," he announced.

Hugo produced one of the white wines, a 1985 Pouilly-Fuissé, opened it and poured some into Oliver's glass. Although his mouth was dry, he tasted it and expressed his approval. Callum and Hugo went to the door and watched as the couple ate their soup. He wondered if they were standing there as waiters or warders.

The soup was excellent and the couple were now beginning to relax and enjoy the unexpected treat. Callum took away their plates and began to serve the Lomo de Orza. This time it came with asparagus tips and stack potatoes.

Hugo gently lifted the bottle of red wine from its basket and proudly announced "the 1945 Chateau Petrus," as he unfolded the napkin to reveal the faded, stained label. Holding the bottle with considerable care, he poured a little of the rare Pomerol into Oliver's glass, then watched as he held it up to the light, sniffed it and finally tasted it, running it round his mouth and savouring it, before swallowing.

He smiled at Hugo. "It's superb Hugo. I can honestly say I've never tasted such a wine. However, Jessica and I aren't experts and we'd like to know what you think."

Hugo looked pleased. He produced another glass, half filled the couple's glasses and poured a little into his own. The couple watched expectantly as he sniffed the bouquet then tasted it and ran it round his mouth. An he held the glass up to the light and moved it backwards and forwards a look of sheer ecstasy came over his face. At last he proclaimed solemnly "Colour beautiful and deep, nose complex and giving off heady aromas, flavour incredibly concentrated and complex, closed at first but followed by an astounding explosion of all things wonderful."

The couple smiled. "We're looking forward to drinking it," said Jessica.

The Lomo de Orza was a new experience for her. When she tasted it she gave an exclamation of delight. "This is absolutely wonderful. It's the most tender and flavoursome meat I've ever tasted."

Oliver tried his and looked at her in astonishment. "It was good last year, but this is even better. The asparagus is perfect with it."

They savoured each mouthful of Alexandre's prize-winning dish. When they had finished Callum began to clear the table. Oliver said "Please tell Alexandre that the Lomo de Orza was wonderful. It was good last year, but tonight it was out of this world. I don't know how he does it."

"I'm sure he'll be pleased. He's always trying to improve it."

"He couldn't possibly improve on that," said Jessica.

Oliver sipped the Chateau Petrus and sighed. "It's hard to imagine better food and wine, but to have them together is a once in a lifetime experience."

Callum smiled at their pleasure and went on to explain "Alexandre insists on selecting all our meat himself and uses several butchers. He's discovered one in Windermere which specialises in pork and goes there when he's going to serve Lomo de Orza. If they have a sufficiently good pork loin he gets them to slice it with the fat on. He fries it before steeping it in the marinade, which is why its so tender and flavoursome, without being heavily scented."

"His perfectionism pays off," said Oliver, picking up his glass and savouring the last drops of the Chateau Petrus.

Callum put a spirit burner on the table and lit it. "Alexandre hopes you like Crepes Suzettes," he said, as Hugo produced a bottle of Courvoisier Louis XO.

"Mmm, I adore them," said Jessica enthusiastically, as Callum poured some mixture into the little pan. Hugo lifted the third wine, a 1980 Chateau d'Yquem premier Grand Cru, from its cooler. Jessica recognised the label and smiled ruefully. "I seem to remember my drunken ex ordering this one last year. It was an expensive mistake."

Oliver reached across the table and squeezed her hand. "There's an old saying in these parts, darling: 'When drink's in, wit's out'. Never mind, you're making up for it tonight."

The brandy was still flaming on the crepes as Callum served them. They were a new experience for him. "Tremendous. I love the sauce," was his verdict.

"All the better for using the best cognac," she remarked.

"The Sauterne goes superbly with them, too."

The waiters looked pleased. When they had finished, Callum cleared the table and served coffee. Hugo poured generous measures of the Louis XO into two enormous brandy balloons and left the bottle on the table.

"I can honestly say that was the best meal I've ever had," said Oliver when the waiters had gone and taken the trolley.

"Me too," said Jessica. "I've been coming here for years, but I've never tasted meat as good as that."

It was almost ten o'clock. They turned on the television and relaxed in the armchairs with their coffee and cognac. The BBC national news was followed by the northern regional news. There was a report about the missing youths similar to the one on the Border news the previous evening.

"It won't be long before the nationals get hold it," he said, turning it off. He went to the radio. "Do you like jazz?," he asked her.

She had slipped off her shoes and was curled up in her armchair with her legs tucked under her, sipping her cognac. "Yes, I love it."

"There's usually a good programme at this time." When he had found it he sat in his chair and closed his eyes as the sound of good jazz filled the room. After they had been listening to it for a while she went to the pie-crust table and returned with a magazine. She began to idly turn the pages then suddenly announced "It says here that a woman needs a reason to make love, but a man only needs a place."

Oliver opened his eyes and considered for a moment before replying. "Quite true when you think about it. Sex is more of an emotional experience for a woman," he murmured, closing them again.

"A woman wants to be talked into bed by the right man." She turned another page. "Did you know that there are twelve different reasons why men seduce women? They're called the Twelve Pleasures of Man."

Oliver's eyes remained closed. "I seem to remember you did most of the seducing last year."

"Don't split hairs. Shall I read them to you?"

He opened his eyes. "You're going to anyway, so you might as well get on with it," he replied, closing them again.

A tenor saxophone was playing an old blues number as she began to read aloud. "One: The Pleasure of Ownership. A man needs the comfort of a possession."

His eyes remained closed. "Perfectly true. You mean more to me than my Lotus, darling."

"I'm glad about that. Two: The Pleasure of Revenge. Dominated by Woman in his childhood and then in marriage, he delights in the chance to humble her."

"Very profound."

"Three: The Pleasure of Conquest. Man likes beating an opponent."

"Some men, perhaps, but I'm not the competitive type."

"Four: The Pleasure of Verification. In a world of confusion, some men need to prove that they are genuine males."

"I've never been in any doubt."

"Five: The Pleasure of Bragging. Men like to tell of their conquests to other men."

"Applies more to young idiots. I haven't told anyone about you."

"Six: The Pleasure of Trespassing. The contrariness of man's nature makes him ignore 'no admittance' signs."

"Definitely. It adds to the fun."

"Seven: The Pleasure of Identification with the Herd. No man wants to be the odd man out, so he chases women as a matter of good form."

"Except the ones who are batting for the other side."

Jessica giggled. "Eight: The Pleasure of Stoking the Ego. Finding a beautiful woman gives a man's ego an enormous lift."

"Not just his ego."

She glanced at his jeans and giggled again. "Nine: The Pleasure of Theft. There is a special pleasure in taking an attractive woman from another man."

"Perfectly true. A small amount of the very considerable satisfaction I derived from our night of passion in The Langdales was the knowledge that I had stolen, or at least borrowed you from your ex. Of course, I regarded him as an enemy, but there's many an erstwhile pillar of society who wouldn't normally steal a postage stamp, who will happily run off with his best friend's wife or girlfriend."

"Quite a speech. Ten: The Pleasure of Compensation. A man who feels a failure in other fields derives comfort from his conquests over women."

"A similar reason is given for men buying sports cars. Success must have eluded me somewhere, but I can't think where."

"Eleven: The Pleasure of Escape. Man finds woman the most soothing of all drugs. In her embrace he can temporarily forget all his troubles."

"Definitely, if she's the right kind of woman, like you."

"Flattery will get you everywhere. Twelve. The Pleasure of Exploration. It's fun undoing the giftwrap and discovering the contents."

Oliver opened his eyes and stood up. She looked surprised as he pulled her up from her chair, held her in his arms and kissed her. When her tongue began to respond to his he picked her up and carried her to the bed, where he lay down beside her. They continued to kiss passionately, then his hand moved to the top of her jeans.

"You look pretty good in your giftwrap, darling. I've been wanting to explore the contents all evening," he said, pulling the duvet over them.

****

They continued to lie on the bed and listen to the jazz. When it ended he went to the radio and turned it off. She watched him without moving. "Under different circumstances that would have been a perfect evening," she murmured.

He returned to the bed, leaned over and kissed her. She looked up at his naked body and her hand reached out for him. When she felt him grow hard again she whispered "It's not over yet, darling, come back to bed."

They had begun to make love for the second time when they heard loud noises coming from the corridor. Oliver flung off the duvet and leapt out of bed. A group of people had gathered outside Scafell, waiting to go in. The twins were holding a stretcher on which lay the unconcious body of a teenager. He had cropped hair, tattoos on both cheeks and was wearing jeans, T-shirt and trainers, while his baseball cap rested incongruously on his stomach.

He turned away from the observation window. She was sitting up in bed, the glow had vanished from her cheeks and she was staring at him anxiously. His face was pale and his naked body was no longer aroused.

"I'm afraid they've captured another one, Jess. They're putting him in Scafell," he said.

Her hand flew up to her mouth. "Oh God! I was hoping they wouldn't."

Twenty

Sunday morning saw the couple up early. They had not slept much through thinking of the youth in Scafell and dreading his inevitable birching. After breakfast they heard the preparations going on in the corridor. Oliver watched as the warders manoeuvred the oak bench into position. He went back to Jessica and told her that as he had already witnessed enough punishments to put Bunny and his gang behind bars for life he did not consider it necessary to watch another. She found Radio One, turned up the volume and they stood by the window.

It was a magnificent morning and the view helped to take their minds off the horrors being enacted outside their room. They watched the boats on Derwentwater and the walkers on Catbells as the loud music filled the room, so if there were any distressing sounds they did not hear them. After forty minutes he went cautiously to the door and looked out. The only indication that a birching had taken place were some damp stains on the carpet. He turned down the radio.

They continued to gaze at the view, trying not to think about what had just taken place. But when this proved impossible they took off their jeans and tops, turned up the music again and did their morning work-out. This time they extended the session to an hour and by the time it was finished they were both exhausted. They filled the bath, took off their underclothes, then revelled in each other's company in the warm water as the powerful jets massaged their aching muscles, until it was time for lunch. Despite their excitement at the prospect of escaping, they dared not discuss it for fear of being overheard.

At three o'clock, they were ready and waiting anxiously, praying that Rafiq and Callum would be the duty warders again, so when the door was opened and they saw Rafiq standing there they breathed sighs of relief. But instead of beckoning them to follow him he stood aside and they stared as Bunny strode in. Rafiq closed the door and Bunny gestured with his cane for them to sit down. He pulled up the chair from the dressing table and sat facing them. "I'm afraid you'll have to miss your run this afternoon because I have something important to discuss with you," he said.

They tried not to let the bitter disappointment show on their faces. "Details of our release, perhaps?," suggested Oliver.

"Possibly, if you decide to co-operate.""What do we have to do?," asked Jessica.

Bunny ignored the question and took a notebook from an inside pocket. He fixed Oliver with his damaged eye. "Exactly where and when were your parents killed?," he asked.

Oliver looked surprised. He told Bunny, who consulted an entry in the notebook. "You say the two scum drove off and have not been caught?."

"That's right. I phoned the Cumbria police a fortnight ago and they still had no idea who they were. They'd stolen the BMW from a village between Cockermouth and Workington and were driving it recklessly when my father swerved to avoid them. There were no witnesses and their fingerprints and other evidence were destroyed when they burnt it." He glanced at Bunny's notebook. "Have you some information?," he asked.

"I think so. As you are no doubt aware, our team captured Scum Ten last night. They brought him in from a car park in Cockermouth, where a number of cars have recently been stolen. He was put in Scafell, then birched shortly after he came round. Kemp decided to give him some time to recover and consider his situation, before interviewing him. I'm pleased to say that for the past two hours he's been singing like a canary, hoping to avoid another birching and possibly the gallows as well. The duty warders tell me you were more interested in admiring the view and listening to some frightful music, than watching the proceedings."

"You might find it hard to understand, but we don't enjoy that sort of thing," said Jessica, sharply.

"Suit yourselves," Bunny shrugged his shoulders. "Scum Ten has turned out to be a very unpleasant individual who's been involved in a lot of criminal activity in the area. He's providing us with a list of his more serious crimes, together with the dates and locations, and the names of his accomplices."

He consulted his notebook again then looked at Oliver. "He admits that on the date and time you mentioned he was the driver of a BMW that caused a fatal accident just below the Forestry Commission's centre on Whinlatter pass. He and the youth who was with him, whose name he has provided, had stolen it an hour earlier from a village near Workington. They went over a bridge at high speed on the wrong side of the road and caused a Rover Metro containing two old farts, as he described them, to swerve. They saw it hit a tree and burst into flames. They made no attempt to rescue the occupants and drove off, then abandoned the BMW in a lane a few miles away and torched it."

Oliver was staring at Bunny. "Are you sure about this?," he asked.

"Kemp has had a lot of experience with his type. He doesn't think he's lying, because he's too terrified. The details tally with your account and there seems no reason why he should invent such a story. He's giving us so much information about other local scum that we're hoping to identify Ginger's attackers, as well as some of the ones who have caused so much misery to my staff."

"What will you do to him?," asked Jessica.

"That's up to Oliver."

The couple looked at Bunny in surprise. "What do you mean?, asked Oliver suspiciously.

Bunny stared at Oliver. His right eye was redder than usual. "It's perfectly simple, Oliver. Scum Ten admits to murdering your parents, so I'm giving you the opportunity to punish him."

"The only punishment that I want for them is the appropriate prison sentence for causing death by dangerous driving, handed to them by a Crown Court judge," said Oliver.

Bunny flushed and struck the table with his cane. "Crown Court poppycock," he shouted. "Perhaps four years in prison, when you know perfectly well he would be out in two. Do you really consider that an appropriate sentence for murdering your parents?."

When Oliver did not reply Bunny leaned forward and looked at him earnestly. "Be sensible, Oliver. This is what I am proposing. I will give you both your freedom if you will join our organisation and assist in Scum Ten's punishment."

"Which is?," asked Oliver.

Bunny stood up. The couple stared at him curiously as his deformed right hand reached into his top pocket and removed the red silk handkerchief. He unfolded it and took out a square of black silk which he placed on his head. Standing ramrod straight he looked down at the seated couple. "If you agree to my proposal

I will go immediately into Scafell and pass sentence on him in the same way that it was passed on Dr. Crippen in 1910."

Oliver was mesmerised by Bunny's watery, red right eye as he began to intone solemnly. "Is there any reason why the sentence of this court should not be passed? In that case I shall pass sentence, which is that you be taken to a lawful prison and thence to a place of execution and that you be hanged by the neck until you are dead." He was a formidable sight as he towered over them with the symbolic black cap on his head, the effect made more dramatic by his hair being the colour of a judicial wig. He put away the black square and sat down.

The couple were horrified. "Is that how you sentenced the others?," asked Oliver. He did not think it wise to mention that he had already heard Bunny pass sentence of death.

"Certainly. The effect on some of them was quite devastating."

"I bet it was," said Jessica. "What part would we have to play in this charade?."

"Oliver will be the executioner and you will be his Number Two. Tomorrow morning at half a minute to nine you will enter the condemned cell with Chief Warder Kemp and another warder. You will be appropriately dressed and will each be carrying a leather restraint strap. "Oliver will approach the prisoner, pinion his arms behind his back and instruct him to follow. By this time the two warders on death watch, who will have been with the prisoner all night, will have opened the communicating door to the execution chamber. Oliver will lead the way through to the scaffold, a distance of seven paces and Jessica will follow the prisoner. As he approaches the gallows he will see the noose ahead of him, at eye level. The two warders already on the cross planks will guide him onto the trapdoors, until his toes are on the chalked T-mark in the centre. They will support or restrain him if necessary.

"The moment the prisoner is in the correct position, Jessica will kneel down behind him and pinion his legs with her strap. As she is doing this Oliver will take the white hood from his top pocket, unfold it and pull it over his head, then quickly pull down the noose, making sure that the knot is under the angle of the left jaw, tighten it to the right and pull the rubber washer along the rope to secure it. Finally, so as to minimise any delay, he will move quickly to the lever, pull out the cotter pin with one hand and push the lever with the other. There will be a crash as the trapdoors fall and are caught by the rubber clips. The prisoner will fall through the opening then hang perfectly still on the end of the rope with only the top of his head visible through the opening."

Oliver glanced at Jessica. She was staring wide-eyed at Bunny and shaking her head. "You're mad. It's barbaric," she exclaimed.

"Nonsense," replied Bunny. "It's the simplest and most humane method of execution. Speed is of the essence. British executioners in the 1950's were so fast that the usual time between entering the condemned cell and the drop was between nine and twelve seconds. The record of seven seconds was achieved by Albert Pierrepoint. I'm afraid my fastest time so far is thirteen seconds, but I'm an old man and you two are young and agile, so you might be able to improve on that."

Oliver noticed that Jessica was still shaking her head. He looked at Bunny and said "Of course we won't do it."

The disappointment on Bunny's face appeared genuine. He leaned towards the couple and pleaded with them. "Oliver, Jessica, please be sensible. I like you both. Surely you must realise that I am offering you your freedom in exchange for the opportunity to join our organisation and avenge your parents' brutal murder?."

Oliver glanced at Jessica and saw that she was still shaking her head. He looked at Bunny and spoke decisively. "The only vengeance that Jessica and I want is to see the two youths arrested and dealt with by the British criminal justice system. We regard your captures as assault and unlawful imprisonment, your birchings as grievous bodily harm and your executions as murder. If this cruelty to young men compensates in some way for your impotence and disfigurement then you really must be mad. We won't condone it in any way and when we get away from here the first thing we will do is go to the police."

For a moment it seemed as though Bunny would attack Oliver, because he raised his cane and stepped towards him. But he controlled himself and when he spoke his voice was cold and businesslike. "If that's your final decision, there's nothing more to be said. You have disappointed me. For the reasons you have just given I daren't release you, and as long as you remain at Surprise View you will continue to be a nuisance to us."

He strode to the door and rapped on it with the gold handle of his cane. As he waited for it to be opened he turned to the couple and addressed them coldly. "You have already heard the words that I use when I pass sentence of death, so I won't bother to repeat them. As of this moment the sentence applies to you both."

As Rafiq opened the door Bunny's parting words to them were "The next time we meet will be at nine o'clock tomorrow morning for our first double execution. Good afternoon."

They stared at each other, aghast, as the door was locked again. "Christ, almighty!," exclaimed Oliver, breaking the silence.

"Oh God, I didn't expect that" sobbed Jessica, holding her head in her hands.

He took her in his arms. "Neither did I, darling. I'm so sorry, it's my fault. I should have agreed to what he wanted, instead of losing my temper. I saw you shaking your head and thought I was speaking for both of us, but I should have considered you first."

She looked at him tearfully. "No, you were quite right, Oliver. We have our principles. I don't think either of us could have done that to the boy next door, whatever he's done." She paused, then whispered "What happens next?."

"From what we saw on Friday they'll probably come for us shortly and escort us to the condemned cell. I expect they'll have to get it ready first and arrange for two warders to be with us."

She buried her face in his shoulder. "You mean until its all over?."

He held her to him and stroked her hair. "Something like that." Then he put his mouth to her ear and whispered "Cheer up, I have an idea."

She looked up at him in surprise. He gave her a wink and continued in his normal voice "Let's have a last shower together. I don't suppose there'll be one in the condemned cell."

She followed him into the bathroom, where they undressed then held each other under the powerful jet behind the closed shower curtain. He moved his mouth to her ear and whispered "Don't give up, darling. I have an idea for escaping in the morning. It will require split-second timing and a lot of courage and strength, but it's our only chance. Will you give it a try?"

"Of course. What do we have to do?."

He moved his mouth closer to her ear. "Bunny's description of a British execution was pretty accurate. I know a bit about it, because soon after I started at the *Star* I had to review the biography of a well known executioner who retired to the Lake

District. They haven't carried out a double execution yet at Surprise View and..."

They leapt in fear as the curtain was torn aside. The uniformed figures of Kemp and the twins were watching them. Jessica let out a cry and flung her arms around Oliver.

"Turn off the water," shouted Kemp.

Oliver did so and continued to hold her protectively. For several seconds the only sound was the dripping of water from the shower. Kemp continued in a quieter voice "Bunny has told us about the death sentence. You have only yourselves to blame. He has instructed me to proceed without delay, so I require you to get dressed and bring whatever you need for tonight. Condemned prisoners aren't allowed to wear belts, braces, ties or shoe laces. We'll wait for you in the bedroom. From now on you'll be guarded with maximum security."

The warders left the bathroom door open and went into the bedroom. The couple were conscious of their stares as they stepped out of the shower and wrapped themselves in the big, soft towels. Oliver wondered if this was to be their last taste of luxury. They got dressed, removed the laces from their trainers, put some toilet things into a sponge bag and went into the bedroom.

The twins stepped forward and told them to put their arms behind their backs, then they handcuffed them. Kemp rapped on the door and Callum looked in through the observation window before unlocking it. "Follow me," instructed Kemp, tersely. The twins gripped the couples' arms and escorted them out of High Stile and along the corridor towards the warders' station, where Rafiq was watching the approaching procession, ready to give assistance if necessary. The first of the two black steel doors stood open and they were ushered inside.

Although Bunny's description had partly prepared them for what to expect, they stopped in their tracks when they saw the condemned cell. To Oliver it looked exactly like ones he had seen in old films. The bare brick walls were painted in two shades of green. In the far wall was a high window comprising squares of thick glass, the top one of which could be opened for fresh air. The window was arched with vertical iron bars on the inside. The white ceiling was bare and the only electric light was a single bulb in a metal cage on the wall near the door. Bare boards covered the floor. In the far left corner was a low, wooden bunk bed on which two thin, grey blankets were folded in military fashion. Three water pipes ran along the far wall below the window. In the far right corner a hand basin and a seatless lavatory, both of cracked porcelain, were fixed to the wall and the floor. Against the same wall, but nearer the door, stood a cheap wardrobe. Just inside the door on the left was a square wooden table, around which were four upright, wooden chairs. Arranged in neat piles on the table were a chess board, some boxed games, a box of dominoes and two packs of playing cards. There was a selection of paperbacks and newspapers on two shelves on the wall.

Jessica gasped as she took it in. The twins did not remove the handcuffs until Rafiq had locked the cell door from outside. Oliver found her hand and squeezed it, as Kemp began to address them.

"As Bunny has already explained, this execution suite is an exact replica of the ones in British prisons up to the abolition of capital punishment in 1965. Until your executions at nine o'clock tomorrow morning you will be treated in the same humane way as were condemned prisoners in those days. These two warders will remain with you through the night. They will do their best to keep you occupied and amused, and, within reason, provide you with whatever you require. As you can see, various games as well as reading and writing materials, are provided for the purpose. Your supper will be brought in at 7:30 p.m. In accordance with tradition, you may order whatever you like for your last breakfast, which will be brought at 7:30 a.m. I advise you to get as much sleep as possible. This cell was designed for one condemned prisoner, so you will have to share the single bed, but I'm sure that won't be a problem. At eight o'clock the chaplain will come and, unless you have any strong objections, will remain with you for your last hour. Any questions?"

"In the 1950s condemned prisoners had the opportunity to appeal and could be reprieved by the Home Secretary. Aren't we to be afforded those rights?," asked Oliver.

"Bunny is the final judge at Surprise View," replied Kemp impatiently.

"Then you're nothing more than a bunch of murdering vigilantes," shouted Oliver.

Kemp's face flushed with anger. He stepped towards Oliver but thought better of it. His face resumed its normal colour and when he spoke his voice was relaxed and reasonable. "My dear sir, executioners aren't murderers, they're public servants. There was never a shortage of applicants for the job before 1965. The most famous were the Pierrepoint family. Henry Pierrepoint became an executioner in 1901 and hanged 107 people before he retired. His brother Thomas followed in his footsteps. But the greatest Pierrepoint was Thomas' nephew, Albert, who became an executioner in 1932 and went on to become Britain's chief executioner in 1940. He hanged over 400 people before he retired, including Ruth Ellis, Derek Bentley, Timothy Evans, John Christie, Lord Haw Haw and many of the nazi war criminals."

Jessica interrupted him. "The Pierrepoints were acting within the law, but you're not. It won't be long before the police catch up with you and when they do, you'll all get life."

Kemp flushed again as he turned on her. "Don't try to provoke me, young lady. Let me tell you something about the execution of women. A hundred years ago one pretty teenage murderess was so distraught that the male warders had to carry her to the gallows. When they came to take down her body they found that her underwear was full of blood. The experience so upset them that condemned female prisoners thereafter were required to wear canvas underwear for their executions." Kemp moved towards her so that his face was almost touching hers. "You'll be the first woman to be hanged at Surprise View," he leered. "Shall I get hold of some canvas and ask my wife to run you up a pair of canvas knickers for the morning?."

"Stop it," screamed Jessica, collapsing, sobbing, onto the bed.

Oliver went to comfort her, then turned on Kemp. "Shut up and get out, Kemp," he shouted. "Can't you see what you're doing? Isn't it bad enough already, without this?."

Kemp flushed again. He grasped the leather strap from under his uniform jacket, withdrew his truncheon and brandished it in Oliver's face. "Don't talk to me like that, you little prig. You're in no position to tell me what to do and you certainly won't again after nine o'clock tomorrow morning," he shouted.

He lowered the polished, wooden truncheon between Oliver's legs and began to move it slowly upwards, making him squirm. "Now I'll tell you something about the hanging of men that you probably don't know. Men can sometimes have erections and even orgasms when they're hanged. Effusions of urine, semen and faeces were all common on the gallows. An early photograph of the Lincoln

Conspirators after they were hanged in 1865 shows one of them to have an erection. One of Albert Pierrepoint's Number Twos was sacked for lifting up the shirt of a hanged man they had just put into a coffin and making a crude remark about his size and performance."

Kemp jabbed the end of the truncheon hard into Oliver's testicles. Oliver gasped and leapt backwards, but the bed barred his retreat. Kemp advanced and, keeping the truncheon pressed into Oliver's body, moved it slowly upwards over his stomach, chest, neck and face. He pushed his own face up to Oliver's and leered into it sadistically "Do you think you'll have an erection when you're on the end of the rope tomorrow morning, Oliver? If so, will it be as big as this?." He waved the truncheon mockingly in Oliver's face. "I don't think so, because we've all seen it on television. Never mind, it seems to keep young Jessica here happy, but not for much longer, I'm afraid."

"For God's sake shut up," screamed Jessica.

Kemp roared with laughter and stepped back, allowing Oliver to stand up. He replaced the wooden truncheon in its long pocket in his trousers and walked to the door. As he waited for it to be opened his parting words to the couple were: "I shouldn't worry too much about what I've just told you. We observe the same strict procedures that were adopted in British prisons until 1965, so I can assure you that your deaths will be quick and painless."

Twenty One

They continued to stand in the middle of the condemned cell, nervously holding hands, uncertain of what would happen next. The Barr twins did not seem at all perturbed by Kemp's violent outburst. They removed their caps, sat down at opposite sides of the table, unfolded the chess board and opened one of the boxes. One of them smiled at the couple. "Do you play draughts?," he asked. His voice was friendly.

Oliver and Jessica looked at them blankly. The afternoon sunlight that streamed in through the high window shone on their golden hair and reflected in the silver buttons and insignia of their tunics. It occurred to Oliver that they were so alike that even if he did survive, he would never be able to tell them apart.

"It's a very good game," said the second twin. "Come and join us. If you haven't played before we'd love to teach you."

Jessica shook her head nervously. "No thanks," she said.

"We've got monopoly, scrabble, ludo, chess, cribbage, dominoes and cards, if you prefer," said the first twin.

The couple sat on the edge of the bed. The thin mattress felt hard. Oliver put a protective arm around her. "We don't want to play any games," he said.

"You'll find it easier if you keep yourselves occupied," said the second twin. He pointed to the shelf on the wall "We've also got some books, magazines and newspapers."

He thought that even their voices sounded the same. He gave her an encouraging kiss on the cheek and looked at them. "Just leave us alone. We can keep ourselves occupied," he replied.

She was nervously examining their new surroundings. The bed on which they were sitting was a low wooden bunk securely fastened to the wall and floor. It occurred to her that they were unlikely to need the two blankets, because the cell was warm. She shuddered as she looked at the primitive, seatless lavatory and wondered how she would manage without privacy. Her eyes moved further along the wall to the cheap wardrobe. It seemed unnecessary, as the only clothes they had were the ones they were wearing.

The twins were setting out the draughts on the board. The first one said "It's nearly three hours until supper time, so we're going to have a game. If you change your minds, you're welcome to join in."

"We have some notepaper and envelopes if you want to write letters," added the second.

"To the Chief Constable, perhaps?," asked Oliver, with biting sarcasm. The twins exchanged smiles and resumed their game. His arm was still around her and he could feel her start to tremble. He put his mouth to her ear. "Don't give up, darling. We'll make it."

"This place is horrid. I couldn't bear it if you weren't with me," she whispered.

"It's impossible to imagine that a year ago this was The Langdales. It was such a beautiful room then."

"I know. It seems a lifetime ago." She looked around the cell, then moved her mouth to his ear. "Do you think there are any cameras or microphones?."

"I doubt it, because it's supposed to be authentic 1950s, but to be on the safe side we'd better wait until we're in bed and under a blanket."

The twins had paused in their game and were watching them. The second one was wagging a finger disapprovingly. "Sorry, no whispering. We have to be able to hear what you're saying," he said.

Jessica stood up and faced them angrily. "You two are from a nice family. We were sorry to hear about your mother, but do you really think that justifies our murder?."

The first twin glanced at his brother and replied "We're not allowed to discuss individual cases." They continued their game of draughts.

Oliver said "The police are bound to catch up with you soon. If you help us to get out of here we'll do what we can to make things easier for you." When the twins did not reply but continued their game he looked at her and shrugged. "Well, it was worth a try."

She took hold of his hand. "Come on, darling. We're not going to get anywhere with these two. Let's go to bed."

He looked at her in surprise, then raised his eyebrows and inclined his head towards the twins.

She shrugged. "I don't care about them. If we've only got a few hours left, it doesn't really matter. They probably saw us doing all sorts of things in High Stile." She smiled weakly and added "Anyway, I don't think either of us could manage anything more than a cuddle just now."

The twins made an effort to concentrate on their game as the couple undressed. When they were down to their underwear they spread one of the blankets on the mattress and lay down on it, then pulled the other one over their heads.

"This mattress is bloody uncomfortable," complained Oliver.

"Yes, but at least it's clean and we can whisper under here." She kissed him, then they held each other as they silently contemplated their dreadful plight. After a while he whispered "I'll see what the twins are up to." He lowered the blanket a little and pulled it up again "They're still playing draughts and not taking any notice of us."

"Or pretending not to. It's time we decided what we're going to do," she whispered.

They held each other a little longer, then he moved his mouth to her ear. "O.K. I have a plan for when they come for us at nine o'clock. It won't be easy, but it's our only chance. We'll both have to know exactly what we're going to do, but before I go into details I'll have to explain what's likely to happen in the morning. Bunny has already given us an accurate description of a straightforward execution, but there are special procedures when two prisoners are hanged together."

"What happens?"

"I'm going to have to describe everything in graphic detail, I'm afraid."

"I know."

"Shortly before nine o'clock Bunny, Thomas, Kemp and one of the warders will assemble in the corridor outside our door. Bunny and Thomas will each be carrying two leather restraint straps. The rest of the execution party will then arrive at the door of the execution chamber. In the 1950's they included the Sheriff, the prison governor, the medical officer and official witnesses. At about half a minute to nine both doors will be unlocked and the parties will enter the respective cells. As soon as the executioners come in here, the twins will slide the wardrobe along the wall to reveal the communicating door."

She gasped. "Is that why it's there – to hide the door?."

"Yes, it's supposed to stop us thinking about what's going on next door. When they've moved it out of the way they'll open the door and we'll be able to see inside the execution chamber. The witnesses will be filing in and the two nooses will be suspended at shoulder height above the trapdoors, held up by a piece of twine.

They'll have to deal with us one at a time, because the executioner always pinioned the prisoners' arms in the condemned cell, then when they got him onto the trapdoors the Number Two pinioned his legs. Bunny will approach us, strap our arms together behind our backs and lead us into the execution chamber, one at a time. As soon as we're both on the T-marks he will face us in turn, take a white hood from his top pocket and pull it over our head, as Thomas pinions our legs from behind. Bunny will then pull the noose down over the hood and, keeping the knot under the angle of the left jaw, tighten it to the right and slide a rubber washer along the rope to hold it in position."

"Why does it have to be under the left jaw?," she whispered.

"So that the knot ends up in front and throws the chin back, breaking the spinal cord. If the knot's on the right side it will end up behind the neck and throw it forward, resulting in strangulation."

"God almighty!." He felt her body jerk in his arms.

"As soon as the nooses are correctly round our necks, Bunny will move quickly to the lever. He will pull out the cotter pin at the base with one hand, then push the lever with the other. The lever will withdraw the bolt from under the trapdoors, causing them to fall, then the weight of our bodies going down will break the piece of twine. When we reach the bottom of the drop our necks and spinal cords will be broken and we will be deeply unconcious. Death from comatose asphyxia will quickly follow. Brain death usually takes six minutes and whole body death between ten and fifteen minutes."

"Are you sure we won't be strangled?"

"Not if the nooses are put on correctly and they have given us the correct length of drop. If the drop's too short it can result in strangulation; if its too long, in decapitation. A famous Victorian executioner called James Berry caused consternation at Norwich Castle in 1885 when he decapitated a prisoner while experimenting with longer drops."

He felt her start again and held her tight. "Twentieth century executioners were required to use a Home Office Table of Drops, which restricted drops to between five and eight feet. The length of the drop in feet was calculated by dividing one thousand foot-pounds by the weight of the prisoner in pounds, having deducted fourteen pounds for the weight of his head. However, experienced executioners also took into account the age and height of the prisoner as well."

"Why did the age matter?."

"Because a fit young man might have stronger neck muscles and therefore require a longer drop than an older man."

"Or a woman," added Jessica.

"The executioner and his assistant arrived at the prison the previous afternoon and were not allowed to leave until the execution had been carried out. Prisons had a room set aside for them and provided them with their meals.

Soon after they arrived they began to make their preparations. The executioner went to the condemned cell and had a surreptitious look at the prisoner through the Judas hole, to check his build before calculating the drop.

Later, when the warders had taken the prisoner to the exercise yard, the prison engineer accompanied the executioner and his assistant to the execution chamber. The executioner checked the equipment in the execution box which had already arrived from Pentonville prison. There was always a choice of two ropes, a new one and an old one. Other items included twine, scissors, copper wire, white chalk, tape measure, restraint straps and the white hood.

Hanging ropes were made to a very high standard by craftsmen at a small factory in south London, from where they were sent to prisons not only in this country but also in British Empire and Commonwealth countries. At the top end was a heavy circular steel eye and at the bottom end a noose enclosed by a pear-shaped brass eyelet and covered with a piece of soft chamois leather. The executioner checked them carefully for damage and selected one, or both for a double execution.

The executioner found the drop from the Table of Drops and made allowances for the prisoner's age and physique. At the noose end of the rope he marked off thirteen inches from the centre of the brass eyelet with a piece of twine, being the allowance for the length of the prisoner's neck. From this mark he measured along the rope the exact drop to the nearest quarter inch and marked it with another piece of twine. Using a pin and tackle, he attached the rope to the chain which was suspended from the hook in the beam above. With the help of an adjusting bracket he adjusted the rope so that the mark showing the drop was exactly in accordance with the prisoner's height.

He took a length of copper wire from the box and having secured one end over the shackle end of the chain he bent the other end to coincide with the mark on the rope showing the drop. Then he put a sandbag of the same weight as the prisoner on the trap, put the noose around it and in the presence of the prison governor pushed the lever and let it fall. If everything operated correctly, the sandbag was left hanging there until the following morning to stretch the rope.

At 6:30 a.m. on the morning of the execution the executioner and his assistant were awakened and accompanied to the execution chamber by a warder. Although the communicating door to the condemned cell was sound-proofed, they worked quietly and spoke in whispers, so as not to be heard by the prisoner. They drew up the sandbag and detached it from the noose, then lowered it into the pit and disposed of it in a corner. The Number Two remained in the pit. He stood on a stool to release the trapdoors from the rubber-clad springs and pushed them up flat. Each leaf was 8' 1/2" feet by 2' 1/2" feet, so they were pretty heavy. The executioner slid in the bolt under the trapdoors and plugged in the cotter pin and its guard, which acted as a safety catch at the base of the lever.

The executioner then placed a ladder against the upper beam and, using the copper wire, re-adjusted the fall to the last half inch, allowing for the overnight stretch of the rope. To prevent the noose from lying on the trapdoors he coiled the spare rope until it was at shoulder height and held it while his number two secured it with a piece of twine. With the white chalk he re-lined the T-mark on the drop where the prisoner's toes were to be, his feet on the join of the trapdoors. Then he placed the cross-planks in their correct positions on either side of the T-mark. Finally, in order to prevent the slightest delay in the execution, he went to the lever and removed the split-pin that held the cotter pin and eased it out for half its length."

"What were the cross-planks for?."

"A warder had to be on each side of the prisoner, to make sure that he was standing in the right position and to support or restrain him if necessary. The cross-planks were to prevent them going down with the prisoner when the lever was pushed. There were ropes for them to hang onto with one hand as they held the prisoner with the other."

"Didn't prisoners ever resist or faint?"

"Not often. According to several eye witness accounts, most of them were co-operative and polite. Some even chatted to the executioner and said cheerio as he pulled the hood over their heads. Women were said to be particularly brave."

"I expect this one will be the exception. What will they do if I faint ?."

"Every execution chamber had a collapse board standing in a corner. It was about the size of a stretcher with straps attached. If a prisoner fainted he would be strapped to it and hanged just the same. However, they were seldom used. Sometimes prisoners' legs sagged on the scaffold, but the warders on the cross-planks supported them until they went down."

"Why didn't they blindfold the prisoners in the condemned cell, to prevent them from seeing the noose as they were being led into the execution chamber?."

"A prisoner who is blindfolded is more likely to struggle, because he is frightened of walking, wondering where he is going and imagining all sorts of things."

"If I don't faint I expect I'll struggle and scream, blindfolded or not."

"When everything was ready the executioner and his assistant went for a cooked breakfast. Shortly before nine o'clock a warder came to inform them that the sheriff had arrived at the prison and had gone to the governor's office. That was the signal for them to go to the corridor outside the condemned cell."

"How will they know our weights and heights to calculate the drops?."

"I'm not sure. They may ask us."

"I usually put on weight when I stay at Surprise View, but this time I'm sure I've lost some."

Their whispered conversation was cut short by one of the twins calling. "Come on, you two, get dressed, it's nearly supper time."

Oliver lowered the blanket. The twins were still at the table with the draughts between them and looking towards the bed. One said "We've had three games while you two lovebirds have been in there."

"O.K., we'll be ready in a minute," replied Oliver. He pulled the blanket up again and whispered "After supper we'll go to bed early and I'll explain what we're going to do."

Still in only their underclothes they got off the hard bed. Jessica looked at the cracked handbasin and said "I'd love a shower or a bath, but I suppose we'll have to make do with this."

"I'm afraid so, darling. I'll hold a blanket up when you want to use the loo."

They had just finished dressing and were sitting on the bed when an eye appeared at the Judas hole and there was a bang on the steel door. The twins stood up and quickly cleared the games from the table as the door was unlocked. Rafiq and Callum came in, each with a tray.

"Cottage pie, sago pudding with jam and a mug of tea for four," announced Callum, as they put them on the table.

When the door was locked again, the couple sat down at the table with the twins. The food on the chipped, enamel plates was the same 1950s prison food they had been given in High Stile, but now there were no knives or forks and each of them had a metal spoon. Oliver saw the revulsion on Jessica's face and gave her an encouraging smile. "Best eat it to keep up our strength, darling," he said cheerfully, but she did not reply.

One of the twins said "This is typical 1950s prison food. We have to eat it, too, when we're on condemned cell duty."

They all began to eat in a silence that was broken only by the clattering of spoons on enamel plates. The couple had little appetite, but the twins consumed theirs with relish.

They had just finished eating and were drinking their mugs of tea when there was another tap on the door and an eye appeared at the Judas hole. The door swung open and the uniformed figure of Callum appeared, followed by Mia. She was carrying two office files and what looked like old-fashioned bathroom scales.

She put the scales on the floor and sat down with the couple at the table, as the twins remained at the door talking to Callum. "I need some information about you for our records," she said. "I'll deal with you first, Oliver."

He was in half a mind not to co-operate, but decided that should their plans for the morning fail, as he knew they most likely would, he wanted the correct drops used. Mia asked them their dates of birth, religion, height, weight, details of illnesses and the amount of exercise they took. When they had given her the information she asked them to remove their trainers and stand on the scales. Jessica went first. She looked down at the dial and as she stepped off said "I thought so. I've lost four pounds."

It was Oliver's turn. He looked down, then at Mia and said "Twelve stone one pound. I estimate a drop of six feet six inches for me in the morning." Mia looked embarrassed and did not reply, but as she was going out she thanked them for their co-operation.

The twins sat down again at the table and the couple went to the window. Oliver stepped onto the top water pipe and pulled himself up by the bars so that he could see out. Although it was still daylight, the sun was going down behind Catbells, the boats had disappeared from Derwentwater and it looked calm and serene. He looked towards Keswick and thought about Ron and Marjory and wondered if they had reported his disappearance to the police. Then he looked up at the evening sky and remembered the aerial photograph he had taken from *Yanky Mike* showing the blurred face. He imagined the terrified youth pulling himself up by the bars and looking out, just as he was now doing. As he stepped down he wondered if he had just had his last glimpse of the Lake District and the outside world.

He lifted Jessica up by her waist for her to see out and for a few moments she held the bars as he supported her. As he gently lowered her to the floor she said sadly "Even from a condemned cell it's a magnificent view. Those poor boys must have pulled themselves up like this. I wonder if any of them came to appreciate the beauty before they died?."

"The one in here last Sunday must have been doing that when I flew past. Perhaps he heard the engine and hoped I would see him. If the photograph hadn't been so blurred I would have taken it to the police instead of coming here and they would have come up for a look round. Bunny and his gang would have been arrested and we wouldn't be here."

He noticed the twins watching them and realised they must have overheard.

"Keep away from the window. You're not allowed to touch the bars," ordered the first.

"How about a nice game of monopoly?," asked the second.

"No thanks," replied Jessica.

"We're going to have an early night," said Oliver.

"Well, we're going to have a game," said the first twin, as he began to set out the board.

"Before you go to bed, what would you like for breakfast?," asked the second. "As Mr. Kemp told you, condemned prisoners could choose whatever they liked for their last breakfast, so the same applies to you."

"Just corn flakes, orange juice and coffee for me," said Jessica.

"The same for me," said Oliver.

The second twin looked disappointed. "That's not much. You could have the Surprise View English breakfast. It's enormous. You even get grilled steak, lamb cutlets and kidneys with it."

"Scum Seven ordered the grilled Manx kippers, but when they came he couldn't eat them," said the first.

"They weren't wasted, because we ate them. They were delicious," added the second.

Oliver interrupted them. "I read somewhere that condemned prisoners had a daily entitlement of a pint of beer or stout and ten cigarettes or half an ounce of pipe tobacco."

"Yes, I believe they did," replied the second twin.

"You can have the beer or stout, but you're not allowed to smoke in here," said the first.

"Why on earth shouldn't we, if we wanted to?," asked Jessica.

"Because passive smoking is dangerous to health and this is our work environment," replied the first.

"The rule wouldn't have suited Albert Pierrepoint because he used to smoke cigars in an amber holder," added the second. "According to Mr. Kemp he would put it down in the ashtray when he entered the condemned cell, then half a minute later pick it up again and, with a look of quiet satisfaction on his jovial face, take a long puff."

Instead of causing Oliver to dwell on the horrors that lay ahead, Pierrepoint's cigars reminded him of his early flying days and he saw himself flying *Yanky Mike* over the Lake District contentedly smoking one again.

His nostalgic memories were interrupted by the first twin rolling the dice.

"Six," he exclaimed excitedly, moving the top hat round the board. "The Angel Islington. I'll buy that for a hundred pounds."

"Come on darling, let's go to bed," said Oliver.

Twenty Two

"Time to get up, you two. It's seven o'clock. Breakfast will be here in half an hour." It was one of the twins, breaking the long silence of the night.

He felt Jessica jump in his arms as the voice startled her into full wakefulness. "Oh God, here we go," she murmured. She was lying on her front with her head resting on his chest and her slender fingers clasping his shoulders, her long, black hair spread all around her. It reminded him of the way she had been lying when they had awoken for the second time in The Langdales. Was that really just a year ago in this very room?

His heart was pounding. "I'm afraid so, darling," he whispered as he released her. He moved his mouth to her ear "Just concentrate and remember everything. We can make it if we keep our nerve."

"I'll do my best, but I'm terrified."

He eased down the blanket. The twins were still sitting at the table, but had put away the Monopoly and now held playing cards. They did not appear to have moved since the previous evening, although twice during the night the couple had heard whisperings and the door being opened and closed.

This time they were naked as they got out of the bed and had to endure the stares of the twins, until they lost interest in them and resumed their game. He held up the blanket as she used the lavatory, before using it himself. Then she filled the basin with warm water and thoroughly washed herself from head to toe with a towel. When she had finished he shaved and brushed his teeth, while she dressed and did what she could with her hair. When they were ready they sat on the edge of the bed holding hands and staring at the green brick wall. Their mouths were dry and their stomachs churning at the dreadful thoughts of what was soon to come.

He glanced sideways at her. She was trembling and nervously jigging her leg. He knew that he was now deeply in love with her and wondered how she could have come to mean so much to him in so short a time. He decided she was everything he had ever looked for in a woman: beautiful, slim, intelligent, sophisticated, feisty, sexy and a little bit naughty. Not only did she look sexy, but she dressed, acted and spoke sexily as well. Furthermore, she enjoyed sex, even, as he had recently discovered, as a condemned prisoner in a condemned cell.

They had gone to bed early to discuss their plans and for a long time after deciding what they were going to do they had lain awake cuddling, comforting and reassuring each other under the blanket. However, shortly before dawn the cuddling had become more intimate, when their hands reached out and they kicked off their underclothes and began the foreplay. As he kissed and explored her body he felt her become wetter than on previous occasions and she began to moan softly. When she could stand it no longer, she threw off the blanket and, not caring about what the twins saw or heard or thought, moved across and straddled him. Her fingers guided him into her and as their mouths met she began to fuck him with an intensity that he had not experienced before. As their thrusts became faster and she cried out repeatedly in her passion, they forgot for awhile their impending fates, but when they finally collapsed, exhausted, into each others arms, Oliver wondered if it was to be for the last time.

His eyes were drawn to the movement of her foot. She had crossed her right leg over her left and was nervously jigging it up and down, balancing her laceless trainer loosely on her toes as she stared at the wall ahead. The sight reminded him of how she had dangled her expensive Italian stiletto by its strap, as she sat opposite her drunken husband in the dining room. When she had noticed the direction of his gaze she had smiled, then deliberately flirted with him. Was that really just a year ago, too?

His gaze took in the jeans and jumper which covered her superb figure, before stopping at her long neck. He gave an involuntary shudder. He saw Bunny towering over her, pulling down the hood, then the noose, taking care to keep the brass eyelet under the angle of her pretty, left jaw, before tightening it to the right and holding it with the rubber washer; his swift movement to the lever, then her trussed body hurtling through the opening, followed by the massive deceleration force at the bottom of the drop, breaking that lovely, slender neck like a matchstick and throwing the laceless trainers to the floor. For Oliver was sufficiently realistic to know that this is what would most likely be happening to both of them in less than two hours, because although he had not said as much, he knew that their chances of pulling it off were very slim indeed.

He closed his eyes, trying to exorcise the awful vision. He desperately wanted to protect her but could do nothing now except hope. He smiled and gave her hand an encouraging squeeze. "You even manage to look beautiful in a condemned cell," he whispered.

She gave him a brief, nervous smile, then glanced at the wardrobe. "I wonder if they're still making their silent preparations in there, or do you think they've gone for their cooked breakfasts?"

He was spared from replying by a bang on the cell door, which startled them and brought the warders to their feet. They hurriedly cleared the games from the table as an eye appeared at the Judas hole and the door was unlocked. Alexandre and Lucas appeared, each with a tray, and began to set the table for breakfast.

Alexandre smiled at the couple seated on the bed. "I'm sorry you didn't want a bigger breakfast this morning, but I hope you enjoy it." As he was going out he said "I was so pleased that you enjoyed the Lomo de Orza on Saturday. You've been wonderful guests, which makes this all the sadder."

Oliver raised his hand in a farewell gesture. When the door was locked again the couple sat down with the twins and sipped orange juice from chipped enamel mugs. The twins were having the same breakfast and began their cornflakes with loud metallic clatterings. Suddenly Jessica began to breathe rapidly and he looked at her anxiously. She had gone deathly pale and beads of sweat had broken out on her forehead. He hoped she wasn't going to faint. She pushed away her cornflakes and said weakly "I'm not hungry."

"Neither am I," he replied. They left the twins to enjoy their breakfasts and took their mugs of coffee to the bed, where they sat staring at the wall, their hands shaking so much that they were in danger of spilling them. He glanced at his watch.

"What's the time?," she asked.

"Ten to eight."

They managed to finish the coffee in spite of their shaking hands. He took the mugs to the table, where the twins were drinking their tea, then returned to her side.

"What's the time now?," she asked.

He looked at his watch. "Almost eight o'clock."

"Oh God, I feel sick. I don't think I'll be able to stand the next hour." She had turned pale again and the beads of sweat had returned to her forehead.

He held her and felt her trembling. He put his mouth to her ear and whispered "Come on, darling, pull yourself together. It's the same for me. We've got to be brave, or we've had it."

The twins were watching them. One of them said "You're entitled to a glass of brandy, to steady your nerves. Would you like it now or just before nine o'clock?"

"We'll have them nearer the time," replied Oliver when she shook her head. He knew that it had been customary to give brandy to condemned prisoners before they were executed and the biography he had reviewed had revealed that the 1955 post-mortem report on Ruth Ellis mentioned the smell of brandy from her stomach.

The other twin said "We're here to make things easier for you, so just say if we can help in any way."

Jessica asked them "Were you in here with any of the others before they were executed?"

The first twin replied "Oh yes. This is the fourth time we've been on condemned cell duty together. It's very interesting and we get a lot of satisfaction from making the last hours easier for our condemned prisoners."

"The trouble is, it's such a long shift without sleep," said the second.

"How sad," observed Oliver.

Another bang on the door made them jump again and their hearts pounded as an eye appeared at the Judas hole. But it was only Lucas. As he hurriedly cleared away the breakfast things he avoided looking at the couple.

No sooner had he gone than another man arrived. He was in his late fifties, balding and dressed in a dark grey suit, black shoes, blue shirt with a white clerical collar, and clasping what looked like a bible and a prayer book in front of him. For a moment Oliver did not recognise him, then he realised he was Mr. Barr from the garage, the father of the twins.

Barr greeted them with outstretched hand. "Good morning to you both. I remember meeting you last year, Oliver." Oliver remembered the deep, rich voice. "And you must be Jessica. I'm so sorry that we're having to meet under such frightful circumstances. Unless either of you has any strong objection, I should very much like to stay with you for the next hour and give you whatever comfort I can."

Oliver glanced at Jessica but she was staring at the floor. He looked at Barr and said. "When we met last year you were a garage proprietor in mechanic's overalls. How long have you been posing as a clergyman?."

Barr looked embarrassed. "Oh dear. You're the first one to question my qualifications. I admit that I have never been ordained. However, I have been doing God's holy work as a lay preacher for many years, so when Bunny suggested that we should have a prison chaplain I immediately volunteered my services."

Oliver looked at him coldly. "I'm sorry, but Jessica and I don't want you. As a party to our murder you're an out and out hypocrite coming here to comfort us. Now please go away, because we want to spend what little remaining time we have alone."

Barr looked as though he might burst into tears. "This is awful. I'm not really a hypocrite, you know. I admit I was in favour of the death sentence on the other eight, but I opposed it in your case because your sins are far less serious. Unfortunately, Bunny sees this as the only way and his word is final."

Jessica looked up at him. "How can you possibly justify the execution of the eight young men who were in here before us?."

Emotion showed on Barr's face as he faced the couple, clasping the holy books. He glanced at his sons seated at the table and when he spoke his words came with difficulty. "Young lady, I have just left my dear wife to come here. If you could see the state she has been reduced to you would understand why my sons and I hate these evil scum so much."

He paused, choking back tears, before continuing. "When I met her she was such a beautiful young woman and after we were married she produced these wonderful twin boys. We became a close and happy family, all of us doing our bit for the family business. As well as running the home and looking after the petrol sales at busy times, she was involved with the Womens' Institute and several local charities, so she was popular and we had a good social life. Every September we closed the business for two weeks, when she and the boys accompanied me on my annual preaching tour. We usually took our caravan to the Highlands or the Western Isles."

Barr paused again as he struggled with his emotions. "Then everything changed on that terrible evening last summer. She was expected to make a full recovery, but shortly afterwards she had the stroke. The specialists have done all they can and now she faces a future of being confined to a wheelchair, unable to speak or swallow. We still meet every evening for family prayers, but now she can't join in, which adds to her frustration and depression. The consultant said she might have had the stroke anyway, but we simply don't believe that."

Suddenly he broke down, sat on the bed beside the couple and buried his face in his hands as he sobbed loudly. The twins were watching their father with concern and were about to go to him when he stood up and blew his nose. "If you could see the tears running down her cheeks and the saliva down her chin as she tries to speak to us, you would understand why we feel so bitter." He looked at the twins "Isn't that so, lads?." They nodded their heads in agreement.

Oliver stood up and faced him. "Mr. Barr, Jessica and I are very sorry about what happened to your wife, but you must realise that the eight young men who have already been hanged here were not responsible, and neither are we."

"They were a bad lot and deserved God's punishment for their sins. If they weren't directly responsible, either they associated with the two scum who were, or their criminal activities have caused untold misery to others," replied Barr.

"You don't know that," retorted Oliver sharply. "As an intelligent, God-fearing man you must know that car theft and trespass aren't punishable by capital punishment and never have been. You must realise that Bunny's hatred of these young men probably stems from his disfigurement and impotence. Jessica and I haven't faced trial under the criminal justice system, so our executions will be murder. Now either do the right thing and get us out of here, or go away and let us spend what little time we have remaining in peace."

Barr looked hurt and disappointed. "I shall go, if that's what you really want. But before I do, may we not all kneel in prayer for a few moments?"

Oliver was about to order him to leave when Jessica stood up. He felt her hand on his arm as she said "Please darling, let's do it. It can't do any harm and it might make things easier."

Oliver looked at her in surprise "O.K., if that's what you want."

Barr looked relieved. The twins stood up and carried the four wooden chairs from the table and arranged them into a semi-circle facing their father, who was standing with his back to the wardrobe. They invited Oliver and Jessica to take the middle two and took the end ones themselves.

"What's the time?," she whispered.

He glanced at his watch. "Nearly quarter past."

They all knelt on the hard floor as Barr opened the prayer book and began to read aloud. Oliver intended to give him a few minutes and if he hadn't finished he would tell him in no uncertain terms to get out and leave them alone. He had never been a religious man and during his adult life had gone to church only rarely, on special occasions. When he had sat in his parents' pew at Loweswater, he had thought about them and his childhood there, but had not prayed to God. Now he realised that he and Jessica had not even discussed the subject.

But as the service progressed he began to find the words strangely comforting. As their father was reading the prayers in his deep voice, the twins were speaking them aloud from memory and to Oliver they appeared to be praying with sincerity. Although Jessica was still gripping his hand tightly her eyes were closed and her lips were moving silently. He bowed his head and tried to concentrate on the words and block out the terrible thoughts.

They continued alternately to kneel in prayer, sit for a reading or stand as they all sang a hymn or a psalm. Oliver began to find Barr's deep, rich voice soothing and hypnotic. After the hymn *Dear Lord and father of mankind* Barr asked them to kneel and repeat after him the words of the Lord's Prayer. Then the twins stood up as the couple continued to kneel with bowed heads, praying in silence. After a while they felt the weight of Barr's hands on their heads as he began to speak the words of the Blessing. When it was finished Barr removed his hands and the couple continued to kneel in silent prayer. For the first time in his life Oliver prayed fervently and sincerely to almighty God.

Suddenly Barr's hands appeared in front of their faces holding two tumblers half full of a golden liquid. For a moment Oliver thought they were being given Holy Communion, but then he recognised the smell of brandy. A quick glance at his watch showed him that it was almost nine o'clock.

"Drink these. It will help," said Barr. The couple looked up at him and shook their heads.

The sudden loud bang on the cell door and the rattle of the key in the lock brought them to their feet. Jessica's hand flew to her mouth as the door swung open.

"This is it, darling," said Oliver, taking her face between his hands and kissing her on the lips. Then their terrified eyes returned to the door as Chief Warder Kemp strode in, followed by Bunny, Thomas and Hugo.

LATER IT OCCURRED TO OLIVER that what happened next was like watching a scene of a play that he had rehearsed in his mind a thousand times. The only difference was that everything seemed to go into slow motion.

Bunny had what appeared to be two white handkerchiefs in the top pocket of his double-breasted, grey chalk-stripe suit. He and Thomas each held two leather straps and as they entered the condemned cell they put one on the table. The twins put on their uniform caps and moved towards the wardrobe. Kemp stepped forward and positioned himself beside Oliver as Hugo locked the door. As Bunny approached the couple Barr opened the prayer book and began to intone the Last Rites. Bunny went up to Jessica and fixed her with his watery, red right eye. "Be brave, my dear," he said, taking hold of her wrist.

Realising she was to be taken first, Oliver moved protectively towards her, but Kemp's strong grip on his arm held him back, as Hugo hurried forward to assist. As the two warders restrained Oliver, he could only watch helplessly as Bunny turned Jessica's arm behind her back. Holding her wrists together, he wrapped the restraining strap around them and tightened it through the brass buckle. Oliver noticed that he had to use the last hole, because her wrists were so slim. As she felt her arms being pinioned she turned to Oliver and whispered "Goodbye, my darling. We'll meet again soon."

"I'll love you forever, Jess," was his anguished reply.

Kemp maintained his grip on Oliver as Hugo released him and took hold of Jessica's arm instead. The Barr twins had shifted the wardrobe along the wall to reveal the steel communicating door. As they swung it open, Hugo turned Jessica towards the opening. Although Oliver knew what to expect, he still felt a shock when he saw inside the execution chamber. He heard Jessica's sharp intake of breath.

The outline of the trapdoors was clearly visible in the floor and the two nooses, one higher than the other and three and a half feet apart, were suspended directly above the two white T-marks. The iron lever, with the cotter pin at its base, was standing upright from the floor near the far right corner. The uniforms of three warders were visible: Callum and Rafiq were already standing on the cross-planks, one beside each noose, and Lucas was beside the communicating door watching Bunny.

Mrs. Kemp and Mia had filed in past the lever and were standing with their backs to the wall near the the stairs leading down to the pit, facing the scaffold and the condemned cell. Each was appropriately dressed in sober colours. Mrs. Kemp was wearing a large hat and sensible shoes and carrying a brown leather handbag over her arm. Mia was wearing a business suit and holding the green medical box by its handle. The twins took hold of Oliver's arms, allowing Kemp to release his vice-like grip. Kemp and Barr walked into the execution chamber and took up positions beside the two women, from where Barr continued to intone the Last Rites.

Bunny glanced round the condemned cell. Satisfied that Oliver was adequately restrained and Thomas was in position behind Jessica, he fixed her again with his damaged eye and said "Follow me."

Hugo's hand guided Jessica forward. She was deathly pale. As she passed through the doorway she turned towards Oliver and for a moment their anguished eyes met. "Jess, I love you," he called to her in a strangled voice and immediately felt the grips on his arms tighten. Jessica did not reply but turned to look where she was walking. Oliver watched in despair as her step faltered and Hugo had to support her. Thomas was following with the leather restraint strap in his hands.

Bunny approached the right-hand noose, the lower of the two, where Rafiq was already standing on the cross-plank. When he reached the far leaf of the trapdoors, he turned to face Jessica. The noose was suspended between them and when she saw it in front of her face she groaned, her step faltered and her head sank onto her chest. From seven paces away it appeared to Oliver that she was about to faint and he called out "Be brave, darling."

Hugo mounted the left-hand cross-plank and guided her forward onto the trapdoors. As he did so, Rafiq took her right arm. Both warders held onto a support rope with one hand as they supported Jessica with the other. When she was on the join of the trapdoors, with her toes aligned on the T-mark, they gently stopped her. Oliver heard her murmur "Please God, I don't want to die," then he saw the two warders having to support her as her legs began to sag and her chin slumped onto her chest. Realising she was about to faint, Bunny quickly reached into his top pocket with his deformed hand. As he withdrew one of the white hoods and began to unfold it, Thomas knelt down behind her to pinion her legs.

The hood was the signal and the couple knew what to do. Oliver shouted and Jessica began to scream. The sudden loud noises coming from different directions caused consternation and everyone looked around in alarm. When Oliver felt the grips on his arms momentarily relax he flung himself forwards and broke free from the twins. He grabbed the heavy, wooden chair which he had recently been occupying and swung it at them, striking one a massive blow on the side of his head. As the twin fell to the floor Oliver jabbed a leg of the chair hard into the face of his brother, who gave a shriek and clutched at his eye as he fell backwards. Like a madman, Oliver charged into the execution chamber with the chair held above his head.

Still screaming, Jessica leaped upwards and freed herself from the grips on her arms, before collapsing onto the trapdoors. Hugo and Rafiq, still on the narrow planks and holding the support ropes, were torn between making a grab for her and protecting themselves from Oliver's chair. Thomas was about to leap onto her from his kneeling position behind, when the chair crashed down on the back of his head, smashing his skull.

Jessica rolled onto her back and found herself looking up at Bunny, towering over her. There was a ghastly look on his disfigured face as his damaged hand reached into his jacket pocket and withdrew a small automatic pistol. For a moment she thought he was going to shoot her, but he was looking straight ahead and when he raised his arm she realised his target was Oliver. Her legs shot up like two pistons and as her feet drove deep into Bunny's groin he screamed and collapsed onto the trapdoors.

Hugo and Rafiq released the support ropes and made a grab for her, but were not quick enough. Oliver's chair caught Hugo on the side of the head as Jessica's legs encircled Rafiq's and pulled him down. Oliver promptly rendered Rafiq unconcious at Hugo's side. Kemp had run forward from the line of witnesses and was rallying Lucas and Callum. The three warders advanced on the couple with drawn truncheons, but were impeded by the four bodies on the trapdoors. Oliver swung his chair at Lucas and struck him with such force that the back broke off. The truncheon flew out of Lucas' hand and he screamed as he clutched at a broken arm.

Oliver dropped the now useless chair, knelt down and quickly unfastened Jessica's restraint strap. She flexed her hands, picked up the strap and stood up to face Callum, now advancing on her with raised truncheon. She swung the leather strap at the polished shaft of wood and yanked hard. Callum tripped over Rafiq's body and as he fell forward Jessica's knee drove into his face with a sickening force.

Only Kemp now remained to prevent the couple's escape. He was advancing on Oliver with his truncheon held high, yelling abuse at him. Oliver, now weaponless, was backing away into the corner of the execution chamber opposite the lever. He had retreated four paces when his back came into contact with something hard and, realising he could retreat no further, he put his arms up to protect himself. He succeeded in deflecting the first truncheon blow and as he did so aimed a kick at Kemp's groin. It missed and contacted his thigh instead, knocking him backwards, but in the process Oliver lost his balance and fell.

As Kemp advanced on him again he rolled over so that he was looking at the object he had backed into in the corner. The collapse board! He grabbed it in his arms and as Kemp rushed at him Oliver tipped the stretcher-like apparatus forwards and thrust it upwards with all his strength. It must have contacted Kemp's solar plexus, because the breath exploded from his lungs as he was thrown backwards onto the trapdoors.

He jumped onto the winded Chief Warder, yanked on the left-hand noose to break the twine, then pulled it down over his head. As he tightened the noose he made sure that the brass eyelet was under the left angle of the jaw, before tightening it to the right and holding it with the sliding rubber washer.

As Oliver was dealing with Kemp, Bunny was struggling to his knees under the right-hand noose, his long, silver hair hanging forward over his haggard, scarred face. Jessica snatched the truncheon from Callum's unresisiting fingers and brought it down with all her strength on the back of Bunny's head. As Bunny collapsed back onto the trapdoors with a groan, Jessica grabbed the noose and pulled it over his head. She tightened it round his aged neck, making sure that the brass eyelet was under the left angle of the jaw, before tightening it to the right and holding it with the sliding rubber washer. Then she jumped off Bunny's back and made a dash for the lever, arriving there at the same moment as Oliver.

Twenty Three

The crash as the trapdoors fell was deafening. In the silence that followed, Oliver and Jessica stared at the opening in the floor, breathless and in awe of what had happened. The doors were now held in the vertical position by the rubber retaining clips, and the two ropes that ran through the opening were taut. At their ends they could see the heads of Bunny and Kemp, three and a half feet apart.

Oliver picked up a discarded truncheon and looked around the execution chamber. The steel door to the corridor was locked, barring their escape that way and he had seen Hugo lock the door of the condemned cell. Of the line of witnesses, only Mrs. Kemp and Mia remained. They had retreated from the opening and were standing with their backs pressed against the wall looking deeply shocked. When Oliver had attacked the twins with the chair, Barr had dropped his prayer book and rushed forward, and now he was kneeling beside them in the condemned cell, tending to their injuries.

Oliver grabbed Jessica's hand and led her past the two terrified women and down the side stairs. The sight that met them in the pit was not a pretty one. Bunny and Kemp were hanging motionless on the ropes, their heads thrown back by the nooses that were already biting into their broken necks. Bunny's long, silver hair had fallen over his forehead, his deformed right hand was hanging limply below his jacket cuff and his feet were almost touching the floor.

Oliver thought that if they were not already dead, they were deeply unconcious and soon would be. Their necks were noticeably stretched and their faces looked grotesque, as they were turning blue, their tongues were protruding and their eyes bulging. It occurred to him that the purpose of the traditional white hood was as much to spare the prison staff from seeing the prisoners' faces after the execution as the prisoners their impending doom immediately before it.

Scattered around their feet were Thomas, Callum, Rafiq, Lucas and Hugo. Thomas had a gaping wound in his head and was clearly dead. Callum and Rafiq were either dead or unconcious. Although Lucas and Hugo both had conspicuous injuries, they were groaning. There was blood everywhere and Oliver thought that some of the injuries must have been caused by the fall.

He looked around the pit, which corresponded in size to the execution chamber above. There was no window and the only light came from a single bulb in a cage on the wall near the stairs. By its dim light he could make out an old wooden stretcher resting on its feet along one wall, a wooden ladder along the opposite wall and two sandbags in a corner. He realised that when The Langdales was converted, a partition wall had been built across Grasmere as well. However, unlike the floor above, a doorway had not been made to the corridor and the only door was a timber one in the partition wall. He tried it, but it was locked. He gave it a hard kick but it had no effect.

"We'll have to get this door open somehow," he said urgently, moving towards the ladder. When she continued to stare wide-eyed at the scene of carnage and did not reply he shouted "Come on Jess, for Christ's sake. We've got to get out of here fast." This time she heard him and understood the urgency. She grabbed the end of the ladder and together they rammed it into the door. At a second attempt the lock gave and the door flew open.

They found themselves in a sunlit room and as their eyes adjusted to the brightness they looked around. It had the smell of a butcher's shop but appeared to be spotlessly clean. The walls and floor were tiled and in the centre stood a pine butcher's table which looked well scrubbed. One wall was taken up by two large stainless steel sinks and draining boards, racks of butchers' knives, meat cleavers and saws, and shelves of empty meat trays and containers. Along the opposite wall was a large stainless steel commercial refrigerator with several doors.

"This must be the hotel's meat store," said Oliver.

The sun was streaming in through a big arched window. He wondered if Jessica realised they were in Grasmere, the room she had shared with her ex-husband. The door to the corridor was the original timber one, but when he tried the handle it was locked. He gave it several hard kicks to no effect. "This one isn't going to be so easy, because it opens inwards. We'll have to use the ladder again, I'm afraid."

She glanced fearfully towards the pit. "That means going back in there."

"We've got to, Jess. Just think about getting away and don't look at them."

Reluctantly they returned to the darkened pit, averting their eyes from the macabre tableau in the centre. They recovered the ladder and manouevred it into the meat store, then had to ram the door several times before one of the panels finally broke.

Grasping the truncheon, Oliver squeezed through the opening and looked up and down the corridor. Turning back to her he said urgently "The coast seems to be clear. I think they all went to the execution, but there may be others we don't know about."

"Let's get out of here before I have a nervous breakdown. The two women weren't injured and at least two of the men are still alive," she whispered as she followed him into the corridor.

As they went cautiously towards the emergency stairs it seemed incredible that only two days earlier they had been using the corridor for jogging while planning their escape. He suddenly remembered the two youths still locked in Scafell and Helvellyn and thought about releasing them. But when he realised that it would mean returning to the pit and searching the warders for the keys, he decided to leave them there until the police came.

When they reached the stairs they looked up and down, but all was quiet. He grasped the truncheon and crept down, as Jessica followed. At the foot of the stairs they looked along the corridor in both directions, ready to retreat, but everywhere appeared deserted. They went to the back door and looked out of the window. "Our cars are still there," he whispered.

"Thank heavens for that. What about the keys?."

They went to the cabinet on the wall. It was locked, so Oliver smashed the glass with the truncheon. He lifted his keys out and Jessica found hers.

"Let's hope they start. Shall I follow you?," she asked.

"Yes. We'll go straight to Keswick police station." He pushed the bar on the door and for the first time in a week they found themselves outdoors in sunshine and fresh air.

"If we had our mobiles we could dial 999," said Jessica as they ran towards their cars.

Oliver noticed that the Rolls Royce had gone from the carpark, but he spotted the Barrs' recovery vehicle. There was a car on its back covered by a sheet, leaving only its wheels visible. He wondered if Barr had used the recovery to drive up from the bungalow and whether the car was the trap car.

As they got into their cars Oliver called out to her "Keep up with me, Jess. I won't stop till we get to the police station."

The relief showed on their faces when the engines started. Oliver put the Lotus into gear and it shot forward. As he sped out of the carpark into the drive he glanced at his mirror, but nobody had appeared from the hotel or the staff building and Jessica was following in her old red Mini.

The wrought iron gates at the end of the drive were closed and both cars screeched to a halt. Oliver peered through the windscreen and shouted in frustration when he realised that not only were they bolted into the ground but they were still held together by the heavy chain and padlock. In his mirror he could see Jessica anxiously watching her mirror for pursuers. He looked towards the Kemps' lodge and seeing no sign of life he jumped out and ran back to her. She had wound down her window and was watching him anxiously. "The gates are locked. We'll have to force them open," he said breathlessly.

"Couldn't we drive one of the cars into them?."

"They aren't big or powerful enough, but Barrs' recovery should do the trick if we can find the keys. They're probably in the cabinet."

She looked horrified. "That means going back. Is there no alternative?"

"If we set off on foot they would probably catch up with us before we reached the main road. There was no sign of anybody as we left the carpark, so I think it's worth a try. If you give me a lift, I'll find the keys and drive it back here. It will only take a few minutes."

"Let's get a move on, then," she said reluctantly.

Oliver ran back to the Lotus and as Jessica was turning her Mini in the drive he parked it on the grass in front of the lodge. He grabbed the truncheon, jumped out and got into the Mini beside her, then watched the tension return to her face as she drove back along the drive to Surprise View. When they reached the staff carpark there was still no sign of life. She stopped near the back door and as he leapt out she called after him "For goodness sake be careful."

In their haste to escape they had not closed the door. Oliver cautiously pushed it open and looked along the corridor towards the kitchen. It was still deserted, so he went to the key cabinet and frantically searched along the rows. He found a set labelled *Barrs' Garage, Keswick*, which he grabbed and ran outside. Jessica had turned the Mini and was looking out for him, and as he ran towards the recovery vehicle he held the keys up for her to see. He tried one in the door and it fitted, so he got in and found that the other fitted the ignition. The big diesel engine roared into life and as he put it into gear and drove out of the carpark he made sure she was following.

As they headed along the drive for the second time he was wondering whether to run into the gates at speed or stop, change into bottom gear and slowly push them down. He decided that pushing them would be safer, but if that didn't work he would reverse and ram them. He stopped short of the gates and looked around. There was still no sign of anyone and the Lotus was where he had left it. Jessica had anticipated his intentions and had parked behind it, leaving room on the drive for him to reverse the recovery if necessary.

He had imagined that the chain or the padlock would break first, but as he inched forwards in bottom gear the gates themselves began to bend. As he applied more power they started to buckle, but still the strong chain and padlock held together. He put an arm across his face to protect it from flying glass and pressed down on the accelerator. As the engine roared and the big vehicle surged forward the gates suddenly collapsed. He stopped and looked at his handiwork. The chain and padlock had still not broken, but the hinges had pulled out of the sandstone pillars and the gates had collapsed onto the road. He reversed the recovery and abandoned it in the middle of the drive, and as he ran back to the Lotus he threw the keys far into the rhododendrons.

They got into their cars and drove carefully over the iron gates, then set off at speed down the hill, slowing only to negotiate Ashness Bridge. Oliver glanced into the little carpark, but now his dark memories had left him and he was thinking only of escaping from Surprise View, bringing the survivors of the gang to justice, then a future of happiness with Jessica. After checking that she was still following he put his foot down and as they hurtled down the steep hill towards the main road, his hopes of achieving all three began to rise.

He left it late to apply the brakes, so the little sports car skidded on the polished bars of the cattle grid and he only just managed to bring it to a halt before it overshot the junction. A glance at his mirror showed that Jessica had managed to stop behind him. He gave her a wave and she waved back.

He had positioned his car to make a right turn for Keswick. He checked for traffic coming from the right and saw a car approaching in the distance, which was signalling a left turn. He looked left for traffic coming from Borrowdale and when he looked right again his heart missed a beat as he realised that the approaching car was Bunny's Rolls Royce Silver Spur. He stared at its tinted windscreen, trying to identify the driver.

The Rolls was still indicating a left turn, but instead of slowing and waiting for Oliver to pull out of the junction, it continued across his front before coming to a halt. The electric tinted window came down and Oliver found himself face to face with Alexandre. For a second the two men stared at each other, then Alexandre's right hand came up and Oliver saw a small automatic pistol being pointed at his head.

Oliver ducked, swung the steering wheel to the left and simultaneously released the clutch. The sports car, already in gear, shot through the narrow gap between the Rolls and the stone wall and onto the main road. He heard a shot and immediately thought of Jessica, but a glance at his mirror showed that she was unhurt and keeping up.

As they sped off towards Borrowdale Oliver kept watching his mirror, but there was no sign of the Rolls following. His intention was to get away from Alexandre, then contact the police as soon as possible. But he knew that this direction would lead them away from Keswick and over Honister Pass to Buttermere, where they would be miles from police assistance. He decided that the most sensible course of action was to go to Keswick via the far side of Derwentwater.

After half a mile he came to a carpark on the right where children were paddling canoes in the lake, then the Lodore Falls Hotel appeared on the left. Oliver checked his mirror again and was horrified to see the Rolls coming up in the distance. He increased his speed and when he saw the sign to Grange he braked and signalled right. In his mirror he saw Jessica do the same. Praying that she had also seen the Rolls and would be able to keep up, Oliver accelerated across the pair of narrow, hump-backed bridges which span the River Derwent, into the little village of Grange.

Although he knew the Rolls' big engine gave it a very high performance, he was reasonably confident that on these twisty roads he could lose it in his Lotus. However, he was not so sure that Jessica could do the same in her elderly Mini and he regretted not having pursuaded her to leave it at Surprise View and come with him. As they negotiated the single narrow street of Grange, Oliver saw that the Rolls was still gaining on them and realised that Alexandre must be a skilled driver. As soon as they were clear of the village he changed down and the Lotus shot forward. For several hundred yards he continued to accelerate, but when he saw that as well as the Rolls he was also leaving Jessica behind, he slowed down again.

The three cars followed the twisty road as it rose and fell towards the west side of Derwentwater. The Rolls was still gaining on Jessica and was now only thirty yards behind her. Oliver braked as another series of bends approached and when he emerged onto a straighter stretch he was alarmed to see that Alexandre had managed to close the gap to twenty yards.

The convoy sped down a hill past some woods and as they began to climb again they passed the big house where Hugh Walpole had lived, which he had seen from the window of High Stile. They continued uphill and when the road levelled out again the blue expanse of Derwentwater appeared below and to the right. A glance at his mirror showed that only ten yards now separated Jessica from Alexandre.

He had to brake again as another blind bend approached. When he rounded it he found himself on a straighter stretch of road cut into the hillside, with a vertical bank on the left and a steep drop to the lake on the right. Instead of accelerating, Oliver continued at the reduced speed, watching his mirror for Jessica's red Mini to appear from the bend. Facing him on the right was a stationary blue Peugeot saloon which had pulled onto the grass above the drop. He had to slow to a walking pace to get past it and as he did so he saw three men inside. They appeared to be looking across the lake towards Surprise View and one of them was holding a large pair of binoculars. Oliver realised they had chosen the very spot where he had stopped to do the same just over a week ago.

He glanced at his mirror again as Jessica's Mini emerged from the bend at high speed and was immediately horrified to see that the Rolls had now caught up with her and was sitting on her tail. The Peugeot was parked so close to the bend that Jessica had no time to brake and shot past it with only inches to spare. Alexandre braked, but the bigger Rolls Royce struck the side of Peugeot and almost toppled it over the edge.

Alexandre did not stop, but continued after Jessica. Oliver adjusted his speed to theirs and watched them in his mirror as he tried to decide the best course of action. If he put his foot down and used all his driving skills he could probably lose the Rolls, but then he would be abandoning Jessica to Alexandre. On the other hand, if he stopped to pick her up they would both be sitting ducks for his gun.

As he was deciding what to do the Rolls Royce suddenly shot forward along the left side of the Mini. Jessica accelerated, but it kept up with her and began to nudge her towards the drop. Realising Alexandre's murderous intention, he banged his foot on the brake and simultaneously pulled up the handbrake, slewing the Lotus across the road in a shower of chippings and smell of burning rubber. He jumped out and had to leap out of the way as the Mini and the Rolls screeched to a halt, inches from his improvised roadblock.

He found himself in a recess in the cliff which he had noticed from the window of High Stile. He had seen walkers leave their vehicles there, before setting off for the top of Catbells. The Mini and the Rolls were completely blocking the road a few yards to his right. Both were damaged with their sides locked together and the Mini's offside wheels on the very edge of the drop. There was no sign of either driver and he realised Jessica would have difficulty getting out.

He was about to run to help her when the passenger door of the Rolls opened and Alexandre emerged brandishing his pistol, his face contorted with fury. He strode towards Oliver and at a range of only a few feet raised his arm, aimed it at his face and screamed "I don't know how you managed to escape, but you certainly won't this time."

Oliver was rooted to the spot and for the second time that morning events seemed to go into slow motion. Over Alexandre's shoulder he could see Surprise View on the clifftop at the far side of the lake. He wondered if the police would ever discover what had been going on there and establish the fate of the missing youths. He glanced to his right again, but there was still no sign of Jessica. He hoped she would manage to get out and run for help, before Alexandre could shoot her, too. His eyes moved back to the pistol and he realised he was looking straight down its barrel. It looked like a small calibre automatic, probably a .22. He watched in fascination as Alexandre's eyes narrowed and his finger began to squeeze the trigger.

He was just wondering if he would feel much pain when he heard the shot. Alexandre's legs folded under him and he collapsed on the road. Oliver looked curiously at the prone figure, as a red patch began to grow at the right temple. He remained rooted to the spot, staring uncomprehendingly at the man who had just been about to shoot him, now lying motionless on the road.

Slowly, he became aware of Jessica's voice saying "It's alright, darling, I think he's dead," then she appeared in front of him and kissed him on the cheek.

Oliver, his face as white as a sheet, stared at her blankly. At last he swallowed and croaked "What do you mean?."

"My passenger window was broken, so I pointed this out and shot him with it. It works very well." He saw that she was holding a small automatic pistol, identical to the one that Alexandre still clutched in his lifeless fingers.

His mouth was dry and he could still hardly speak. "Where did you get that?," he croaked.

"I picked it up when Bunny dropped it. I thought it might be useful."He began to laugh.

"You thought it might be useful! Oh, you little darling, you thought it might be useful!." Tears began to roll down his cheeks.

If his laughter had not become hysterical, they would have heard the running footsteps and the man's voice shouting urgently "We're police officers. Drop that gun."

Twenty Four

"What made you suspicious about Surprise View"? asked Oliver. They had been at Keswick police station for three hours and were being given a break from the interviews, having a late lunch of sandwiches and coffee in the Detective Inspector's office.

The DI finished his coffee and looked at Oliver. "When Ron Formby reported you missing he told us that it had been your intention to go there last Monday. He explained about your visit last year to research your article and your concern about the hotel's closure. When you didn't return that evening he and his wife were concerned about you, then when you didn't turn up for your appointment at the *Cumbria Star* office the next morning they became very worried. However, they left it another day before informing us.

The missing persons report landed on my desk on Thursday and when you still hadn't turned up by Friday I decided to make some enquiries. The two officers I sent up there found the gates closed. The woman from the lodge told them about the owner's illness and denied all knowledge of you. When they asked her to open the gates to let them speak to the manager she told them she was under strict instructions not to admit anyone, but after a bit of an argument she agreed to phone him. When he eventually came to the gates he more or less repeated what the woman had said, adding that although he recalled meeting you last year he had not seen you since. There was no reason to disbelieve him and we had insufficient grounds to apply for a search warrant."

Oliver interrupted him. "That would be Thomas. I killed him this morning when I hit him with the chair. The woman was Mrs. Kemp, the wife of the chief warder. She saw her husband get hanged."

The DI stared at Oliver for a moment before continuing. "Yesterday evening the Dumfries police phoned to say they were making enquiries into Jessica's disappearance. Her sister had reported her missing when she failed to return from a visit to Surprise View last Monday. When asked the reason for the visit she reluctantly told them about Jessica's annual visits with her ex-husband and her hopes of meeting a certain good looking man called Oliver, whom she had met there last year. Unfortunately, she didn't know his surname." The DI smiled at Jessica "I take it you were successful?." Jessica nodded and Oliver was intrigued to see her blush furiously.

"Our colleagues at Dumfries asked us if we knew anything about Surprise View. We told them about its sudden closure, our enquiries into Oliver's disappearance and our suspicions when we couldn't get past the gates. We also filled them in on what we already knew about the place, including its history, the owners and their notorious New Year's Eve parties, as well as the unusual circumstances of Ginger Rutherford's death.

They agreed that it was a remarkable coincidence that you had both gone missing after expressing your intentions to visit Surprise View on the same day. When we checked the dates, we realised you'd both been there at the same time last year. They asked us if we thought it possible that you'd gone off together without telling anyone, but I said that in view of Oliver's appointment on Tuesday it seemed unlikely. I promised to take a look at the hotel myself and if necessary obtain a search warrant.

This morning I went in an unmarked car to the opposite side of the lake, accompanied by my Detective Sergeant and the rural bobby who covers that area and knows the hotel and some of the staff. We had taken some powerful binoculars and immediately noticed the alterations to the bedroom windows and what appeared to be bars on the small window on the top floor at the north end. I had just announced my intention to apply for a search warrant when a yellow sports car drove past. Then a red Mini shot round the corner with a Rolls Royce on its tail, both going like bats out of hell. The Mini only just managed to get past us, but the Rolls hit us and nearly toppled us into the lake."

"Even if you had arrived with a search warrant, you would have been too late to save us," remarked Jessica.

"Yes, I'm afraid we would. However, it was fortunate that we were on hand to witness the events that led you to shoot Alexandre. The three of us can testify that he was about to pull the trigger and that you did the only thing possible to save Oliver's life."

The telephone rang and the DI answered it. He stood up and said "I'm afraid I'll have to leave you for a few minutes." He went out, leaving the couple to remember the extraordinary events of the morning.

****

When the DI had carefully removed the pistol from Jessica's unresisting fingers, unloaded it and put it in an evidence bag, the other two officers knelt down beside Alexandre and confirmed that he was dead. The sight of the police uniform and the authority in their voices made the couple pull themselves together and Oliver's hysterical laughter quickly subsided. When he was thinking rationally again he asked the DI to send immediate police and medical help to Surprise View, then gave him a brief account of what had happened there.

As the Detective Sergeant spoke to the control room on his personal radio, the DI got throught to the Head of CID on his mobile phone. The couple heard him mention the missing youths and numerous fatalities. When he had finished speaking he assured them that police and medical assistance were on the way to both locations and the Head of CID was setting off immediately for Surprise View.

Soon they saw the blue lights of the emergency vehicles on the opposite side of the lake as they sped along the Borrowdale road. Within ten minutes an ambulance with paramedics, more police and two scenes of crime officers had arrived at their own location. The area around the shooting was sealed off and the minor roads between Grange and Portinscale and the one leading up to Watendlath were closed to the public. Oliver and Jessica sat in the back of a police car and watched as photographs were taken of the scene of the shooting, including Alexandre's body which hadn't been moved and the three cars which still blocked the road.

Oliver spotted the Cumbria Police aircraft approaching at low height from Bassenthwaite Lake and wondered if they were having a look at Surprise View and the scene of the shooting from the air. Then a uniformed PC got into the car and drove them to Keswick police station.

On arrival they were seen by a police doctor, who questioned them about their experiences, before giving them a checkover. Apart from a gash on Jessica's knee where it had driven into Callum's face, and grazes on Oliver's arms from when he had broken free from the twins and a bruise on his shoulder from Kemp's truncheon, they were unhurt. After the doctor had treated these he was able to give them a clean bill of health.

A PC took them along a corridor to the DI's office, where a sergeant pulled up two chairs and ordered some coffee. He explained that the DI was on his way back from the scene of the shooting and wanted to interview them personally.

They did not have to wait long. The DI gave the couple a friendly smile as came he in and sat down at his desk with a woman detective beside him. "I'm glad to hear you're little the worse for your experiences," he said. "Our people and the medics are now up at Surprise View in force, under the command of the Head of CID. I've left my Detective Sergeant dealing with the scene of the shooting on the other side of the lake. Now, when you're ready, I'd like you to tell me everything that happened to you after you arrived at Surprise View."

They spent the next hour giving a detailed account of their experiences, as the DI listened and the woman detective made notes. Oliver did most of the talking, with Jessica occasionally adding or correcting something. When he got to the events on the scaffold the DI frowned. Finally, Jessica gave a description of their escape and the car chase that culminated in her shooting Alexandre.

The DI told them they would have to make written statements, so two Detective Constables took them to seperate interview rooms where they spent another hour giving their individual accounts as the detectives wrote them down. They began with their stay at Surprise View the previous year, including their late-night assignation in The Langdales, and ended with the shooting of Alexandre. When they had finished the DCs were each holding several closely-written statement forms as they led the couple back to the DI's office.

AFTER THE LUNCH BREAK THE DI picked up the statements from his desk, then there was a long silence as he read them. When he had finished he looked at the couple and said "Well, that explains the mystery of the missing youths. Our lack of progress was becoming embarrassing. You've both had incredible experiences and are extremely lucky to be alive."

Oliver took Jessica's hand and smiled at her. "We certainly wouldn't want to go through it again, would we, darling?."

"Heaven forbid," she replied with feeling.

The DI was not smiling. "What I'm not clear about is why you hanged the two injured men this morning. Was it absolutely necessary to save your lives?"

A feeling of doubt was coming over Oliver. He replied cautiously "As we have already told you and have put in our statements, we didn't hang them. Although we put the nooses around their necks and went to the lever, we changed our minds at the last moment because we couldn't go through with it. I don't know why, but the trapdoors simply collapsed."

The DI was shaking his head. "I find that hard to believe. You admit putting the nooses around their necks and going to the lever. Now you're telling me that you didn't push it and the trapdoors fell of their own accord. Do you seriously expect a jury to believe that?"

"A jury?" Jessica was looking bewildered.

"Yes, a jury," said the DI. "I'm not happy with your explanations and might have to arrest you on suspicion of murder."

Oliver began to protest. "Surely we were justified in hanging Bunny and Kemp, even though we changed our minds at the last moment. Up to then we had been fighting for our lives against odds of twelve to two. They were the ringleaders and although we had injured them there was a danger they would recover sufficiently to kill us or prevent us escaping. Killing them was the only thing to do to ensure they wouldn't."

The DI looked at them sternly. "To have the defence of self-defence the force you use must be necessary and reasonable. From what you have told me and have now put in your statements, both men were already incapacitated when you put the nooses over their heads. Then you went to the lever with the intention of pushing it. I don't believe you didn't push it and I don't think a jury would either. Neither would they consider your actions to be necessary and reasonable in the circumstances."

Jessica looked incredulous. "You mean that after everything they'd done to us and the danger we were still in, we shouldn't have hanged them?."

"Not unless it was absolutely necessary to save your lives. You were probably justified in overpowering and incapacitating the other men to prevent yourselves being hanged, even though you killed three of them in the process. You might also have been justified in putting the nooses round the necks of Bunny Liddle and Kemp to restrain them. But you were not entitled to push the lever and deliberately kill them when they presented no immediate threat to you."

There was a knock on the door. A uniformed PC came in and whispered something to the DI, who excused himself to the couple and went out, leaving them with the constable.

They looked anxiously at each other. "It seems we've jumped out of the frying pan into the fire, Jess," said Oliver.

"Perhaps we should ask to see a solicitor before answering any more questions," she replied.

Reluctant to discuss their new predicament in the presence of the constable, they continued to contemplate it in silence.

****

When the DI returned he was accompanied by a smartly dressed man in his late forties, whom he introduced as Cumbria's Head of CID, a Detective Chief Superintendent.

The DCS smiled when he saw their anxious faces. "I have some news for you that should cheer you up. When we examined the execution chamber we discovered that the lever had not been pushed and the safety pin was still in position. On further inspection we found that the bolt which withdraws from under the trapdoors when the lever is pushed had broken. It seems that the weight of everyone was too much for it and the trapdoors collapsed not because you pushed the lever, but because the bolt had sheered. I had a look at it myself as the photographer was taking some pictures. It had snapped clean in two leaving half in the slot under each leaf."

Oliver breathed a sigh of relief. "Thank God for that," he said.

"Quite," said the DCS. "This seems to confirm your story and gets us out of a very difficult situation. We would have had to charge you both with the murders of

Bunny Liddle and Kemp. The charges might have been reduced to manslaughter, but you could still have been looking at prison sentences. In view of this the hangings can now be attributed to an unforeseeable accident."

The detective continued as the couple smiled with relief. "Well, now we've got that unpleasantness out of the way I thought you might like to know how we're progressing at Surprise View."

"We certainly would," replied Oliver. "Have you accounted for everyone?."

"I think so. The first four officers to arrive there this morning found the gates lying across the road, then they had to push the recovery vehicle off the drive to get past. Halfway along they came face to face with a car being driven by a young woman, who turned out to be the hotel receptionist trying to escape."

"That's Mia. Her young child was killed by joyriders near here," said Jessica.

The DI interrupted. "Yes, I remember. It was a terrible business. Unfortunately we never arrested anyone for it."

The DCS continued. "Well, she's now in the cells downstairs. When they entered the hotel there was nobody about, so they split up and carried out a quick search. On the first floor they found a locked door with a hole smashed through it, which they assumed was one of the bedrooms, so two officers squeezed through. From what I can gather they came out pretty quickly looking pale and immediately called the control room for more assistance.

When our main team arrived they were directed to the execution suite by the first officers. In the pit under the scaffold they were met by an appalling sight. Five of the men were dead. Two had been hanged and were still on the ropes. Another four had serious injuries. There's very little ventilation down there which made things worse. Wandering about amongst all this mayhem in a state of shock was a smartly dressed woman wearing a large hat and carrying a handbag."

Oliver interrupted him. "That's Mrs. Kemp. She went as a sort of modern day tricoteuse to witness our execution and ended up witnessing her husband's instead." Oliver coughed, then hastily added "accidental hanging that is."

The detectives exchanged glances. "Well, apparently she was quite traumatised, so the doctor gave her something and now she's in the cells as well. They also found the owner of the local garage dressed as a clergyman. He was kneeling beside his injured sons reading passages from the bible to them," said the DCS.

“He was the prison chaplain. He was reading the Last Rites when we launched out attack,” said Oliver.

“Well he’s now in the cells as well, minus his dog collar. By this time five ambulances with paramedics and a doctor had arrived. They did what they could for the injured men before taking them to the Cumberland Infirmary under police guard.”

“Did you find the two youths?,” asked Jessica.

The detectives exchanged glances again. The DCS replied “Yes, they were still locked in their cells. We had to search the dead warders for the keys. When we got the doors open the one in Helvellyn was severely traumatised and the one in Scafell had back injuries from his birching. They’ve both been taken to the Cumberland Infirmary as well.”

Oliver explained “The one in Helvellyn was the first to be captured. He’s been in there for over three months.”

After another exchange of glances the senior detective continued. “The experience seems to have had a profound effect on him. When we went in he was looking very smart in a navy blazer, grey flannel trousers, white shirt with detachable collar, collar studs and cufflinks, dark tie and highly-polished black shoes. He was well-scrubbed, the rash on his face had gone, he had a short back and sides with a neat Brylcreemed parting and was wearing spectacles. When he saw us he jumped smartly to his feet and placed an encyclopedia on his head. Then, while standing to attention and balancing the encyclopedia, he said in a cut-glass accent “Good morning, sir. The rain in Spain falls mainly in the plain.” When we just stared at him he cleared his throat, adjusted his tie, fiddled with his cufflinks and looked at us expectantly. Apparently, Monday is his day for elocution and deportment lessons.”

The detectives exchanged further glances. Realising they were struggling to keep straight faces Jessica smiled. “The training seems to have done him some good then?.”

As the DCS was studying the floor the DI took up the story. That’s a matter of opinion. The police surgeon had a look at him and diagnosed shock and post traumatic stress disorder, so a sergeant who knows him said he would drive him to the psychiatric unit at the Cumberland Infirmary. On the way he sat bolt upright in the back of the car staring straight ahead and between clearing his throat, adjusting his tie and fiddling with his cufflinks kept repeating 'How now, brown cow', in a most refined voice without a trace of a Cumbrian accent."

The couple smiled patiently as the detectives tried not to become unprofessional by giving way to their black police humour. The DCS continued. "When they arrived at the hospital he greeted the chief psychiatrist with 'In Hertford, Hereford and Hampshire, hurricanes hardly ever happen. How kind of you to let me come'. He was still clearing his throat, adjusting his tie and fiddling with his cufflinks as he was escorted along a corridor to a secure ward by two male nurses. The sergeant thinks he prefers him as the thieving little toe-rag he was before he went to Surprise View and doubts if his family will have him back if he's not cured."

"Will you be informing the families of the other eight of their executions?," asked Oliver.

"Not until we've found the bodies and have more information about their deaths." The DCS was composed again.

The DI interrupted. "I expect that will be my job and I can't say I'm looking forward to it. Knowing their backgrounds, some of the families will be upset but others won't give a damn."

The DCS stood up. "Well, I think that brings you up to date with events at Surprise View. I don't think we need detain you any longer. We'll have to know where you'll be staying in case we require more information and to keep you posted with developments."

Twenty Five

"To the happy couple," toasted Ron.

"To the future Mr. and Mrs. Mills," echoed Marjory, raising her champagne glass as the happy couple kissed.

Jessica laughed. "Hang on a minute. I need an engagement ring before anyone can call me that."

"All in good time, darling. The shops aren't open tonight." Oliver could not conceal his pleasure. He turned to Ron. "I'm thrilled to bits about the job, Ron. Are you sure the MD doesn't want to interview me?"

"He said that anyone who can survive what you've been through must be capable of running the *Star.* He also said there'll be a job for Jessica too, if she wants it."

Oliver turned to her "Are you sure you won't mind moving to Cumbria, Jess?."

"As long as I never have to go up that road to Watendlath again," she replied with feeling.

Marjory was beaming at them. "You're welcome to stay here until you've found somewhere of your own, you know."

Oliver caught Jessica's eye and they exchanged smiles. When Ron heard they had turned up safe and well he had telephoned Keswick police station and after a delay been put through to Oliver. After expressing his relief he said that he and Marjory were looking forward to meeting Jessica and invited them both to stay. The couple had accepted gratefully and when they were finished at the police station they were given a lift to Threlkeld in a police car, as their own cars were still needed for the inquiry and Jessica's was damaged.

On the way Oliver told Jessica about Marjory's reputation for her old-fashioned views. They were, therefore, intrigued when, after the introductions in the hall, she had led them upstairs and shown them into the larger of the two spare bedrooms which had a double bed.

Now he replied "Thanks, that's kind of you both, but we don't want to outstay our welcome. A couple of days should give us time to decide what we're going to do."

There was a ring on the doorbell. Ron went into the hall and when he returned he was accompanied by the DCS and the DI.

"Sorry to interrupt your celebrations, but we've got some news for the couple which they might prefer to hear now rather than tomorrow," said the DCS.

Ron invited the detectives to sit down. "Marjory and I have to get dinner ready so we'll leave you to talk. You're welcome to join us, if you have time," he said.

"There's plenty to go round," added Marjory.

"It's very kind of you, but we've got to get back to Surprise View," replied the senior detective.

When Ron and Marjory had disappeared into the kitchen the four of them sat down. The DCS said "We've made some more progress since I spoke to you this afternoon. When scenes of crime had finished in the execution suite we began to make a search of the buildings and the grounds. Everything we've found points to an operation that was both well planned and extremely clever.

We examined the recovery vehicle and the trap car. The Barrs must be very skilled engineers, because they'd made a superb job of them. The locks and the mechanisms in the seats for firing the tranquiliser darts were pure genius. We've taken another look at the CCTV recordings from the different towns and the recovery vehicle appears on them on four occasions, but it's such a commonplace vehicle that nobody suspected it.

Another clever device was made by Hugo and Thomas for capturing intruders. Inside the old shed in the kitchen garden they had installed a TV camera on a moving pan stand. Attached to the camera was a compressed air pistol loaded with a dart containing the same tranquiliser. They had chosen that location as the most likely for an intruder to enter the grounds. When someone climbed the fence an alarm was activated at the warders' station. A warder could then keep the intruder in view on the monitor and when in range fire the pistol by remote control. Simple but clever."

"Painful, too," said Jessica with feeling. "While I was unconcious someone pulled down my jeans and put a plaster over the spot."

The DCS smiled distantly as he pictured the scene, before continuing. "When we took Bunny Liddle down from the scaffold we searched him and found, among other things, his notebook. It appears that after condemning you to death he returned to Scafell and continued to interview the last youth they caught."

"That would be Scum Ten," said Oliver.

Jessica gave him a disapproving look. "I hope you're not going to start using that horrid word, now," she said sharply.

"Yes, Scum Ten. That's what was written," confirmed the senior detective. "Apparently he told Bunny that the two youths who had run Ginger Rutherford down in Workington were two brothers who later went missing from the town. Bunny realised they must have been the brothers they'd captured in Workington and the first ones they hanged."

Oliver's eyebrows shot up. "They were Scums Two and Three. That certainly is interesting. They were lucky Bunny hanged them before he found out." Jessica gave him another withering look.

"That's what I thought," replied the DCS. "If he'd known what they'd done he might have given them a short drop and let them strangle, which is the way Ginger Rutherford died according to the pathologist's report."

"If he didn't torture them first," put in the DI.

Jessica grimaced. "What an awful thought."

The DCS was looking at Oliver. "The last youth they captured is still too ill to be questioned about the deaths of your parents, but we've arrested the one named in the notebook as his accomplice. When we told him his friend had grassed on him he admitted everything, so we stand a good chance of getting them both convicted of causing death by dangerous driving."

Oliver breathed a sigh of relief. "That certainly is good news," he said, as Jessica found his hand and squeezed it.

The DCS continued. "We were puzzled about where they'd put the bodies of the youths they'd hanged, so we interviewed Hugo and Lucas in hospital. They told us that as no-one else had wanted the job it had been left to Alexandre to dispose of them. However, they had no idea what he'd done with them. We got a dog handler to search the grounds and I got the force aircraft to take some aerial photographs, but there was no sign of any graves.

While some of the team were looking for graves, others were searching the staff quarters. Most of the rooms revealed nothing of significance, but when they got to Alexandre's room they found evidence of some very perverted tastes. There were books, cuttings and videos on male asphyxiation, necrophilia and coprophilia. There were also hundreds of pictures on these subjects, downloaded from the internet. Our experts at Headquarters have examined his computer and discovered that for several years he's been repeatedly visiting websites showing brutal images of male rape and strangulation."

"Yuck! What some people do for kicks." Jessica's face was screwed up in disgust.

"What's coprophilia, for goodness sake?," asked Oliver.

The DCS glanced at Jessica. "You'll have to look that one up, I'm afraid."

"It's means having a preoccupation with faeces," explained Jessica, still pulling a face.

Taken aback, the three men stared at her for a moment before the DCS continued. "We had discovered a bunch of keys in Alexandre's pocket. One was for the padlock on the entrance gates and another for the door of the meat store, which you smashed as you were escaping. They searched the refrigerator and in the deep freeze section found some beef and pig carcasses wrapped in muslin, hanging from hooks. Concealed behind them and also hanging from hooks, were the bodies of the eight youths. Several had parts missing. They had been decapitated, skinned, gutted and cleaned. In another section they found some of the missing parts on trays, but the heads and genitals are still unaccounted for."

Jessica shuddered. "As if we haven't heard enough horror stories already."

"In an attempt to find out what had been going on we spoke to Hugo again. When we told him of our discovery his reaction of shocked surprise seemed genuine enough. He explained how Surprise View had lacked a special room for meat preparation and storage, so when the execution suite was built Alexandre pursuaded Bunny to allow him to use the room next to the pit. After that Alexandre always attended to the buying and storage of the meat himself and became unusually secretive about it. Hugo also told us about Alexandre's obsession with perfecting a pork dish which has won him several prizes. It has a Spanish name which slips my memory."

"Lomo de Orza," said Jessica.

"That's it!," exclaimed the DCS.

"Lomo means pork loin and Orza the terracotta dish in which it's traditionally marinated," added Oliver, helpfully.

"Alexandre must have known that human flesh tastes very much like pork and thought he could improve his Lomo de Orza by using it instead. Unknown to everyone at Surprise View, instead of best loin pork he was dishing up slices of Cumbria's delinquent youth as the Saturday treat following an execution. Did you have some, by the way?"

The couple were staring at the DCS with expressions of revulsion, as the significance of this sank in. Jessica was the first to recover. "Yes we did, unfortunately. We even said how much we enjoyed it and sent our compliments to Alexandre."

"I tried it last year, on Alexandre's recommendation," said Oliver. "It was wonderful then, but I have to admit that it was even better this time. The thought of it now makes me feel sick."

"It seems you are lucky to have escaped being on the menu yourselves this Saturday. Jessica would have been the first woman to be executed at Surprise View and the first one available to Alexandre for his Lomo de Orza"

"I didn't like the way he used to stare at me, but now I realise his interest might simply have been culinary," said Jessica.

"I don't think he was interested in women in the normal way. His perverted tastes have made us wonder what he did to the bodies after he took them down from the gallows. We've collected some samples for DNA testing, not only from the bodies but from the butcher's table as well, in case he had an unconventional method of tenderising the meat."

"He must have thought that all his birthdays had come at once when Bunny gave him the job," observed Oliver.

"That occurred to us, too," said the DCS. "Suddenly he was able to act out for real the things that previously he had only been able to fantasize about – and was being paid to do it. What on earth's the matter with you?" This question was directed at Oliver, whose jaw had fallen open.

"My God! I've just remembered the food display in the middle of the dining room last year," he said.

The detectives looked mystified. "What about it?," asked the DCS.

"The centrepiece was a highly decorated boar's head glazed in aspic, with an apple lodged in its mouth. I stopped to admire it as I went in for dinner and remarked to Callum how unusual it is to see such displays in restaurants nowadays. He told me that Alexandre had taught himself the art soon after he started at Surprise View. When I replied that it must be a dying art, I didn't realise how near the truth I probably was."

Now it was the detectives' turn to be taken aback. "You don't mean?," asked the DI.

Oliver nodded and for a moment even the DCS seemed at a loss for words. There was a short silence before he asked "And instead of the apple?." Again Oliver nodded.

There was a longer silence as the three men conjured up pictures of what Alexandre might have been up to. Oliver saw a row of eight glazed and decorated human heads with gaping mouths staring at him with bulging eyes from a shelf in some undiscovered chamber of horrors. The faces of the detectives told him they were having similar visions.

Eventually the DCS said "Well, I suppose we must consider every possibility."

"Where do we start looking?," asked the DI.

"Fortunately, that's something Jessica and I don't have to worry about," replied Oliver with a smile, reaching for her hand.

Jessica was looking mystified. "What's an unconventional method of tenderising meat and what have the boar's head and the apple got to do with it?," she asked.

The detectives exchanged glances. Oliver was saved from replying by the reappearance of Ron and Marjory with the Hostess trolley. On it, surrounded by steaming dishes of vegetables and a gravy boat, was a large joint of meat. As the detectives rose to leave Ron announced "Dinner's ready. Are you sure you won't join us?."

"We'd love to, but we still have a lot to do at Surprise View," replied the DCS. He went over to the trolley and looked at the joint. "Mmm, it smells delicious. What are we missing?."

Marjory looked pleased. "Roast loin of pork with stuffing," she replied.

www.ingramcontent.com/pod-product-compliance
Ingram Content Group UK Ltd.
Pitfield, Milton Keynes, MK11 3LW, UK
UKHW040556210726
13854UKWH00007B/770